The Killvein White

By

Ralph Reynolds

Order this book online at www.trafford.com
or email orders@trafford.com

Most Trafford titles are also available at major online book retailers.

Printed in the United States of America.

ISBN: 978-1-4269-5104-6 (sc)
ISBN: 978-1-4269-5105-3 (hc)
ISBN: 978-1-4269-5106-0 (e)

Library of Congress Control Number: 2010918333

Trafford rev. 01/06/2011

www.trafford.com

North America & international
toll-free: 1 888 232 4444 (USA & Canada)
phone: 250 383 6864 • fax: 812 355 4082

Also by Ralph Reynolds:

Growing Up Cowboy...Confessions of a Luna Kid. FULCRUM PUBLISHING, 1991

For Gabriella,
and heights traversed.

Buried deep
And cold alive
The Killvein Slide
Swept away sixty-five

Rue the day
Of mines and men
The Grim White Scythe
Will reap again

Hark brave lads
Still hammer and drill
Lest your last breath on earth
Shall be the Lord's will

When beyond the dark storm
The Killvein glows white
Pray God for deliverance
All through the night

...**Old Miner's Stanza, Lucite, Utah**

Chapter One

Samantha shuddered. Her free hand moved upward by reflex to a sensation of coldness at her throat. Still clutching a roll of maps, she bent to shut off the computer. Its job was done. Hers was just beginning.

Get hold of yourself, Sam!

The storm had suddenly become something more than a mere red X on her charts; bigger and scarier than the abstract apprehension that had dogged her mind for days. The dreaded fronts had emerged at last, and they were reeling like drunken monsters toward the Wasatch Mountains. Their timing could only be described as God-damn-awful. Tomorrow would launch the busiest ski weekend of the year and the North America Alpine trials were right around the corner.

Gripping the maps and charts ever tighter, Samantha reached nervously toward the telephone, wishing she had done it sooner. She must tell Chap. Her fingers trembled at the dial.

Relax, you dip stick!

Of course she couldn't have told anyone, even a boss as trusting as Ted Chapman. The cycles had been a crushing weight to bear alone, but only theoretical until now. Well, they weren't a theory anymore. The storm was here and it was angry and dangerous. The time had arrived, finally, to thrust the whole craven nightmare onto broader shoulders than her own.

The voice at the other end was that of Ken Touey, the bureau's crop specialist. "Chap left early today and will be out of town 'til Monday."

"Oh damn... Ken, I've got to talk with someone about getting a warning out. Who is here?"

"Buford is the only forecaster. I think he's ready to leave. What are you talking about anyway? We've got no data..." Samantha dropped the phone and whirled toward the door.

Hell's afire! Storm coming, Chap gone. Now only Buford!

A sense of panic hastened her steps down the hall. Whether she liked or disliked a guy didn't make any difference now. She had to have a forecaster, and quickly.

Buford was buttoning his overcoat when Samantha burst in. He eyed her curiously from behind a tidy desk, equally-tidy salt and pepper eyebrows, and a blackened mustache.

"We have a problem here Buford."

He grimaced. The mustache twitched. "It's martini time. Can't it wait 'till Monday?"

Samantha paused. Always at the Weather Bureau she'd treated Buford, who fancied himself a ladies man, with vacant professionalism. Always he had resented that. Now they were uncomfortably face-to-face. This would be a hard sell, and no occasion for pride or professionalism. It was time for an instant turnabout, some patience, and a woman's wiles.

Samantha laid the papers on a chair, stepped behind Buford's desk and took his overcoat. Her arm brushed the back of his hand as she smiled into his eyes and said lightly "You can't leave yet, big guy. Your martini will have to wait." Hanging his coat back on the rack, she sensed his gray eyes watching her. Today's flex pants and silk blouse had always seemed uncomfortably and unseemly tight. But just now she judged the outfit as perfectly appropriate, even provident.

She turned slowly to face Buford. He may have been waiting for her to speak, but his attention was clearly riveted to the lean curves of an athletic woman's body: a delicate jutting at the breast, slight curving of stomach and thigh, a clinging softness of fabric.

Good. His balls are roped and tied.

"I need an expert." In other circumstances, Samantha might have blushed after saying that. But she pressed on, "I need a forecaster that people believe in." Buford's teeth gleamed white below his mustache. "How can I say no to that?"

Samantha had guessed that her appeal to vanity would work just as well on Buford as it did on most men. Or better. She'd learned long ago that men who ignore brains in a woman will usually make the quickest response to beauty and femininity.

She unrolled her maps and was taping them to Buford's desktop as he bent deeply to peer over her shoulder. His educated eye would not fail to see the startling weather anomalies she had charted: low-level winds of dangerous velocity at Flagstaff, Las Vegas, Houston and Calgary, all moving toward the Great Basin. One air mass pushed sharply northwest out of the upper Gulf of Mexico, skirting the southern Rockies. Yet another was flowing across Baha from the Pacific and into the south of Arizona. Most ominous of all, a deep cold front came spearing out of Winnipeg toward the Wasatch Mountains as though locked-on by radar.

A tall man, Buford bent nearly double for a closer look, then straightened and smiled broadly. "That's pretty imaginative charting."

"It's not imagination. The systems.are real. What will happen as they come together?"

"You mean *if* they come together."

"Okay, *if*." Samantha again felt the chill at her throat This was taking a bad turn.

"The Wasatch would get clobbered with snow."

"Like, how much?"

"Maybe a foot per hour."

"For How long?"

Buford shrugged. "Who knows. Several hours I guess."

He clearly wasn't interested

Hairy bastard!

She felt the irritation that always came with impatience, then collected herself.

"What's the absolute longest?"

"As long as the northerly flow keeps bringing up moisture. Until upper winds tear the system to pieces. This kind of storm could hang in there a long time."

"Dropping a foot an hour?"

Buford's eyes strayed to the window and the gathering darkness beyond. "Theoretically."

"Buford, would you believe that could happen in the Wasatch?"

His smile was indulgent "I guess it could; but it's not going to. What you're showing me here is about a foot of powder on the Wasatch tomorrow night."

Samantha blinked rapidly, fearing her hazel eyes might reveal a rising anger. She detested the condescending note. "How come some of you are so smart and the rest of us so stupid?"

Buford seemed to take her sarcasm as a compliment. He glanced at his watch and mumbled something about experience and judgment. He was obviously showing off for Samantha and enjoying it. Then he sternly shook a finger in her face. "Number one: Atlantic systems almost never get as far west as you've drawn this. Their winds can't counter the jet stream." His tone was more professorial than conversational. Then he leaned back to the map and studied it a moment. This time two fingers came up. "Number two: That Pacific system is going to move faster while the Atlantic system slows. There's not a chance in hell they'll converge like that."

Samantha felt herself slipping. She couldn't deal with this bastard. She said coldly, "I'm a statistician. Don't lecture me about chance."

"Well, almost no chance."

"Buford, please relax. Will you believe that what I'm telling you is important?"

"Well, maybe you should relax."

They glared at each other in hostile silence. Finally, he gestured, palms out. "Okay, okay. If you say it's important, it's important."

Samantha breathed in deeply. Finally she continued: "Can you visualize a twenty-foot snowfall in the Wasatch?"

"No."

"It has happened."

"I doubt that." Buford glanced at his watch. He appeared to be getting nervous and rattled. Buford couldn't bear to learn from a woman; even a woman statistician.

"Back in 1861 something like ten feet of snow fell at Bear Lake in one day."

"That's not twenty feet. Anyway, how do you know?"

"Diaries left by prospectors in winter camp there. They also wrote of a much bigger snow early in the century, described by Ute Indians."

Buford snorted. He moved around the desk to sit, contemptuously it seemed, on the maps taped there. "I'm not impressed by your sources."

"Please, Buford. Give me time. During the nineties, nineteen feet of snow caused an avalanche in the canyon below Lucite that buried a whole herd of elk. Indians were still eating them in July. A second avalanche caught 65 miners. None were saved. Early last century, ten feet of new snow fell at Lucite just before an avalanche killed forty-two miners. After that disaster they abandoned the mines."

"Okay, okay." Buford looked at his watch again. He clearly wanted out of this, but on his terms. "Say what you want, just validate. Don't waste my time with hearsay."

It was too much for Samantha. "Damn you, Buford. If I'm wasting your time just go on home to your martini!" She gestured as if chasing away an errant bull. "Shoo, go on. Get Out."

"Well, golly; excuse me."

Prick with ears.

"Buford, I told you this is important."

"I'm sorry. Proceed."

"All right, here's your precious validation: Samantha raised her voice, but her words came out measured and slow. "In 1921, the Forest Service reported eleven feet of snow from one fall in the Wasatch south of Elk Basin. In 1951 twenty feet fell in two days at the head of Giant Oak Canyon, causing a half dozen severe avalanches.. Luckily the eye of the storm only skirted Lucite. You want validation! That storm is in the records of your own dear, damned Weather Bureau. It wasn't publicized because nobody lived up there then."

Her emphatic, defensive delivery seemed to startle Buford. He relaxed. "Okay, I lose. I like to see my people do their homework. Now. can I go home?"

She rolled her eyes in disbelief. "What in hell do you think I've been telling you all this for?"

"I've no idea."

"Well, you're about to find out."

It was time to come right out with it. "Buford, There's a statistical relationship between these dates that has to mean something." She paused and motioned, palm up. "Now if you'll kindly get your butt off my maps..."

Buford blushed and stood awkwardly.

Samantha regretted her impudence, and sensed that any chance of success with this man had just slipped away.

Stupid, Sam. Never humiliate a man who has power over you.

She looked up and reached out to touch Buford's arm. "Forgive me. I guess I'm too close to this stuff." Buford answered with a nod and a crooked smile.

There was a moment of strained silence. Samantha bent over her maps and began writing with her quick hand. It was the only thing she knew to do. Buford stood stiffly by, tall and intimidating. Finally Samantha held up her map and said softly. "It's as simple as this, Buford. Once every thirty years someone has recorded a massive storm with very deep snowfall in the Wasatch. And every second snowfall, or every sixty years, that storm has been mind-boggling. Really huge and dangerous."

"So what does it mean?"

"We're due for one of those super snows and it's on the way now."

"You're talking cycle. I don't believe in weather cycles. The bureau doesn't accept them. Neither does the Meteorological Society."

It was the boss speaking.

"I understand you, Buford," she said. "But look at this:" The moment was urgent and the time was now On a map she quickly placed a series of dates inside a band angling through New Mexico, across the Four Corners region, and on into central Utah.

"I was doing snowfall correlations a few months ago when I noticed something really spooky. The deepest snows outside this corridor are random, but within the band they happen every thirty years."

Buford seemed startled. "Is there a pattern of deeper snows every sixty years?"

"Nope. Every thirty years all those reporting sites get a big snow. That's all. The repetition is uncanny it's so damned precise. Snowfall in central New Mexico has measured within an inch of sixteen inches every time."

"Do these coincide with your big snows in the Wasatch?"

"Perfectly."

"I guess that proves that big Atlantic storms can move all the way into the Great Basin."

"Right, Buford."

"Well, maybe I'm kind of stupid here, but if this is the front that hits the Wasatch, why are some Wasatch storms bigger than others? I mean, how do you explain the super snows?"

Samantha patted Buford's arm. "Good boy. Good question." He was snared at last. She drew another corridor, starting at the Gulf of California, across Mexico and into Arizona. "Every sixty years, a big storm moves north from southwestern Arizona, up across the Grand Canyon, southern Utah and into the Great Basin. I'm talking big-time snow: Four feet at Flagstaff. Eighteen inches at Cedar City and Gunnison, heavy amounts at Provo."

"Salt Lake City?

"No. At Provo the storm always moves into the Wasatch."

"Buford frowned. His lips contorted beneath the mustache. "When did these big storms come down?"

"Simultaneous with the super storms in the Wasatch."

"That's unbelievable."

"Every storm in these cycles is well documented."

"You're losing me. How many damned cycles are you talking about?"

"Just two. Every thirty years a very moist system moves northwest out of the Gulf of Mexico along a hundred-mile-wide corridor. It hits the Great Basin and bends easterly again, encountering the Wasatch Range. As the system rises to cross over, it is enveloped by a Canadian front, and really heavy precipitation results. That's one cycle. The other repeats every sixty years, simultaneous with every second storm in the thirty-year cycle. Saturated winds move up through Arizona bringing rain and flooding on the Gila River, and dumping heavy snow at higher elevations. It drives into northern Utah and converges with the Atlantic system. The two fronts pump an ocean of moisture into this part of the country. When it collides with a Canadian low, the precipitation is simply fantastic. Buford, I guess it can only be described as all hell breaking loose. That happened in 1831, 1891 and 1951.

Samantha looked up from her map. Buford was staring at her with, for him, an unusual expression. Maybe admiration.

"Buford, I have checked tree-ring records. They track both these cycles back to the sixteenth century."

Buford turned to sit again at the edge of the desk. This time he respectfully moved the maps aside. "That's fascinating. I want you to write it up and we'll get it published in the meteorological journal."

Samantha reached out to take his hand in both hers. "Buford, a terrible storm is coming into the Wasatch. You've got to warn people."

"We've forecast possible snow for tomorrow at higher elevations. We can't do any more. There's no reason."

Samantha dropped his hand. "God in heaven, Buford. I've just given you a reason."

"You mean this? Oh, I don't see it at all now. The systems won't converge. The Pacific front doesn't carry that kind of moisture. Anyway, your Atlantic system will be turned back by the jet stream in just a few hours."

"Even if it's just something that could happen, we have to put out a warning. Will you do that as a favor for me if nothing else?"

"That's no favor for you. The bureau will be embarrassed, especially me. Everybody will say I came under your spell or something."

"Stop it Buford. You make me sound like some kind of sorceress or bimbo. You know I don't deserve that."

Damned piss ant!

"Gimme a break. I didn't mean you're anything other than a top-notch professional. You may look the part but ...I...I just mean it's a....well....it's just a matter of perception. The rare person who doesn't know how smart and competitive you are might think along those lines."

Samantha flushed. She groped behind her for a desk chair and abruptly sat, staring at Buford. She finally answered in a calm voice, her calmest of the day: "I guess I wasn't aware that people here think I'm competitive. Buford, I only compete against myself. I don't think you know me at all."

"I know you dress better, ski better, run faster, bike farther, serve harder, read more books. You win at everything oftener than anybody else. You even invest smarter. They tell me you've built up the biggest tax deferred account in the bureau." He glanced down, "You've also got the nicest..." He paused, saw the hot fury in her eyes, and blushed. "Sorry. That has nothing to do with being competitive."

In one fluid motion, Samantha stood and reached for her maps, ripping them away from the tapes. As they curled into her arms, she whirled and stalked stone-faced out of Buford's office, slamming the door. No matter that life or death may hang in the balance. She couldn't take any more of this bastard.

The Bureau was empty. There was no one else to talk to. It was dark outside.

She found a bench and sat quietly until she heard Buford leave. She didn't know whether to laugh or cry or scream. Yes, she would scream, except for the old janitor working down the hall. It would scare the pants off him. Finally, she put her things away and started out. As she passed him, the janitor stopped sweeping and leaned on his broom. "Cheer up, honey."

"Give me one good reason."

"Well, we ain't got it so bad. The radio just said there's a flash flood in Phoenix and Albuquerque has got knee-deep snow on the ground. Think a that. Poor devils."

Chapter Two

For those who claim success can't be measured, Matthew had an engineer's answer. Anything can be measured. Even nothing .Of course success was hard to quantify and not easy to define. But it's the kind of thing that if you have it you have ways of knowing. So when Jason phoned and asked him to come to Utah, Matthew simply walked into the office of Petrocain's president to announce that he was taking a week off. "It'll cost us ninety thousand if we lose those gas leases," Bernard Baker grumbled. "Hell, Matt, we can't spare you any other time either so you may as well go now."

That's success.

At four-thirty Friday, Matthew had barely dropped his itinerary in the out box when Bernie's secretary called to say that Baker was on the way to tell him good-bye. The president came in shortly and gripped his hand. "Now Matt, you can twist every joint and bust every damn bone from your neck down. Even your pecker." He burst into a hearty Texas laugh. "Just don't fall on your head. That's the only part we need around here."

That kind of success didn't need to be quantified.

Gloria called just at quitting time to suggest that they meet for dinner at the race track. "If we eat early you can be home packing by seven."

Matthew protested it wasn't enough time then added, "Well, maybe that's enough time, but the wrong place for what I had in mind."

Gloria answered, "Whose fault is that? You're the one who booked that barbaric five o'clock flight. Besides," she pouted, "My Mother always said, he who plays alone might just as well sleep alone."

"Your Mother did not say that."

"Well, she would if I told her how you run off on vacation and leave me behind."

Matthew deserved her barb. On Tuesday at lunch, a bright and pretty anticipation had rounded Gloria's always glowing eyes when he told her about the trip to Utah. But she pursed her lips and pretended to lose interest when it became clear that she wasn't invited. Of course, she didn't know how to ski and Matthew had no toleration anymore for ignorance in anything. Gloria hated his impatient streak and would quickly drop out if he tried to teach her. But there were better reasons for not taking Gloria to Utah.

Matthew's personality, like his profession, had its rigid systems and compartments. There was a proper slot for everything. Jason had been one part of his life and Gloria quite another. There wasn't any common ground for blending the two and no need for it anyway.

But Matthew had another reason for not wanting to take Gloria to Utah. Jason needed him there and it was unheard of for Jason to need anybody. Here was a breakthrough. Gloria would never understand that, even if Matthew tried to explain. Something beyond the ordinary was on Jason's mind, something maybe unwound and tangled or dark or desperate. It would not be a thing that Matthew wanted Gloria mixed up in.

Driving to the track, Matthew fell in behind a Toyota with a ski rack, incongruous here in hot and sunny Houston. Skiers, like St. Bernards, had proliferated into all kinds of unlikely places. Seemed everybody was either into skiing or wanted to try. As a Colorado native and expert skier who hadn't skied in nearly 15 years, Matthew reversed that trend. He used to love skiing but times and people change. Prospecting for oil was a lot more interesting than skiing. Anyway, splitting with Jason had spoiled skiing for Matthew. He didn't care to ski with someone else and he had never enjoyed doing it alone. When Jason called, they talked mostly skiing, but Matthew sensed something else was really on Jason's mind. Jason had said, "I need to see you, Matt, but we're getting ready for the winter contests and I can't get away just now to come to Houston. Isn't it time you took a vacation?"

"I'll be there Saturday," Matthew told him. "Save me some powder." Mathew had been surprised by the gratitude in Jason's voice:

"Matt, it's great of you to do that for me." Here was a confounded puzzle. Matthew had never known Jason to ask favors from anybody, not for himself. It was as out of character as a tiger barking. The mystery was less intriguing than worrisome. The worry of it was causing perspiration where Matthew's hands touched the steering wheel. Why would Jason, in his serene little ski resort world, be seeking help from a friend of 15 years ago? And what kind of help? And why Matthew? Everybody always admired and enjoyed Jason. He would have no scarcity of friends. So it must be something Matthew had that others didn't. What? For whom? That was the question.

It was troubling to recollect that in college days Jason never had shown any sense of possession. In Jason's view, everything belonged to the person who wanted it most. Well, maybe who needed it most. That kind of soft-headed-ness proved to be fateful. Jason got so much into the habit of giving that he finally gave it all away; his career, his dreams, his actual self and very soul. That was the limit, but maybe he was still giving.

In primitive times or societies, when man lived by the rule of feelings, a person like Jason would have risen to the top and stayed there. But times change. It wasn't enough anymore to be fearless, loyal, clever and strong. Those traits would carry a Jason to the top among primitives, but in today's society, soft-hearted guys get eaten alive.

All the same, years of separation had not dimmed the attractions of Jason in Matthew's mind. The steady hazel eyes, bronze-tanned face, Jupiter profile, a body at once powerful and graceful. Each spontaneous motion had seemed practiced and dramatic. Jason used to ski the way a great dancer would ski, and he danced that way too. Smart! He used to dash through trigonometry and calculus faster than anybody in class. He could have achieved any heart's desire but for that softheaded sentimentality.

So look out. What Jason gave away might even be yours. Sure, Jason was proud and self-sufficient when it came to himself, but he had no such inhibitions if the cause was someone else's. He had been capable of groveling like a beggar. He would solicit the world until he got what somebody was after.

Pulling into the parking lot at the race track, Matthew looked for Gloria's white Audi. It wasn't there yet. He hoped she would arrive soon because he did want a quiet and restful night's sleep, regardless of what he had told Gloria. The flight was early. Lucite was a high place. He needed to acclimatize quickly. Only God, and Jason, knew what was in store for him there.

Chapter Three

Merlin swung feet-first out of bed and cursed as his feet touched the icy floor. He quickly pulled on long handles, a sweatshirt and the heavy wool pants from his missionary suit. He would have preferred Levi's but no way could he get them over the long handles. Anyway, better to wear something warm for these mountain deliveries. When it stormed in Middle Aspen Canyon you could bet fifty-fifty on spending time standing around waiting for some yeahoo to get pushed or pulled out. Or you might be doing some of the pushing yourself.

He glanced out the east window. Clear and sunny but with wind. He heard a whistle around the air conditioner cowling. Probable storm today. All the more reason to haul ass. He had just enough time to get over to the shop, load out, and head for Middle Aspen Canyon before swarms of skiers hit the road. Then he could unload and high tail out ahead of the mob coming back. The Forest Service didn't like Saturday deliveries in the canyon because of crowds on the road. Merlin didn't either but there wasn't any help for this one. Anyway he would get time-and-a-half, plus pay for the whole day whether he put it all in or not. Good duty so long as the road stayed dry, but tricky when it didn't. Too damned many of these kids like to drive the way they ski. All out.

Hulda was at the sink. He tiptoed until he could reach out to her waist. His hands clutched. She jumped. "Gotcha, Mamma."

"Ha. I heard you."

"Dammit. Feed me. I ain't got time to be held up by the kitchen help." His chin pressed against her ear. His hands moved to the roundness of her plump thighs and up.

"Filthy buggar."

"I said feed me." His hands were fumbling inside the split of her housecoat. "Wish I had five minutes more."

"Promises, promises." She twisted deftly in his grasp and planted a wet kiss on his cheek. Her hands arrested his fingers, then cupped his face. "Naughty. Time for breakfast. Brush your teeth."

"Who wants breakfast?"

"You. And you'd better eat it 'cause that's all you're getting."

"I'd rather had a piece of Mamma."

Merlin ate quickly. The weatherman was giving the same forecast from last evening. A front promised to bring bits of rain off and on during the day to Salt Lake Valley. Light snow a possibility at higher elevations, with some locally heavy snow in spots along the Wasatch front.

"Shit, hon, you know where that local spot's gonna be:"

"Of-course. When they need snow at Lucite they ring you up for a gas haul."

"It always works too, don't it?"

"Be careful Merl. I worry about that big tank in the canyon."

"Oh, now, you know I been there a few times."

They were at the door. Her arms curled under his elbows and hooked around his burly shoulders. "The radio said yesterday they've had three wrecks a week in the canyon this winter."

"Don't worry. Those gearheads stay clear of a rig like mine."

Hulda kissed him whispering, "Enough breakfast?"

"Plenty."

"Want anything else?" The front of her was pressing against him.

"You'd better believe it."

"Then take it easy in the canyon. Mamma don't sleep around with corpses."

"You'd bring 'em to life."

"You just drive slow. It'll keep."

Driving to the terminal, Merlin turned on the radio, hoping to hear some Clint Black, or maybe his favorite, Merle Haggard. Instead the newscaster was giving a revised forecast. Damned ski-happy town's hung up on weather. He turned it off. No matter what the forecast, there would be snow by noon in the Wasatch. Just concentrate on making good time and getting to hell back home before the crazies started sliding all over the road.

It was smack ten o'clock by the time Merlin slid behind the Jimmy's wheel and eased out of the lane toward Interstate 80 east. The road was dry but the sun had disappeared behind a cloud bank that seemed to be moving in awful fast from the west. Snow was a lead-pipe cinch on the way home. Nothing to sweat about. Tires good, the truck in first-class shape. Merlin glanced at his gauges. All's well—vacuum, oil pressure, alternator, temperature. He knew this truck like he knew Hulda. He recalled their morning banter and smiled, but his mind was still on the truck.

No big deal to make an up-canyon run, even in snow, with a rig like this. Butane was never a real heavy load, and the trailer caused him no worry except sometimes the brakes. Coming out of Middle Cottonwood, Merlin liked to slow down with the trailer brakes when there was snow on the road. That way the tank wouldn't outrun the truck. One of these days some dumb shit would jackknife all the way into the bottom of Middle Creek. Be a chore just to get the corpse out. The truck would stay down there.

On the Interstate ramp he let off on the gas pedal and pulled the air lever sharply downward. The rig slowed instantly. Trailer brakes okay. Merlin eased up on the lever and accelerated. A drag behind—damned brakes sticking. Finally the truck lurched up the ramp. Good, they sprung loose. Should get the brakes checked. They ought to cut quicker.

There was practically no traffic on the interstate as Merlin steered into the outside lane eastbound. In spite of clouds to the west the sky was clear over the mountains. The Wasatch loomed rough and white and stern above the valley floor

The mountains were almost as much a part of his life as Hulda and the kids. If you know the Wasatch and the moods of those peaks, you didn't need a calendar. Not even a watch. You could read seasons, tell time, even predict weather in the play of light and color on the mountainside and in the haze and desert dust around the peaks. There was neither today. Must be lots of moisture in the air to settle all that Nevada dust and Utah smog. A hell of a storm was moving in for sure. Merlin felt the sting of urgency even as he noticed that the Jimmy had crept above the speed limit. He throttled back and turned his attention again to the great range ahead.

To a Mormon like Merlin, the Wasatch was the most conspicuous of all things sacred. It towered by thousands of feet over the great temple and the beloved tabernacle, both somehow elevated by the thrust and pull of the brooding peaks. The Wasatch was security. The great barrier had sheltered and protected the early Saints from dangerous outsiders. And it was from high in the Wasatch that Brigham Young himself looked down into a dead land and pronounced, "This is the place."

Merlin had been around a little, first in the army and later to Canada to fill a mission. He knew that the Arabs had their Mecca, the ancient Greeks their Mount Olympus. The modern Christians had Bethlehem and the Jews Jerusalem. Of course Mormons were Christians, but no Mormon would dream of going to Israel, or wherever, before his pilgrimage to Salt Lake. This was where the sea gulls ate the crickets that ate the crops of starving Saints. And God sent choice angels here to whisper instructions to clumsy immigrants so they could make sand dunes bloom like the rose. And it was the crystal waters of the Wasatch that irrigated the crops of Mormondom so folks could feed themselves, pay a ten-percent tithe, even send grain back to Iowa for emigrant Saints waiting there to cross the plains.

It was ten-thirty as Merlin approached the entrance to Middle Aspen Canyon. Making good time, but the clouds had closed overhead. The first dry flakes were drifting aimlessly onto the hood even as he turned sharply at the forest road that entered the canyon. Lord Almighty! He'd never seen a storm come up so fast. He shifted down and revved. High time to get moving. He'd take the curves a little faster than usual. Wouldn't hurt the Jimmy to wind up a little. Shit, if a real big storm hit they might close the lifts. He'd be stuck with the mob coming out and late getting home. Hulda would worry. No sense to worry little Mamma. Merlin pressed harder on the gas pedal. Being from Canada, Hulda couldn't get used to the idea of people moving around when it snowed. She liked the snow when everybody was home but she got frantic when Merlin or the kids were out driving in it.

Merlin was now halfway up the canyon road. It was getting steeper. He geared down. The sky was overcast all across the Wasatch now. Surprisingly dark for eleven o'clock, but the canyon walls were steep here so only a good bright sky could lighten up the road. Stray flakes of snow started hitting the windshield but they glanced off, leaving no water drops. It was really going to be a dry fall. Nice snow for the skiers. But he would almost sure be coming out on a snow-packed road. Hustle!

The Jimmy didn't like the altitude. He geared down again and revved.

He was coming up on Helix Creek. Tourists considered this the hairiest part of Middle Cottonwood because of the sharp blind curve leading into the culvert, then an even sharper open curve over the culvert. Merlin figured it really wasn't the worst stretch of the Canyon. It just scared people because there wasn't any guard rail along the outside of the south lane.

Drivers tended to hug the bank, so fender-benders always happened here when there was un-sanded snow in the canyon. Kind of a bad place for trouble, what with Helix Creek being an avalanche course. It wasn't a real bad one but bad enough that the Forest Service closed the road two or three nights a year so they could shoot the slide down with artillery.

It was eleven-fifteen when Merlin pulled over Clementine Ridge. Lucite lay only about a hundred feet below on the valley floor, but he could barely see it through a sheet of swiftly falling snow.

Day of the Wren

The wren was out of patience. Once more he trilled a plaintiff signal. Again her answer was a careless "cluck."

He hopped along the branch to a place near the end where his anxious eyes could see a world far away. He was measuring the warning in the dampness of the mountain air, the cool breezes that pressed against his up-thrust tail feathers, the crescent of color that curved halfway around the horizon. It was more urgent now, but he had found a place and he called again, the notes rising in pitch, beyond impatience to a sharp command.

Her response was the same as before, except a little cross this time.

Fury propelled the wren back to the ledge. He perched there near the crack in the rocks and his white throat pulsated with a barrage of angry, high-pitched chatter.

Nothing came back except a sleepy cluck.

Seeing another squirrel hair on the rock below, the wren flitted down to get it, returned to the ledge and commenced scolding again. This time his demand was lowering in pitch to an ominous threat.

Her answer was three contented peeps.

He picked up the hair along with a fragment of leaf and flew back to the little cavity in the high snag. He flitted there a moment then slipped inside to drop his burden, but quickly returned to perch on the branch below and hurl an angry taunt toward the crack in the rocks, "stupid 'n lazy, stupid 'n lazy, stupid 'n lazy."

She didn't answer, but there was no time to wait. The warning was in the air around him and the north breeze was teasing his tail feathers with an urgent supplication. He slipped inside and hunkered there. He slept awhile and when he woke great white stars were swirling around the cavity.

Chapter Four

The jet took off to the south at Stapleton and wheeled back over Denver, climbing steeply to cross over the craggy spines of the Front Range with a comfortable four-thousand-foot gap between its fragile fuselage and Mount Evans. Matthew thought about moving to an empty seat across the isle for a look down at Golden, but the seat belt sign was still on and he didn't like to break rules. Anyway, Denver had grown prodigiously but Golden probably won't be so different from twenty years ago. And if so he didn't care to see it because he remembered the old Golden with pleasure. The big brewery would still be there with its rich aromas and his Alma Mater, The School of Mines, or Tech Institute, or whatever they called it now.

The pilot throttled back. They were approaching cruising altitude. As far north as Matthew could see, the Rockies gleamed a cold white. Golden was far behind, at about the snow line. No chance of seeing it today. He loosened his seat belt. The stretch at Denver had been welcome, but he was never one to sit still for long, and this day had started hours ago. He reached for the newspaper, a tabloid. The splashy front page made no impression. Golden was still on his mind.

Matthew recalled the hangout with the cafe in front and the bar in back A freshman got the clap there once so they used to call it the Red Pecker. He and Jason favored the place because the bartender was a skier and never asked for ID. He would see them often together on weekends at Winter Park and admired the way Jason could ski (who didn't?) The friends frequented the bar, drinking Coors draft by the pitcher, and dancing with the foothills women who hung out there. Now and then they took one out to Matthew's pickup, which he always left in a dark corner of the parking lot. Whether they scored or not (usually they didn't) each would confide all the details later on. Occasionally a brawl would break out when the place filled with lumberjacks. Matthew always stood aside, but Jason liked to wade in, usually on the side that seemed to be getting the worst of it. He would hug his adversaries when it was over and buy a round of beer, sometimes at Matthew's expense.

Although smaller, Jason had been much brasher and, admittedly, much tougher than Matthew—better-looking, too. Matthew conceded that. Jason's unruly, ash-blonde hair and chiseled features would be hard for any guy to top. Still, Matthew had held his own when it came to eyes and chin. A girl from Matanuska told him that the blue of his eyes reminded her of a glacial stream. That meant cool. Matthew liked the thought. And women seemed intrigued by the deep cleft in his chin. One date said she had yearned for months to finger it. Then too, Matthew's voice was more resonant than Jason's. Girls went for that. But in many ways the friends hadn't been much different. They both liked cowboy hats, Chevy pickups, tennis, swimming, girls, history, math and Tchaikovsky. They had loved movies, beer, popcorn and skiing, but hated politicians, cigarettes, whiskey and fraternities.

The jet bucked, nearly spilling a cup of coffee just delivered brimful to Matthew. Strange to find such strong winds aloft on such a clear day. He studied the striking terrain below. To the north a great arc of mountains encircled an undulating snow-covered prairie, North Park. In minutes the jet would be over Rabbit Ears Pass, then Steamboat Springs. Damn it, wrong side again. He wouldn't get to view the vast ski area expansion paid for by big corporate money. Matthew shrugged. He'd seen enough progress. He would just as soon remember Steamboat, like Golden, the way it was twenty years ago. At times he and Jason used to tire of Winter Park with its serpentine waiting lines and swarms of apprehensive skiers. After the powder got deep enough to cover logs, they'd head to Steamboat. Jason loved to dart through Mt. Werner timber. For days after his passage or until the next snow covered them, his tracks were a conversation piece among lesser skiers, and that included just about everybody. Not quick or bold enough to keep up, Matthew would follow along in the clearing. But on the lower mountain he and Jason would ski together, seeking out moguls of the steepest runs, carving across the top and down the face, then leaping to the next. Jason used to ski his best at Steamboat, maybe because his fluid, floating style, drew less attention there. Jason hated grandstanding on skis.

Matthew glanced at his watch. Forty minutes to Jason. They had met only once since Jason quit college. A great pity, because Jason had been a special friend, unselfish and devoted, full of life and joy.

A big winding river came into view on the right, with white water and gaps of ice where it slowed—the Green. The airliner was over Utah. The Uinta Mountains would loom momentarily. Matthew didn't know this region but he knew its geology from his studies in mining engineering. Ironically he'd never made a dime out of the discipline that absorbed so many years and beers at the School of Mines, then grad school at Kentucky. Of course, metals were more interesting than oil, but how could you regret success? His accumulated stock from options alone was worth millions. His nieces and nephews liked to kid that he was rich enough to get married now. But Matthew had no such intentions. A family would be nice, but the trouble was he liked kids better than he liked women. Gloria might be an exception. They had been lovers for years but they were both too set in their ways to start raising kids, so why marry? Matthew had what he wanted of Gloria.

Any regrets had mostly to do with Jason. The study of mining attracted Matthew partly because he loved mountains. Jason had majored in field geology for the same reason. At Golden they used to plan a business venture, a consulting partnership to serve some of the small uranium mines still operating.

To test their ideas and learn more about uranium, the friends had worked hard for poor pay in a western slope mine the summer before their senior year.

Matthew knew he would regret it always because in a Grand Junction bar they had met Ellen. And that was the beginning of the end of their dreams, their partnership, even their friendship. Long ago Matthew stopped worrying about what might have been.

Matthew guessed that the disaster of Ellen must surely be behind Jason now. During their contacts over the years her name had never been mentioned. Jason's life had been interrupted. His dream of becoming a field geologist failed. Jason would never join Matthew in the millionaires club, but what Jason was doing and what he could do well seemed to have come together for him. Jason's talents were compromised talents, but they would serve him well as snow ranger for the Forest Service and specialist in avalanche control.

Matthew fished sunglasses from his breast pocket. The Wasatch range was coming under his side of the airliner and he could begin to see why a Jason was needed here. Although streaked clouds were layering to the west, the early morning sun had followed the jet in from Denver and was shining on the tips of the highest peaks. They glowed like embers in a bed of ash. The heights were barren of snow, with only an occasional tuft of vegetation clinging in sheltered places. Perhaps the weak sunlight from the southeast exaggerated the depth and pitch of canyon walls, but Matthew's educated eye told him instantly that in any light the slopes would be starkly sheer and precipitous. Here there were few of the rounded contours of the eastern Rockies, the two ranges having been created by different forces. A shrinking of the earth formed the Front Range of Colorado, with its cobweb of wrinkles and ridges. By contrast the Wasatch arose from a cataclysmic fracture of the earth's crust. To one side of the rent the land began to sink, pushing the other ever higher. At one point the Wasatch might have been just an awesome granite cliff. Thrust ever higher; that cliff began to break into massive blocks to relieve the tensions. Even after millions of years of weathering and erosion, the Wasatch still showed the effects: massive rocks, great wedge-shaped cracks thousands of feet deep, sheer cliffs and dark irregular canyons.

The pilot throttled back. Again there was turbulence. High winds seemed to be curling upward, deflected by the great rocks below.

Matthew drew his eyes from the spectacle to glance ahead. The layer of clouds to the west was getting darker and thicker. Some kind of front was moving in, which would explain the wind. But weather didn't interest Matthew today. He looked quickly back to the terrain below and noted an obvious fault and vein in the rocks. The basin beyond would be Middle Aspen Canyon. At its floor, where the mineralized vein narrowed, he would see Lucite.

The pilot came on to announce their Salt Lake City landing. And added, "On the right side of the aircraft you have an excellent view of one site for the upcoming North American Ski Trials. That's world-famous Lucite Ski Resort."

Matthew barely listened. He glanced at the network of lifts and runs and noted some anxious skiers already milling around the lower chairs. But it was the lay and slope of the canyon itself that caught and held his attention. A great U-trough perhaps four-thousand feet deep, the canyon at its base pinched to little more than a few hundred yards between the looming walls. It headed not far to the east of Lucite, where Matthew could see white columns indicating the frozen convolutions of a high waterfall.

From aloft it was easy to understand why miners abandoned Lucite even before the veins played out. Destroyed once by avalanche, it burned to the ground in 1895. Several avalanches struck again in the next century. Finally miners left it alone for good after the great slide of 1912 killed scores of them. Matthew knew this history because Lucite was a classic case of a great silver lode no longer accessible for ecological and recreational reasons. By the time the Forest Service learned how to control avalanches, Lucite was on its way to becoming a world-class skiing center. Re-opening the mines was unthinkable.

Making such a place safe for skiers would require a man like Jason who knew skiing, geology, physics and snow. A perfect fit. Matthew counted five avalanche paths leading directly into the scattering of lodges and stores. One flowed from the ski area itself, but Matthew reasoned that the major threat would come from the north, away from the ski runs. Walls were steeper in that direction, with less timber and other obstacles to sliding snow. Here were all the ingredients of avalanche: narrow canyons, granite slopes offering little friction or holding power, heavy falls of dry snow. It would be interesting to see how Jason managed such a lethal combination to make the canyon safer for skiers than it ever was for miners. The scene below was more rugged than pretty, but Matthew viewed it without apprehension. To a skier of his ability it was purely seductive. Matthew had no thought of danger, but there was something unpleasant about the scene, an irritant like a discordant note in a symphony or a billboard on the lee side of Old Faithful.

The jet was losing altitude even faster than the canyon. Matthew saw a great line of cars creeping uphill along the ribbon of blacktop: day-skiers from the valley. Of course, Lucite would be always crowded on weekends because of its proximity to the largest towns of the Great Basin. Here were thousands of commuter-skiers along a road that ended at Lucite. Now Matthew understood. The configuration below would offend the instincts of any mining man. This was a road to nowhere, a great inclined shaft fifteen miles long into dead end. A blind shaft with one way in and the same way out. A cave-in here and…Damn, it was the same wherever he went. An engineer cursed with an engineer's training. Too fastidious, too general, too much oriented to principles rather than situations. Matthew instructed himself in a whisper—*what we have here is a canyon. It is not the shaft of a mine.* Ten minutes later Matthew and Jason were hugging each other in the Salt Lake terminal. It was 8:45 a.m., Mountain Standard Time.

Chapter Five

Samantha slept scarcely at all. She awoke at dawn, ate a quick breakfast, then hurried to the office, finding it strangely quiet on Saturday. Down the hall she could hear the computer printer of the secretary assigned to George Rose, the only meteorologist on duty. Both George and the secretary would get days off next week to compensate for weekend duty. Samantha would get nothing beyond the surprised stare from Rose. Statisticians were expected to do their work during the week. What didn't get done one week could wait until the next.

Samantha smiled at George, waving and calling out something about lazy people who get behind. George had a tender streak. If Samantha didn't speak every time she saw him, his feelings would be hurt. He was a pretty good meteorologist, but carried a professional scar. Five years ago, he read incoming data and predicted a dangerous storm with high winds over the central Wasatch. The systems weakened. The storm never came in, but George's ominous forecast aborted a Forest Service rescue mission on Clementine Ridge. A lost hunter froze to death. At the federal hearing, one agency blamed the other. They exonerated George but stigma remained. Because of the fuss, he had become the most conservative forecaster in the bureau's mountain division. Rose would never again predict a violent aberration in the weather, even if it stared him in the face.

Well, this morning the signs of just such a beast were eyeball-to-eyeball with anyone who dared look. Even Rose had revised the snow forecast upward. It was 7 AM and TV Weathermen were saying 'locally heavy snow in the mountains.' That could mean anything from eight inches to eight feet. Whichever happened, nobody would criticize the Bureau.

Samantha quickly set to work reading tapes and collating the data.

Snow was still falling at Albuquerque, Gallup, and Farmington. Heavy snow had started at Cortez. In less than three hours the Atlantic front would spill into the Great Basin, its wet winds mixing with the vanguard of the Pacific storm. A river of moisture was flowing through the sky. Its clouds would soon dam up to rise over the Wasatch against icy winds of the Canadian front. That cataclysmic encounter would center over a little ski town crammed with wall-to-wall visitors. Lucite would soon be lashed by the most dangerous storm in sixty years and folks there hadn't a clue.

The ski lodges, always fully booked, were one worry. Those people ought to be evacuated before noon and brought to safety in Salt Lake. Leaving them there under the storm was asking for it. But the thousands of day skiers already heading up canyon road into the eye of the storm—that was a calamity. Either get them reversed and on their way home quickly or there would be hell to pay. Within the hour, Samantha must convince somebody with clout that what lay ahead for the Wasatch was something more than locally heavy snow.

Damnation!

She huddled for a moment with George Rose, showing him the system maps she had drawn that morning. Samantha didn't mention cycles. There wasn't time. Anyway, George sure wouldn't buy into them if Buford hadn't. George listened politely, asked a few questions then promised to take Samantha's concerns into account, but "I believe I've got us covered okay with locally heavy snow."

"Can't you at least say something like, signs point to a very dangerous storm in the region of Middle Cottonwood and Lucite?"

George was already shaking his head before Samantha finished. "No, no, Sam. You're going overboard. That Atlantic storm will stall out any minute. We don't want to scare folks unnecessarily, do we? Why don't you just get out of here. Drive to Lucite for a little skiing. Lord knows that's what you like to do."

The uselessness of saying anything more snuffed Samantha's anger before it could surface. After the bruising session with Buford she felt only futility. But she had a parting shot: "I'm not that stupid, George. When this storm is finished every skier in Lucite will be buried. And you'll have a lot more to answer for than one lost hunter."

George blushed all the way to the top of his bald head. He had become stiff as a cadaver while she spoke. He stared at her a moment, then relaxed and managed a smile. "Sam, you're tired. You're too close to this. Go home and get some rest, I'll forget you said that."

Rotten crotch asshole!

Samantha was still hugging the rolled-up charts and maps as she walked past Rose's secretary without speaking. Her bridges at the bureau were not only burning, they were down to embers. Before long George would be phoning Buford, "Sam's getting into stuff that's none of her business. Has she lost her marbles, or what?"

She dialed the local Forest Service office. A secretary answered, telling her "It's Saturday, Mr. Hext, the super, and all the rangers are gone til Monday."

"This is Samantha at the Weather Bureau. I just wondered if they know there's a big storm on the way and they should be thinking about getting the skiers out of Middle Cottonwood." It was a desperate long-shot but what else could she do?

"Well, like I say there's nobody here. I can telephone the supervisor at home and have him call the Weather Bureau."

"No, no! Don't do that."

"Well you might call Jason Stemple, our snow ranger at Lucite. His number is..."

"I have it. Thank you."

So it had come down to that. Somehow, she'd known from the start that it would. No fairness here. People who got paid to make that kind of decision should make it, not Jason...just because he had the power. Not with so much at stake. She'd rather swim in swill than put Jason on the spot, especially without an official forecast, but there was no way to duck this. Everybody thought of Jason as good man, a real rock of a guy. Now was the time for him to prove it.

Samantha picked up the phone, paused a moment, then set it down. How could she possibly expect so much trust from this or any man. And the personal thing made it harder. It hurt that she hadn't talked to Jason or heard from him since the improvised funeral for the little girl whose last days they shared almost a year ago.

Samantha rummaged in a desk drawer and took out the postcard a nurse had let her keep. She hadn't thought of it in months. It was the kind a nickel or dime could buy at the payout counter of any truck stop along the Interstate. Its montage of photos included an oil well, a great pile of coal, a refinery, and a cowboy riding a bucking horse, all from "Rawlins, Wyoming, Energy Capitol of America." The note itself was written in shaky script, as if composed in a car traveling a bad road or a badly worn car on a good road. Judging from its coarse line, the pencil had been sharpened by fingernails picking away the wood to expose a millimeter or so of graphite.

The salutation: *Dear Kind Nurse* seemed too elaborate for the terse message: *Please take care of our baby. We can't pay no more for her.*

Orderlies found the girl with the postcard in her hand in the lobby at LDS Children's Hospital. Tests confirmed what the nurses guessed. Transfusions would prolong her life, but it was only a matter of time. She lasted until either March or April of last year, a date that didn't make any history books (not significant at the five-percent level or any level.) It must have been April, because Jason couldn't possibly have spent such a lot of time away from Lucite during the big ski month of March.

Samantha stirred at her desk. She picked up the map and rolled it back tightly against its warp. Three times she had done that already and the cursed thing still wouldn't lie flat. She felt nervous enough to scream and she hadn't screamed of nerves since the day she opened her final calculus exam at Rutgers.

She should have rested more. Samantha had scarcely thought of the child in months. She had rather quickly forgotten, an act of will on her part but one that didn't require any heroics. The tot had never been whole to Samantha, because she hadn't been anything but dying. There couldn't be regrets where there had never been hope. No one grieved for the girl except silly Jason, who seemed to lack tolerance for finality. Samantha pitied the child but reserved her pathos for the person who penciled the crude note. The four hours from Rawlins to Salt Lake, was it time enough to say good-bye?

Samantha glanced beyond the map in her hands to the telephone. She must call Jason, but not just now. In a moment.

Jason had been with them the night the girl dropped into a deep sleep and never woke. They took turns sitting up by the bed. Afterward they drank coffee at an all night cafe across the street and watched the sun rise behind the cold pink Wasatch. Jason wanted to talk, so Samantha listened. He told about another time and another death, the loss of a hired man, only a farm worker but a beloved friend. His recollection was so vivid that Samantha felt as though she had shared that experience too.

That was nearly a year ago. It seemed wrong that they had shared the experience of the dying child, then gone their separate ways without a word between them. Samantha had come to care deeply about Jason, and maybe she loved him a little. Almost any woman who knew him well would do the same. He couldn't know that, of course. She never expected Jason to respond. Their friendship, generally warm and trusting, had been flawed by an attraction for one another that could only be called physical. Once they clutched hotly in Jason's car, their kisses wild and probing, bodies pressing without tenderness. It might have been release or escape. And it was Jason who objected.

"This isn't right for us."

"I know, Jake. We'd better go." She had been breathless as the lingering vacuum at the eye of a hurricane.

"I can't explain how good you are for me," said Jason.

"I'm glad I mean something to you. Just don't forget me."

"That won't happen."

But it did happen. Or so it seemed. It mattered, of course, that Jason was married. Much of the attraction of the man could perhaps be attributed to the pain she sensed inside. Jason would never abandon a soul that needed him. The helpless insanity of his wife, of whom he never spoke, bound Jason irrevocably. Samantha regretted their moment of passion. She thought it had driven them apart. It hurt deeply that Jason dared not trust himself and Samantha together.

Samantha had come from New Jersey to ski, and especially to learn the graceful art of powder skiing, with its nuances of the ethereal in human motion, floating and free. She first met Jason when he guided a helicopter tour into virgin powder.

By then she was an accomplished powder skier, but even she had thrilled to the rippling power and daring abandon of Jason's powder technique. A friend employed at Children's Hospital told Samantha about the child over lunch one day. After that Samantha would visit the girl every evening, except for rare days when she arranged a substitute and stole away to ski. Then one evening the child insisted, "I can ski too."

"Well, we'll ask the doctor."

The doctor nodded approval, so she phoned Jason and asked him to help. It had been perhaps the most joyous day of the tot's life, for Jason put her on his shoulders and skied all day in the warm sun. She loved it and loved Jason, so almost every night until the end, Jason would drive the long road down the canyon to Children's Hospital where the dying girl awaited him, giggling joy at his arrival.

The time had come to call Jason. It wasn't fair, but that's all she could do. A furious storm was descending upon Lucite. It would put him in a terrible spot, but Samantha couldn't help that. From now on the whole dreadful business would rest on his shoulders, not hers.

Chapter Six

Merlin turned right, following the gentle curve past Clementine Inn. It was partly cut off from the rest of Lucite by the ridge, but that didn't keep the Clementine from being about the nicest lodge in Lucite. They were customers of the Service Company but they wouldn't need gas today. Even so, Merlin was tempted to stop and josh with old lady Martin, the owner. She could out-cuss any Mormon in the valley, which was saying quite a bit. But there wasn't enough time today. Merlin had five stops. Better to get them done quickly and get the hell out of here.

He swung past the big day lodge on the right and turned into the service entrance of the sprawling new Jackhammer Motel. He noticed a big crowd in the day lodge, which was usually almost deserted at this time of day. Skiers figuring to pick up a quick lunch now, then go back to ski after the light got better. Dumb shits didn't realize it was going to get a lot worse before it got better.

Merlin rapped the counter at Jackhammer Lodge. '"Where's your lazy boss?"

Three pretty faces looked up, recognizing the voice.

"Hey, the gas jockey," said a girl he knew as Jean. "Hey, don't talk to us about lazy."

"I didn't say you was lazy."

"Where've you been? We're about to freeze."

'"Pay your bills and you'd get better service."

"Well hey, stop your leaking and we might pay the bills."

"Shouldn't talk dirty like that. Ham might hear."

"Well just think, you wouldn't have to climb out of a warm bed on Saturday."

"That old valve trick sells lotsa gas."

Jean put her hands on her hips and glared in mock anger. "Here comes Ham. You're in for it."

Hamilton Burkart had managed nearly every lodge in Lucite at some time or another. He'd be a little irritated anyway, so Merlin piled it on. "The energy shortage just don't mean a thing to rich folks."

'Well, the brain shortage does."

"You running short?" The girls giggled.

"What gives with your stupid gas company. Damned valve leaked out two-hundred pounds in ten days. If I ran a lodge that way we'd both be broke."

"That's lots of pollution. Government may close you down, then you won't have to worry about going broke." The girls giggled again, Merlin was getting the best of it.

'What's broke and better get fixed is your goddamn valve." Although a thin man, Hamilton had a strangely plump face with prominent jowls. He loved to josh, but could be hell on wheels if he became irritated. So keep it light.

"Well, what you expect. You turn the heat down to sixty, freeze these pretty girls here." He waved in their direction. "Means we're stuck with all that gas. We invented that leaky valve for bad guys who try to freeze people."

The girls cheered and clapped. Hamilton came close to a grin but Merlin could see that his friend wasn't much into the banter. Something besides a leaky valve was on his mind. He spoke soberly, "To tell the truth I was glad to see the old Jimmy. I think we're going to need that gas. The Weather Bureau don't seem excited but I say one hell of a storm is moving in." He lit a cigar and took two puffs, blowing them away from the girls. Ordinarily he would banter on and on with Merlin. Today he seemed a little wound-up and tense. "How's it look to you?"

"Like both barrels," said Merlin. "Those clouds are dark and the wind is from the southwest." He nodded grimly toward the girls. "If you're not over-booked, you're out of luck. I say the canyon will be avalanched-in by midnight."

"That's no problem. Every room in Lucite is booked. Most guests will be in by dinner. The lodges are in good shape."

"Then what you worried about?"

"I don't like a lot of snow when the canyon is full of skiers."

"Avalanches, eh?"

"That's part of it."

"Are they bad for business?"

"Hell no. Tourists love avalanches. Everybody who comes here wants to get cut off. No secret about it. They can hardly wait to get stranded in Lucite. It's part of the mystique of the place. Coffee?"

"Better go. I've still got stops at two lodges and Jake's place."

Hamilton frowned and seemed to hesitate, then he blurted out, "If you see Jake tell him what you told me about the weather I think he'll listen to you."

Merlin looked questioningly at Hamilton, who went on: "If it gets really bad we've gotta get these day skiers out. Jake hates to close early because Lucite Corporation doesn't much like taking back all those lift passes. I'd hate to make the decision, but when there's a big weekend snow we get one hell of a mess moving day skiers out and guests in. That's bad for the lodge business. It's tough enough to baby sit guests even with nobody else around."

"You baby sit adults?"

"Have to. They go nuts out here. Even the most respectable people go nuts. It's the macho thing. Everybody is out to prove something. Skiers are wild people."

"So relax. Let em raise hell?"

"You can't. Just this morning five dudes from here took off up Red Diggings Road on cross-country skis."

"Isn't that where those Boy Scouts got caught in a rock slide?"

"Exactly. It's been restricted ever since. No skiing allowed."

That's sure no place for flatlanders on a day like today."

"Not a damned thing I could do about it. A big redhead who claims to know the road took them out. He's a smart-alecky, real nasty bastard. We may all be out looking for those monkeys tonight."

"Tough shit. Just don't call me."

"You better get going. If you see Jake, don't say anything about those guys on Red Diggings. I don't want to cause trouble for my guests."

Merlin shivered as he filled the Jackhammer tanks. A great dark blanket had suddenly been drawn across both walls of Middle Aspen Canyon. The snow wasn't just falling, it was pouring from a gray sky. He could see barely fifty feet ahead as he groped for White Powder Lodge. Even as the road disappeared ahead he was getting a clear picture in his mind as to why Hamilton wanted to close the area early on such a day.

Merlin quickly filled the tank at White Powder then headed for Bluebird Lodge. He wished now he hadn't stayed so long at the Jackhammer. At the Bluebird he saw at least an inch more snow on the valve than he had brushed off at the White Powder. The stuff was really piling on. Well he was nearly finished. He'd make a quick call at Jake's house, then beat it to hell out of here. A couple of miles down the road and a few hundred feet lower should get him out of this shit. He'd never seen a big storm come up so fast.

It was getting surprisingly lighter as Merlin steered around the upper circle. There could be trouble pulling up the lane toward Jason's place so it was nice to see the storm lift a bit. Claim Jumper Road angled sharply right off Circle Drive to climb toward Clementine Ridge. No place to turn around in there, so Merlin had to drive past the skating rink into Jake's place, then back up all the way out again. If they knew it, the Service Company would make him stop deliveries there, so he kept his mouth shut. That was the least he could do for Jason Stemple.

Merlin remembered when he first started making deliveries in Lucite and Jason had begged a ride to town for a scruffy runaway kid from back east. It was against Service Company rules, but if Jason could go out of his way to help the kid, what the hell. The boy said Jason had given him bus fare to Denver and sent his Mom gas money to drive there and meet him. Merlin asked the kid if he really wanted to go home. The kid said, "Yeah. And I'll work for the rest of my life if I have to, so I can pay him back." Merlin doubted that, but the kid had said it like he meant it. He said Jason had taught him to ski powder and the experience was like discovering Jesus on a TV show.

Jason had that magical effect on people. He was sometimes a rough talker and nobody ever took Jason for a gentle person, but he had saved more souls than any two preachers or bishops around.

Seemed a shame that a guy like Jason had had such bad luck as to get stuck with a crazy wife.

The snow had eased almost to the point of stopping by the time Merlin came up to Jason's lane. Although there was little chance, he hoped Jason would be there so he wouldn't have to see Ellen. Merlin understood she looked pretty bad since getting back from the hospital. A pity. She had been a beauty once. Jason was foolish to keep bringing her home. They said she'd threatened the boy with a butcher knife before they put her away the last time. Now she was back home again.

The truck climbed nicely through the dry snow. As Merlin pulled up even with the tank a tall figure stepped out of the front door. Good, Jason's boy. Merlin wouldn't have to go inside. He grinned at the boy, who was already taller than his dad. He was clean-cut in appearance, but seemed to take after his mom, rather than Jason. "Okay, you ski freaks always want snow. I brought you some."

"Well, take it back. We only want snow at night."

Pleasant kid. Quick in the head. "Is your dad here?"

"No. There's a snow emergency in the village. Mother can write you a check for the gas."

"Forget it. We'll send a bill. I don't want to trouble your mother." Merlin watched a flush darken the face of the boy and was sorry he'd said that.

"Mother is okay."

"I mean on a day like this I don't want to bother anybody. Besides, it's best for me that I just hightail it on out of here."

The small tank filled in no time. Merlin quickly folded away the hoses and climbed into the truck.. Suddenly it was dark again. Snow was falling in big blinding flakes even thicker and faster than before.

Merlin checked the time: Fifteen past twelve.

The boy offered to guide him out but warned, "Take it slow. I can't see much."

It was slow going because Merlin could barely see the tracks he made coming in. The boy expertly waved him along: left, right, straight ahead. At the end of the lane, with Merlin safely back on Canyon Road, the boy waved. Merlin stuck his head out of the truck window and hollered, "Thanks a heap. Say hi to your folks for me."

"Sure will," the boy shouted back. He paused a moment, then ran up closer to the truck. "Be real careful. I never saw a storm like this." He was blinking away giant flakes in his face. "Maybe this is the time for a Killvein White."

Kind of a strange thing for a kid to say, thought Merlin as he pointed the Jimmy downhill and went through the gears. Maybe he's a little tetched like his mom. Killvein White. Merlin had heard the phrase. That was how old-time miners used to describe the Killvein Basin when snow bridged all the way across the draw and the trees disappeared. Merlin looked up. He could barely see the lowest part of Killvein even though he was at the base of it now. If that big draw ever filled with snow it would be something like old Lake Bonneville filling with water all over again. It would kill all the nearby world.

Merlin was still musing about it when he rounded the first S-curve at Helix Creek and saw a Ford Escort moving slowly toward him. It was almost at dead center in the road and turned slightly sideways, the wheels spinning wildly. There were two girls in the car. Their mouths open. They were terrified. The scene, through streaks of whiteness, hit Merlin like a hammer in the pit of his stomach. He expelled a sharp cry. In two seconds those young heads would be under his axle. Merlin swung the wheel sharply left. The trailer followed. Thank God: The Ford seemed to be floating by on the right. Merlin could hear the screams of the girls now. All wheels were locked. Suddenly the trailer was beyond the Ford but the road was all used up. There was only the canyon and empty space. Merlin thought of Hulda as he spun the wheel to the right. Jesus: The truck was skidding. It was still on the road but the trailer wasn't following. The trailer was pushing the cab toward the bank. Merlin spun the wheel again and cut the brakes. The rocks at the bank kept coming to meet him.

It was a slow, groaning crash that kept happening. The left front end seemed to melt away as the hood flew over the windshield. Then there was a wild breaking of glass as the trailer pushed the right rear of the cab toward Merlin. It was coming so very close. Any closer it would crush him. Then it stopped and everything stopped.

The silence was awesome. Only a sizzle, as great clouds of steam came rising out of the engine cavity, stretching up to meet the falling snow.

Chapter Seven

Matthew had barely finished putting his things away at the Jackhammer Lodge before Jason telephoned him. "Matt, heavy weather is on he way. I should stay around the station. Do you mind if we don't ski today?"

"That's okay. I'm already panting from the altitude."

"Come over to the station. I'll show you how we stay alive around here."

Matthew was astonished to step out into a swirling shower of big dry snowflakes. The air had about it an eerie feeling for winter: the heavy, clammy consistency of a summer cloudburst, except it was cold. A brisk wind blowing from the west caused Matthew to turn up the collar on his down jacket. A strong smell of impending storm had come into the air. It nagged his senses with a primordial alarm: *Gather the necessities of life. Seek shelter*. This was cockeyed weather. The sun shone brightly in Denver only a few hours ago.

The ranger station, a modest log veneer building, was set out of sight in a clump of spruce and aspen about forty steps from the base of chairlift number two. Its roof bristled with antennae. As Matthew approached he heard Jason on the telephone. "That's funny. I called George a half-hour ago. He didn't say anything about two fronts—only said we could expect snow from the southwest today."

Jason saw Matthew and motioned him inside. Matthew warmed himself by an old wood-burning stove that seemed incongruous beside the space-age communications gear spread on a bench along the south wall. A battery of dials showed above.

The stove, cherry red, radiated exuberant warmth, the kind one never feels from a heat register. Matthew enjoyed the feeling as he listened with little interest to bits and pieces of the conversation between Jason and a woman. Her soft, precise voice seemed to quicken as the conversation proceeded. The stove was throwing too much heat. Matthew guessed that explained the open door. Jason showed a keen interest and pried with questions. He was quite laudatory toward the woman. "Fascinating stuff. Good work on your part." Finally Jason said, "I understand. Thank you, Sam. I'm convinced. But of course I can't justify closing without some kind of an official forecast. I want you to talk with George. Tell him what you've told me. Say it's snowing hard up here. I'll call him again in a few minutes. Maybe he'll issue a realistic forecast."

A quick exchange followed. The woman apparently had Jason on the defensive. "Oh sure, I could do that," he said.

And then again, "Well, it's really not just a matter of guts." Followed by, "In a way, yes. But I'm also responsible to the tow operators." And finally, "I'm sorry to disappoint you." There was a brief final outburst, then the other party hung up just when Jason was about to say something.

Jason turned slowly to Matthew. "What color is skunk spray?"

"Yellow. I got a face-full once in scout camp."

"And what does mercenary mean?"

"Somebody who'll do anything for money. What's this all about?"

"I've just been called a skunk-piss mercenary."

"The voice sounded like a woman. Some lady."

"She grew up with six older brothers on a hill farm in New Jersey. When she gets irritated, look out. Right now she's mad as hell and really excited. I'd do almost anything for her, but I can't close the area just because she wants me to."

Jason sat by the stove looking glumly out the window. Matthew could see his friend had been in a conversation with someone he cared about and was distressed by its abrasive ending. Jason also seemed worried. Deep in thought, his eyes intently watched the falling flakes. "That's the kind of snow that causes me the most trouble," he mused. The flakes are big and dry but they're branched."

"That's bad?"

"Both good and bad. We don't need much dry snow to have avalanche conditions here. But branched snow resists sliding. It's more stable when you get a lot of weight on it. Makes you uncertain. Either way I don't like to see heavy morning snows in this canyon." Jason walked to the window, glared out for a moment then returned to warm his hands at the stove. "If Samantha is right we're in real trouble." He walked back to the window, peering intently at the buildup of snow outside on the sill. "I guess I'd better close the place."

He picked up the telephone and dialed quickly. "Hell, after all, she works for the Weather Bureau."

Matthew heard the other party answer with an explosive. "Hello."

"Ernie, this is Jake. Listen Ernie, something hellish is moving in. I hate to do this but I think you'd better close."

Jason listened a moment. "Ernie, all these day skiers have to get home tonight." There was a pause. Matthew could hear a rumble. Then came a longer pause then some more rumble. Finally Jason spoke again. "I'm responsible for these people, not the Weather Bureau. Ernie, I don't give a shit what they told you. We're about to get plastered. I'll alert the ski patrol. I want the slopes swept by one o'clock."

Another rumble, Jason listened then hung up and turned to Matthew. "Ernie said I'm rattled."

"A rattled yellow mercenary," Matthew smiled. "You got any friends at all here?"

Jason shook his head. "They're both credible sources. You want this job?"

Matthew studied his old friend for a moment. It was startling that he had changed very little in appearance over the years. A hint of gray in the sideburns, a squint in the eyes that wasn't there before, maybe an inch more waistline, and a slight droop at the shoulders. Other than that, it was the youthful Jason he remembered. His bearing was different, though. This Jason moved in a more measured and cautious way, as though burdened. His countenance had a gravity about it that didn't used to be there. His voice, more precise and steady now, had lost its dashed-off, lighthearted tone. This Jason was a more serious person, accustomed to taking control of himself and those around him.

"Does this kind of trouble always come up so fast?" Matthew asked.

"No. We usually have more time and better information. The bureau really blew this. It's going to be a big one. Three hours ago they were forecasting snow showers for the mountains."

"Why does this woman want you to close?"

"She has records that big dangerous storms have hit the Wasatch in a cycle of every thirty years and every sixty years that storm is twice as big. She says the worst kind skirted Lucite last time, but now another one is on the way and we are right in its path. Her theory seems weird but she's right about one thing. There's a little cemetery in the canyon just below town. Everybody there died on the same date 120 years ago this month."

"Well, was she right about the cycle?"

"Samantha is smart. She wouldn't be very far wrong about anything, but I think she's gone overboard this time. Twenty feet of snow—I just can't buy that. It would kill everybody in Lucite."

"You do see signs of a big snow?"

""No question. We could get three or four feet out of this."

"Enough for avalanches?"

"That's the main reason I want skiers off the slopes and day skiers out of the canyon. There's a slide course at Helix Creek just west of here that crosses the road to Salt Lake. After a big snow we try to shoot it in the early morning, then get debris cleared so traffic can move again by daylight. Another course runs parallel to Clementine Ridge. In a heavy snow the wind sometimes curls around from the north and a cornice wants to build up there. We don't let it happen because Clementine Lodge sits at the base of the avalanche and homes are in its path, including my own."

"Are those the worst?"

"No, not the worst, only the ones we worry most about. The worst ones don't slide very often. Wildcat Mountain used to be real dangerous, but it hasn't caused trouble in years. An avalanche on Savage Ski Run could hit Lucite if it built up. It's on the ski area anyway, so we don't let that happen. The biggest avalanche by far is Killvein Basin, but it's nothing we worry about. Legend says it sleeps for thirty years, wakes up and burps, then goes back to sleep. It's last burp was before my time. But even that wasn't much of a slide, at least it didn't kill anybody. The last big slide was more than a century ago, before the First World War. I know that because it was a killer. According to the law of averages we don't have to worry much about Killvein. The miners were plenty scared of it, though. I guess with good reason. That big one killed a lot of 'em."

Matthew stood and walked to the door. The snow was streaking down. At least six inches had built up on the step since he entered the station. The flakes were also bigger, sliding past the eye like textured white paper on a printing press. As Matthew watched, the top inch of a stubby spruce disappeared under a layer of white.

"Jesus," he said over his shoulder to Jason. "I've never seen snow come down this fast. It surely can't keep this up?"

Jason nodded. Matthew didn't know if that meant he agreed or not, but Jason was clearly. worried. Suddenly Jason stood, eyes narrowing, to peer at something in the dimming light. He reached for the telephone and snapped into the receiver, "Ernie, why are you still loading chair number two?"

A short pause, then Matthew heard his friend growl angrily into the telephone. It wasn't like Jason. "Son-of-a-bitch. Close those lifts and don't ever do anything like that again."

He slammed down the receiver. Maybe Ernie was right. Jason did appear just a little bit rattled. Jason sat scowling for a moment, then picked up the short-wave mike and called out a code that included a headquarters designation. A female voice came in: "That you Jake?"

"Yeah, Vera. Get me Bruce."

"Jake, he's on the telephone. I think it's the Weather Bureau." Then she lowered her voice almost to a whisper. "You're mad, aren't ya?"

"A little, but not at you."

Her voice picked up. "Well, be nice to Bruce. He shouldn't even have to work today. I think somebody from the ski corporation called him at home." Then she whispered again. "Hey, this is the second time he's called the bureau."

"Thanks, Vera. Get his attention. I want to talk, now."

A man's voice came in. The accent was southern, not south Texas, but southern. Matthew could tell the difference instantly. These were inflections of a man born and raised a southerner, then long removed. "Jake boy, I was about to call you."

"Instead you called the Bureau."

He seemed to ignore what Jason was saying. "I heard that you were thinking about closing the area."

"Well, what you heard isn't accurate. I did close the area."

"I talked with the corporation. They couldn't understand it. Not a bit. like I say, I was going to call you."

"I've been right here."

"Jake, the Weather Bureau told me this front dropped most of its moisture across Arizona. It could lift almost anytime. Now Jake, the Forest Service will look pretty foolish if we have four thousand skiers driving back home in the sunshine. Don't you think so?"

"You reversed my order."

"Well, I had to. I just told you why I had to do it."

"The bureau can't make these decisions, Bruce."

"They didn't. I made the decision."

"It doesn't matter what decision you made. The tows are closing."

Again the man seemed to ignore what Jason was saying. "What's the weather doing now?" he asked. His voice, amplified through the speaker, was starting to sound more southern.

"The snow has stopped," Jason answered.

Startled, Matthew turned to glance out the open door. It wasn't snowing anymore. Shit. This could mean trouble for Jason.

"That's what I thought." said Bruce, the accent diminishing again. "Now for God sake settle down Jake. We all know you have a lot of responsibility there and sometimes you get rattled a little. We can all forget this. Call Ernie, verify that he can keep the lifts moving. You don't even need to tell him we've discussed it."

"I'll tell Ernie that if he doesn't stop the tows in five minutes I'll arrest him."

"Jake, now listen Jake. You stay right there at the station. I think you're wore out. I'll drive to Lucite and take over. Don't you dare talk to Ernie." His accent was getting very southern again.

"I'll be at the station," Jason told him.

Jason hung up the mike and walked to the big topographical map on the east wall. He studied it intently for perhaps thirty seconds, then spoke without turning around. "Well, Matt, I guess it wasn't a very good time for you to come."

"I'm glad I was around to hear the way you handled that son-of-a-bitch. Is he going to be a problem?"

"He'll never make it up here. It just means I'll have to follow his orders until the snow starts again. It means Ernie can stay open for a while longer. It means I can relax and visit with you without having to worry about a goddamn thing." Regardless of what he said, Matthew could see apprehension in Jason's eyes and he knew his friend wasn't anxious about the man called Bruce.

Jason dropped some fresh wood into the cast-iron stove and filled the coffee pot. "We've got a long afternoon to kill. May as well have some coffee and take it easy."

In a moment the coffee was ready. Jason poured, then collected a scattering of papers on his desk and put them into a neat pile. He checked the dials over the radio bench and made some notes. He sat across the stove from Matthew and put his feet on a stool. "Matt, I need your help with Ellen."

Matthew was startled. He hadn't expected that. He thought Ellen had disappeared into a rest home or sanitarium years ago, but he quickly recovered.

"How is Ellen?"

"Ellen has mental problems. They keep coming back."

Matthew stood to put a hand on Jason's shoulder. His friend had thrown away a lifetime of dreams because of a promiscuous girl. Just now he had been set upon by two friends, overruled and insulted by his boss. A dangerous storm threatened Lucite. But here was Jason sipping coffee and worrying about an old whore gone crazy. Matthew had a fleeting thought that he wanted to help. There was something almost epic here, beyond compassion, even beyond love. That was only for a second. He was too sensible to become a part of this. These were Jason's problems and they were Jason's kind of problems.

"I'm really sorry, Jake."

"I guess you've heard that Ellen has been committed, off and on."

"Well, yes. But I thought the commitment was permanent."

"It looked that way. She stayed three years once. Then a very bright doctor got interested in her case and worked miracles with Ellen. But I better back up a little." Jason's voice sounded clipped as if he suffered from pain or fatigue. His face was averted so Matthew couldn't see his eyes, but he guessed they were closed.

"Right after we got married I had an awful time with Ellen. I worked as edger-man at a sawmill in Dillon. It was damned hard. Before I toughened up there were days I didn't think I could hack it. You and I, we thought we were pretty tough, but we didn't know the meaning of tough. I learned all about that on the sawmill. Ellen hated the mill and hated me working there. Once she ran away. I had to take a week off to find her and almost got fired for it. Another time during the spring, she tried to drown herself in the Blue River by walking across thin ice. She was saved by a big dog that crawled out on the ice and grabbed her shoulder in his jaws. It was incredible, and even more incredible that the baby survived, because Ellen was eight months pregnant.

"Matt, I'm only telling you this because the doctor said I should."

"Go on," said Matthew, suddenly on guard.

"After the baby came, Ellen was a new person altogether. She loved the baby, she loved me and she loved being married. It was a new life for us both.

"Jesus, what happy years we had. You couldn't know how great it was to be married to a happy woman like that. I had a summer job with the Forest Service and a ski school job at Arapaho for the winter. It was something different, winter and summer. I enjoyed that. We got by just fine and had a hell of a good life together.

"Ellen's problems came back when David was about eight years old. For weeks at a time she wouldn't talk to either of us. After about a year of that, I came home one day and she had tied David to a chair and was holding a mirror in front of his face. She had forced him to look at himself for hours. It was weird and terrifying.

"She finally asked to be committed.

"She was gone three years. When they released her we had great hopes for Ellen. For a while she was good and beautiful again but then she started staring. Matt, she would sit and stare at either David or me. If we moved, she would follow us and never say a word, only stare. One day she threatened David with a knife. After we put her back in the institute she was hysterical for days. That's when they brought in the new doctor and he started helping Ellen.

"Matt, it was beautiful to see the old spirit come back to Ellen. This doctor helped her because he told her what was wrong and she believed him.

"He helped me understand it too. He was the first to really tell me what was wrong with Ellen. One part of her mind hated our son. The other part loved him.

"I've never told this to anyone, Matt."

"Go on."

"It was a tug and pull between love and hate that killed her mind. She was insane with it." Jason paused then. Matthew thought he wanted to continue but didn't quite know how. A burned-out log crumbled inside the stove, shooting a noisy shower of sparks.

"I'm really sorry for Ellen and for you," said Matthew.

"Matt." The voice very tired and not sounding like Jason. "Please take our boy to Houston for a while. The doctor said if you'll do that we can save Ellen."

"I'm surprised, why me?"

"Ellen told the doctor about you. He said no one else could help. That's why I asked you to come."

"I'll help any way I can."

A few scattered flakes were falling outside. It was still darkly overcast but lighter than a half-hour ago. Jason shoved another log in the stove and poured two cups of coffee. As he sat the pot down, someone hailed him from outside the cabin. Jason opened the door, "Come in, Ernie." A stubby man came inside. He was wearing a wolf-skin coat and he tugged off a Cossack cap as he approached the stove. Jason introduced him to Matthew. The man was eager to talk.

"Jake I didn't call Bruce Lerner. You know I wouldn't do that."

"I know." Jason said. "Who did?"

"Doc. Tartor. He's on the board of directors of the stockholders group. He was standing over my shoulder when you called."

"I know Doc. I'm surprised he'd go over my head that way."

"Ordinarily he wouldn't. But he's a friend of Buford Harris at the Weather Bureau. He called Buford and Buford told him you were getting unauthorized forecasts from a girl at the bureau."

"Sorry to hear that," muttered Jason. "I guess Sam is in trouble, too."

"Why do you say too?"

"I've been told to rest. Bruce Lerner is coming up to take over."

"That's a joke. Lerner, he don't know a ski pole from a pitchfork."

"We'll find out. You and your boss really fixed things up pretty well."

"Okay Jake, I should have tried to stop Doc. But anyway you were wrong to take what the girl said as gospel. She must be some humdinger to influence you that way."

"It wasn't just what she said. From the start I never liked the looks of this."

"Then you were both wrong. Just like Rose thought it would, the storm is lifting."

"You'd better take another reading," said Jason softly.

Ernie and Matthew had their backs to the open door. They turned to see that it was dark again, even darker than before, and giant flakes were pouring down, pushed swirling by a chill breeze. They all three walked to the door and peered out into the lost world of Lucite. Even the big Jackhammer Lodge had disappeared into the swirl of white.

Finally Ernie spoke. "Shit. I'm closing right now." As he walked beyond the threshold the telephone rang. Jason answered, listened a moment then hung up and stepped quickly to the door.

"Hey Ernie. Just a minute." Ernie heard and started back. "Ernie, a truck just wrecked on Helix Creek. They say the road's blocked."

Ernie stood motionless. It was like one frame of a movie out of context, except he kept blinking as the onslaught of flakes hit him squarely in the cheeks and forehead. He wasn't so far away but what Matthew could discern on his face something beyond apprehension. Call it fear or panic. But only for the moment just before he wheeled and disappeared running, into the sea of snow..

Chapter Eight

Jason was talking on the short-wave when Matthew left the station to grope his way to the day lodge. He wanted a cigar and thought he might buy one there. Anyway, he knew it would be filling with skiers and he would enjoy eavesdropping on the kind of disaster stories skiers always tell on stormy days. At this hour the crowd would be jovial. He could escape the atmosphere of crisis that had descended on the station as it suddenly filled with an assortment of tense ski patrolmen, instructors, tow operators, and lodge owners.

It would be pleasant to pass the time with a bit of solitary girl watching, something he always enjoyed doing in a crowd. Of course being slightly shy, approaching middle-age, and very much executive, he knew he shouldn't get kicks out of watching pretty girls. But in a crowd, Matthew could do as he pleased and he happened to be very pleased when his eyes could caress pretty skiers. Matthew remembered skiing as the most Freudian of sports, perhaps because male and female were equally adept and seemed to enjoy it most together. It was the rites of winter. Its sensual atmosphere was enough to turn even half-blind, crotchety old men into hot-eyed girl watchers.

The day lodge was certainly the most impressive structure in the village. Its roundness reminded Matthew of the Astrodome in miniature. On a clear day the view either south or north would be magnificent because of the great floor-to-ceiling glass walls on both sides. Even to the east and west, glass transoms would allow marvelous views of the main ridge of the high Wasatch and the rugged outcroppings on Clementine Ridge as it plummeted toward the canyon bottom.

But today there wasn't a view, only a great dark blanket enveloping the lodge. This is what a caged canary would see if it were wrapped in crepe paper for a Christmas present. A great white tongue crept up along the glass wall. The wind-blown snow had snaked upward nearly twenty feet in one place. Matthew shuddered.

The lodge was filling fast. Maybe five-hundred skiers, maybe more, were already tramping about, duck-like, heavy-footed in the rotunda. Many were sitting at the massive steel tables, sipping drinks, removing boots, moaning, combing, snapping, wiping, rubbing, all the things that skiers at rest always do, and piling the tables high with trappings of the sport: gloves, parkas, scarves, caps, belts, goggles, liners, warm-up suits, after-ski boots, maps, and of course the pharmaceuticals, lotion, salve, bandages.

It was a great and colorful example of the American devotion to outfitting, which was okay with Matthew. *This snow keeps up they may need every piece of it.*

Matthew lit the cigar he had stood in line to buy, enjoying the animated, excited sounds around him. A girl at the end of the bench where he was sitting was giving a companion, who had just arrived, the "situation report."

"The lifts are all closed but nobody can leave yet because there's a wreck in the canyon. A guy is trapped in a truck. His foot is caught in some kind of mangled stuff. They have to cut it out with torches but they can't start 'cause the gas tank was smashed in the wreck. There's gas all around so they have to wait until it's evaporated to cut the poor guy out."

Matthew was surprised at the accuracy of her information. He thought they had been trying to keep the worst part quiet, but this kid seemed to know everything the rangers knew.

"So, what's the deal?" her companion asked.

"Well—they've blocked all the exits from the parking lots. They're not letting anybody out. Cars can't come up the road either. That's kind of exciting?"

"Hey, great, this should be over pretty quick. We can get back on the slopes with some nice powder to bust."

The young couple moved on, jostled by the growing crowd. Their place was quickly taken by a striking black girl, who piled two sets of mittens on one stool and sat gracefully on the next one. Nicest rump Matthew had seen today. In a moment she was joined by a slender, well-formed man, very dark and impeccably dressed for skiing. He carried a small canvas bag with CREW stenciled on the side. This handsome couple would scarcely have been noticed at a Houston restaurant or discotheque, but here they were drawing attention. They weren't just skiers but the only blacks in a colorful but very white crowd.

Matthew was musing that Utah skiing was pretty much a lily-white Nordic sport at just the moment when a huge Nordic type came through the crowd toward him. The man was close to six-six, with short-cropped, blond hair and wildly freckled face. He would weigh at least two fifty. His frame carried a little thickness around the girth, otherwise it was bone and muscle—quite a specimen. Matthew judged him a farmer or maybe steel worker. A covey of boys followed the giant, about age fourteen, dodging and pushing through the crowd, trying not to get left behind. Each seemed tiny in comparison to the rather eccentrically dressed giant, who probably was derived from the Danish race.

Big Danish asses are bad for girl-watching. Matthew was silently fussing even as he realized that the big guy was addressing him. "I hear the road's shut down."

Matthew wasn't at all sure he wanted to be the bearer of bad news in this case, but he told the giant what he knew. The boys gathered 'round. Their occasional expletives as they listened drew withering stares from the big Dane. When Matthew finished he said, "Sounds pretty bad." Then he addressed the kids. "You heard that. We'll hang together and leave here as soon as the road opens up. Conference tomorrow, can't chance getting stranded." To Matthew he said, "I worry when it starts to snowing like this up here. Not for myself. I've been skiing here for twenty years, but about being responsible for these young folks."

"You from Salt Lake?" asked Matthew.

"North of there, a little place by Ogden."

"I take it you're a scoutmaster?"

"Nope. These boys are mostly scouts but we're all Mormons. I'm bishop of the Henderson ward. That's out in the country a piece."

"I guessed you were on a scout outing."

"Not that. These boys are all deacons in the ward." He scanned the young faces encircling Matthew, put a burly arm around the unlucky ones on each side, squeezed and beamed. "This is the best crop we ever had. Not a one of them smokes or drinks."

"I guess that's kind of rare nowadays," ventured Matthew, feeling a bit embarrassed that the conversation was attracting attention.

"You bet. I'm real proud. That's why I brought the whole bunch to Lucite for today. Everything paid, by me." And he squeezed again until the two trapped under his burly arms grimaced. "We'll get out of here, don't worry," he told the boys.

As they wandered off looking for a place to sit, Matthew glanced in the direction of the black couple. He was startled to see that the slim man had assumed the insolent stance of a ghetto black. He was sitting on the table, feet wrapped around his chair back, staring contemptuously into the face of the passing bishop. Matthew wondered, searching his memory. There was something here, a kind of doctrinaire animosity between Mormons and blacks. It was maybe similar to the trouble between Arabs and Jews. He would ask Jason.

The day lodge was nearly packed now, chairs long since taken. Skiers were standing between tables and around the walls. The great windows had fogged from the multitude of respirations. Snow frosted incoming skiers, so clearly the storm continued.

Matthew stood and stretched. Maybe Jason could use some company. By now the congestion might have cleared out of the ranger station. He started out, weaving through the steaming mass. The mood of the crowd wasn't so festive anymore, but there was no sign of impatience or apprehension. Skiers were used to storms.

Near the door, a young man in a dripping parka had drawn a crowd. As he talked to one group they melted away and others took their places. Matthew drew closer and heard him say that the truck was out and the road cleared. "They're plowing it now. All the day skiers have to leave the area. They want the parking lots empty by three, only forty minutes from now. Ten miles downhill the highway is plumb dry."

Matthew stepped out of the day lodge into a different world than the one he had left less than an hour ago. The porch and steps had disappeared under a white pathway, itself packed nearly four feet beneath two rising walls of snow. The scene was halfway between light and dark, an eerie kind of dusk with afternoon light reflecting upward from the great fields of white, giving illumination and dimension to the falling flakes.

Was there no end to this? He wondered about the woman in Salt Lake who had predicted much worse. Matthew pitied the day skiers. Thank God he didn't have to drive out in this. An army of skiers crowded the walkway leading toward the big parking lots, moving slowly, loaded with skis and gear. Imagine the mess in the parking lot. He missed where a trail forked toward the ranger station, so re-traceed his steps. On the way back he noticed two of the bishop's deacons standing, heads together, where the walks forked, screened from the day lodge by the great pile of snow scraped from the lodge deck. They were taking turns puffing a cigarette, carefully shielding each draw inside cupped hands and blowing the smoke downwind.

Matthew could hear loud voices as he approached the station. It seemed Jason was still catching hell, but talking back with a good deal of authority in his voice. Maybe even Jason had come to realize that kindness might not be compatible with crisis.

"We don't need calculus to figure this." It was Jason. "At rush hour the slide will hit one car for every two feet of cornice. That calculation is from ten years ago when cars were bigger. By my reckoning, the cornice is about twenty-one feet now. The avalanche will release at some point between twenty and twenty-eight feet. Some of the cars will be close enough to the bank on the outside S-turn that the avalanche will slide across the top of them. If we're lucky and quick, we can save those people. At least ten cars will drop into the canyon with the slide. On Saturdays in March there's an average of two-and-three-eighths people per car out of Lucite. Nobody is going to live through that dive. There's no way I'll open the road unless the storm lifts and we can get a better reading on the Helix cornice."

Jason noticed Matthew standing at the stoop then and motioned him inside.

Matthew shook hands with a uniformed deputy and a very tall, somewhat weather-beaten, gray-haired woman. "Alice Morton. She owns the Clementine Lodge." He'd met the third visitor that morning, Hamilton Blake of the Jackhammer Inn. They exchanged nods and a quick handshake, but Hamilton wasn't interested in Matthew. He was angry and venting that anger at Jason.

"I can understand why you didn't shoot the Helix avalanche. It might have killed Merlin. But Merlin has been out for a half hour already. Why haven't you just shot the goddamn slide?"

"When they got him out, it was too late to shoot. The cornice would spill over the highway. It takes two hours to clear the road, and by then there's another cornice. Ham, our only chance is for the weather to lift."

"Have you faced up to what can happen if we get four thousand day skiers trapped here in the canyon?"

"Well, have you? I warned the association two years ago that it could happen."

"Let's forget that a minute. I don't believe this doomsday bull shit about twenty-five dead people in a Helix avalanche."

"Hell no you don't. Day skiers are expendable anyway."

"Well, we've heard enough of your theories. I've got some reality. You'd better get four thousand people out of Middle Cottonwood damned quick, because there isn't any place for them here." His voice was rising.

"Well," said Jason, "they're sure as hell not going down Canyon Road. Not with that cornice hanging up there."

""Look," insisted Hamilton, "I've got a theory of my own. I say the Helix avalanche is a Forest Service plaything. You can shoot it with artillery and bring down lots of snow. But not one of us in this room has ever seen a natural avalanche on Helix Creek."

"Ham, that's a dangerous notion. You've never seen a natural avalanche there because we don't wait that long. We bring them down. Have you ever seen a busted appendix?"

"Once."

"What happened?"

"The guy died."

It was grim humor, but a chuckle went around the room, breaking some of the tension. Jason didn't smile. He sat in stony silence, eyes focused beyond the window.

"What do you think, Alice?" he asked, without looking at her.

"I think it doesn't make any goddamn difference what I think. You, you stubborn son-of-a-bitch, you'll do what you want to do anyway."

"Do you think the Helix avalanche is a delusion of mine?"

Alice sighed and threw up her hands. "Yeah, probably."

"What about the Clementine Ridge avalanche?"

A long, uncomfortable silence followed. Finally Alice answered, "You win, Jake. None of us wants to take a chance that might kill somebody. Some of those day skiers can stay at my place. Of course I'll have to charge a little."

Jason turned to the deputy. "I understand most cars in the day parking lot have been dug out and started."

"That's right."

"How many deputies are in Lucite?"

"Just me."

"Okay. Here's what you do: Deputize some ski patrol. Circulate around to every lane. Get those people out of their cars. Tell them they can go home as soon as the weather improves enough for their personal safety."

"That's a tough job, Jake. Everybody wants to be first in line. There's no space for them in the day lodge. Why do they have to leave their cars?"

"Because every hour there's another foot of snow. We might not be able to get them out later. These young skiers have old cars and combustion isn't good at this altitude. I don't want any dead kids in those cars. You see to that. You're responsible for those kids."

"But I told you, Jake, there's not enough room in the day lodge for them."

"I didn't say they all have to go there."

"Where, then?"

"Tell them they're welcome to use the lobby and dining room at the Jackhammer and Clementine Lodges."

Alice gasped, "Hey. I said they could sleep at my place. That's all."

And Hamilton roared, "Nothing doing."

Ignoring them, Jason spoke directly to the deputy. "You're to arrest anyone who interferes."

Hamilton interrupted, stammering. "Jake, you'll ruin my business. The lodge guests won't stand for this."

Jason waited calmly until the outburst ended, otherwise seeming to pay no attention. He addressed the deputy again. "Have you any handcuffs?"

"In the patrol car."

"Good. Bring anyone arrested to the station here and handcuff them to the drain Pipe in the back room. Now go clear those cars."

Hamilton cut in: "Do me one favor, Jake. Before you give these kids a blank check to take over the lodges, let's call the Bureau once more. This could lift."

"I'm willing." Jason dialed a number, then spoke into the receiver. The occupants of the ranger station made no attempt to hide their interest in the conversation, which was punctuated by long pauses as the unseen party talked. Matthew gathered a secretary was telling Jason something about a reprimand. Jason kept asking about Samantha, so Matthew concluded that Jason's friend the statistician was into some trouble with her boss.

Finally Jason said, "Keep trying to get her and tell her to call me here at the ranger station. Now let me talk to George Rose."

He was crisp and abrupt with Rose. "I hope you know what's going on here. How much more of this can we expect?" Jason questioned him sharply about the two fronts, pointing out that the Bureau must have known about them yesterday. At least Samantha did. Then Jason seemed to soften, telling George that of course Samantha should have discussed the two fronts in detail with him instead of Buford. And he added in a friendly and compromising tone, "Uh, George, this business of a letter of reprimand That could be awful embarrassing to the bureau.You'll talk to Buford and get it stopped of course."

Then he asked if Buford were at the Bureau, and after hearing the answer barked angrily into the telephone "That figures. Well, here's a message for you to pass along when you do see him. Tell that son-of-a-bitch to come to Lucite and sit under these avalanches and do his forecasting from here. He'll get smarter quick. And he'll start listening to... hello... hello?"

Jason looked around questioningly.

"Goddamn phone's dead."

There was a startled silence around the room. Then Hamilton observed, "Lights are out too. What the hell is wrong here?" He moved to the door to peer out into the whiteness. "All the lights are out. I can't see a damned one."

The short-wave emitted a rumble of static, followed by a voice, hoarse and nervous. "Come in Jake." Jason moved quickly to the radio and picked up the mike.

"I'm here. That you, Barney?"

"Yeah, I'm at the plow station." There was excitement in his voice. "Jake, Helix just slid. It's really big. Some of the snow went over the east fence. I think it took out the hi-line the relay station, and the phone wire."

"Is everybody okay?" asked Jason.

"Yeah. We're all together here but a little shook. That's a bad one Jake. It brought a chunk of mountain along with it. There are some big rocks and trees in there."

"Barney, stay where you are. Don't start any clearing until you hear from me. Is your phone working?"

"Jist a minute...Yeah, we get a buzz."

"Make sure somebody stays with the radio. You'll have to relay to Salt Lake for us."

Jason turned to the stunned trio in the station. Nobody seemed ready to say anything or hear anything. Jason crammed some wood into the stove. It emitted a sparkling roar, a warm comfortable sound, breaking the silence of the room. Matthew thought that none of them had ever projected beyond the possibility of avalanche. These were practical people, never really believing in the unexpected. They would have to think about the avalanche for a while before talking about it. Finally Jason spoke, almost to himself. "We've never seen spill even close to the plow station before."

"Jake, I'm scared as hell," said Alice.

"So am I," said Jason. Then he turned to Hamilton. "Get some help, Ham. Round up all the lodge execs. I want everybody here in half an hour."

Hamilton nodded. He stood to leave, then approached Jason. He put a hand on Jason's shoulder and squeezed. "You know how big I feel right now."

"Just get going," said Jason. Then he was on the radio calling someone at the ski patrol. "This is Jake. Get over here quick."

Chapter Nine

A husky young man came out of the storm, jogging toward the station. He had heavy eyebrows and a Wyatt Earp mustache. He nodded to Alice Morton and shook hands with Matthew. Jason introduced Edwin Laverne, head of the ski patrol.

"Ed, you know the Helix avalanche just released?"

Edwin nodded, "I heard Barney on the radio."

"How many drive-in skiers are here today?"

"At last count, Ernie had refunded money to about three thousand. Another five hundred were standing in line, and you have to count on about five hundred season ticket holders. I'd say around four thousand."

"There are seven hundred beds here and the lodges are full. Would eleven hundred guests be about right?"

"I'd say so."

Jason shoved a paper pad at Matthew. "I want a quick inventory of all the food in Lucite. Go with Ed. Start at the Jackhammer. Tell the cook that I have ordered you to confiscate all food because of the emergency. Make a list, and do it quick, of everything edible in his locker. Have him sign the list. Tell him it's prison for anyone who uses food without written authorization from me. Then go to the Clementine and do the same thing. As quick as you can, inventory every lodge and the cafe. Now for God's sake hurry. I don't want any food to disappear. We may need every bite of it before this is over."

Matthew and Edwin trotted to the intersection. They were slowed by a host of skiers moving toward the parking lot, compressed into a crowd by walls of snow. The path was getting narrower as the snow banks rose higher. Where the day lodge trail intersected with the main road, Matthew could see the heads of only the tallest skiers across the high snow bank. But a forest of ski tips moved through the falling snow. These people couldn't know yet that they were trapped in a shaft. They would learn soon enough, perhaps too soon.

When Matthew and Edwin reached the Jackhammer, the lights had gone on again. Edwin explained that a standby generator was maintained for such emergencies. At the Jackhammer, the chef was surprised but cooperative. They counted twenty boxes of twelve pork chops each, thawed for dinner. There were thirty-two frozen turkeys, and a hundred pounds of trout from Green River Fish Farm. They found about a hundred-and-fifty pounds each of ham and bacon. Altogether, it was about a three-day supply for lodge guests, the chef told them.

Edwin admonished the chef to keep his mouth shut for a while to avoid a panic. Then they hurried to the Clementine. Matthew expressed surprise that the lodge had only a three-day supply of food. Edwin shrugged. "They store it in Salt Lake. Electricity and space are costly here."

"That's why Jake is worried?"

"Absolutely. We'll be lucky to find enough for even one good meal all around. Goddamn storm better lift quick or we're in a heap of trouble."

As Edwin and Matthew left Clementine Inn, day skiers started pouring into the lobby, grumbling that the patrol wouldn't let them start for Salt Lake, or even let them sit in their cars. Somebody wanted to know why neither land or cell phones were working. Edwin lied that he didn't know and they moved on quickly. Matthew's watch showed four o'clock when they finished the inventory at the Downhill Cafe. They paused near the door to wrap up and heard the owner tell a customer, "They're closing me down. The Helix avalanche slid. The road's blocked. Everybody's gonna spend the night in the village."

It didn't seem to matter now. They had only one call left. At the day lodge, they had to walk through hip-deep snow to get to the service door in the rear. The door was locked. Edwin knocked until it opened and a small nervous man greeted them. He seemed to know Edwin but there was no friendship between the two. He told them that he had nothing left. "The crowd cleaned me out," he said. "I've already closed the kitchen."

"We'll have a look anyway," Edwin informed him.

They found nothing in the locker, but a long deepfreeze was filled with cartons of hamburger patties and three-hundred pounds of frozen wieners. Under a shelf they counted fifteen five-gallon cans of chili beans. "Why didn't you tell us?" demand Edwin.

"Let's face it," said the man, "I know the road's blocked. I can get a lot more money for that stuff tomorrow than Jake will pay. You guys forget you saw this and there'll be plenty here for us all. No matter how long the storm takes."

Edwin gripped the man and shook him until his spectacles fell off. Matthew had to separate them. He admired Edwin for refusing to be put off. In an emergency like this Edwin could be a good man to have around.

They left the day lodge and hurried toward the ranger station. It was four o'clock but the darkness of night was descending on Lucite. Matthew could see bright pyramids of falling snow under each light along the path. Beyond that he could only feel the flakes as they continued to pelt his face and neck.

At the station they were surprised to find Jason alone. The meeting with lodge executives had been short and much was decided, Jason reported. Women and children would be sheltered in guest lodges. They would sleep at least eight per room. Men and boys age twelve and over would occupy the day lodge and the Clementine Inn. A medical center with volunteer doctors had been set up at Bluebird Lodge. It was already occupied by three patients with broken legs from skiing that day. Merlin Landis was also there with his mangled foot.

Each lodge was to furnish four blankets per room for use in the day lodge, which would be crowded, very crowded, but there was no alternative. The guest lodges would also be dangerously overcrowded. A committee of lodge owners would determine food allocation based on Matthew's inventory. All liquor had already been ordered locked away from the public. Jason had appointed an old powder skiing friend, name of Olsen (also known to Edwin) to organize a detail of volunteers from the day lodge. They would shovel trails and roads to be sure of free passage between all the stores and lodges of Lucite. Ski patrol and ski school people were not to be assigned any detail. It was necessary to keep them available for rescue and avalanche control. Jason had dispatched a second man to the artillery site on Grizzly Peak with sleeping bags and enough food so both men could spend the night and tomorrow too if necessary.

The short-wave interrupted Jason. "Come in Jake."

"I read you, go ahead."

"Jake, I've got a message from Bruce Lerner. He says tell you he tried to drive up today but got stuck. He didn't make it back to Salt Lake till just now. He says in an emergency like this you should go ahead and take charge without him. What's he talking' about, Jake?"

"A long story. Is Lerner still on the phone?"

"Yeah."

"Tell him he's badly needed here. I think he should try again to come up."

After a pause, Barney was back on the radio. "Jake, he wants to know when."

"Tonight," said Jason, and hung up the microphone.

At four-fifteen the deputy reported in that all day skiers had vacated their cars and were gathering in the lodges. Everybody seemed to know about the Helix avalanche. But most didn't know yet that they were trapped for the night.

Jason wanted to shoot the Clementine Ridge avalanche before a lot of movement started between the lodges. It was a Forest Service policy not to shoot the south facing slopes when skiers were massed below. Unlikely, but possibly a piece of shrapnel could fall among them, or the shock could set off an avalanche directly above the main concentration of lodges. The Clementine avalanche was no threat at this stage. Jason calculated it would dissipate or pile up on Higgins Flat after only about 1500 vertical feet of travel. It was the most predictable of the Lucite avalanches. So long as artillery kept bringing the cornice down before it reached critical depth, the slide would drop to the flat and pile up harmlessly.

In the years before wealthy businessmen and Salt Lake City doctors started building cottages and summer homes along lower Clementine Ridge, nobody worried much about the avalanche. Then one night, twelve years ago, it inadvertently released from a shot on Wildcat. There was more snow in it than anybody believed. By the time the avalanche came to Higgins Flat it had so much momentum that it scooted across the flat, hooked around the western slope of the ridge and slammed into the south wing of Clementine Lodge. It collapsed an empty bedroom, crossed the corridor and crashed into the room where Alice Martin slept.

Rangers and ski patrolmen laughed about it now, but it had been terrifying at the time. When they dug Alice out she was unconscious. She was also naked. Suspecting a bed-partner, they dug further and found the assistant bartender, young, very slender and very shy. He too was naked but conscious, through slightly stunned and very frightened. Legend had it that when they explained what happened he was wildly relieved. "Thank God," he had sobbed. "I thought I'd been sucked in."

Legend also had it that old Lady Martin, once the hot mamma of Lucite, had been an ascetic ever since. She told somebody that having experienced the heights of ecstacy the only thing left was poor anticlimax.

Jason had instructed the rangers on Grizzly Peak to shoot the Clementine cornice at four-thirty. Then they were to allow forty minutes for inter-lodge movement before shooting the Wildcat Mountain avalanche.

The movement of men out of the central lodges and women in must go quickly and smoothly because the Wildcat shot shouldn't be delayed beyond five-thirty at the latest. If the snow kept falling at the current rate, by six-thirty there was a mathematical chance that the avalanche might spill all the way to Bluebird and Angel Lodges, in which case everybody would need shelter before the shot. Because Bluebird Lodge wasn't equipped with a basement, they would have to move people from there to the Blue Spruce basement, which would be perilously over-crowded. Anyway, Jason didn't want inter-lodge movement after dark, a dangerous procedure when avalanches threaten. It was bad enough to be moving people in the semi-twilight of the storm. He instructed, even lectured, each lodge owner by radio on the importance of the schedule.

Matthew accompanied Edwin to the day lodge, where Edwin stood on a table with a bullhorn and told a hushed audience what had happened and what would be required. Instructors from the ski school were standing by to guide the women in groups to the guest lodge just as soon as the avalanche was down. A strange silence fell over the great room. They waited, shuffling and whispering, perhaps thinking they might hear the announced shot. Finally, Edwin asked the women to begin gathering at the north door, and for the first time that day, Matthew sensed an uneasy tension among the skiers. This was not a lark anymore. Nobody would be going home tonight. A fierce storm was threatening, literally, to bury them, and in minutes families, friends, loved ones would be separated. It wasn't fear; these skiers were self-reliant and confident people. It wasn't a feeling of insecurity that fell upon the crowd, but an attitude of isolation and helplessness in a world that had risen up to dwarf them, diminishing each by the minute.

It spontaneously swept the hall—a compulsive touching and embracing, people clinging together. Young men and women who had perhaps merely shared a casual ride that day were suddenly melting into each other in the crowd. Matthew observed that regardless of what the storm may finally do, it had at least brought a thousand kisses to people who might otherwise not have been kissed that day.

On the way back to the ranger station, one of the ski patrolmen came charging out of the snow, nearly running into Matthew and Edwin. "Thank God you're here," he blurted. "Ed, all hell's broke loose. Four guys from Jackhammer are lost on Red Diggings Road. We can't shoot the Clementine avalanche."

"I wondered why we never heard the shot," said Edwin. Then he was quiet for a moment, processing the information, his eyes sober and thoughtful. "Are Ellen and the boy at Jake's house?"

"Yes. Jake's trying to talk to them on the phone or the radio."

"We've got to bring them out."

Jason met them at the door to the station, pale and drawn, in contrast to the confidence of half hour ago. Something had indeed gone wrong, but Matthew couldn't grasp just what it was.

Jason seemed to anticipate a question from Edwin. "I just talked to Ellen. She and David are drifted in but they'll be okay."

"We're going in after them," said Edwin.

"No. I can't allow that. We have men enough for only one mission. Take your best people, a portable stretcher and extra snowshoes. See if you can bring in the Jackhammer party. But don't stay out longer than six-thirty."

"Shouldn't we go ahead and shoot the Clementine cornice now?"

"Can't risk it." Jason walked to the map and pointed. "The lost party probably took refuge somewhere along this limestone outcropping that spans from Higgins Flat to the upper part of Red Diggings Road. A slide on Clementine or Wildcat could reach that far."

Ed was insistent. "We have to worry about later on."

"I understand. Ellen and David are okay. They've got plenty of food and the fuel tank is full. Now please, Ed, get started."

Edwin wasn't buying it. His blue eyes shifted from Jason to the map, then darted around the room to the door with the darkness beyond and back to Jason. His air was that of a man who had something to say that nobody would want to hear. "Well, Jake, I was thinking: What if we have to shoot Clementine slide before the night's over to save the lodge? Shouldn't we get Ellen and David out now?"

"Christ sakes, Ed. just do what I'm asking you to. If you find the lost people quickly we can shoot the avalanche before it gets any more dangerous. Anyway this storm has to lift sometime. It'll be hours before Clementine is in danger. The damn storm just can't last that long."

Edwin touched Jason on the arm and turned to leave. "Okay, I'll pick up the crew at the rescue hut. They should be ready. We'll be back no later than six-thirty."

"Take a radio and report in every thirty minutes," said Jason.

After Edwin left the station, Matthew and Jason were alone together for the first time in hours. But Matthew felt that Jason, already fussing with his instruments and gauges, would not be in a mood to talk. Something was wrong with Jason. He was behaving like a person in physical pain, but Matthew knew that Jason wasn't hurting in that way. Jason was either worried or afraid.

Matthew couldn't bear the silence. "Jake, what can I do to help"

Jason seemed startled at the question. "I'm afraid not much, Matt. I've been a bit slow to take action. My wife and son are in some danger and I guess it's affecting me. Matt, I don't want to concern you, it's not such a big deal, but I still worry."

"Let's go get them, you and me."

"It wouldn't work. They're drifted in, which means more digging than even a big crew could do. And I can't leave here even for a minute. Do you know how many people there are in six thousand?"

"But most are safe. At least we could try."

"Matt, I'm doing the best I can. I don't want to hear another goddamn word about my family."

It had the effect of a slap in the face. Matthew was shocked. Then he felt Jason's hand on his shoulder. He looked up into Jason's face which had relaxed and softened. There was no remorse there, only concern and kindness. "Forgive me, Matt. I had to say that to somebody. I feel better now." He patted the shoulder. "There's something you can do for me. We've got to maintain communications. Go to the day lodge and find somebody who knows about radios. Just in case ours goes to pieces, try for a guy who can use the Morse code."

Twilight of the Wren

The light was nearly gone when the tiny eyes of the wren peered again into the white world of great white stars. He waited for the stars to fall clear, but they wouldn't and now the light was going so he tried to dive onto the ledge before it was too late. He couldn't dive through the wetness so he fluttered down toward the ledge, following the great stars, but the ledge was gone. He swooped powerfully upward against the pounding current, overshooting the branch then struggling back again to land near the cavity. He flitted inside, turned to peer at the place where the ledge should have been and hurled an anxious cry of alarm into the fading light. Again and again the cry, until finally there was a time of silence.

Then from deep inside the wren, a full-throated wail of despair and anguish burst out to lose itself without resonance among the falling stars.

Chapter Ten

The dry snow squeaked underfoot. The sky was now dirty black. It had poured flakes for nearly five hours with pausing. Before the let-up it had snowed for more than a hour. Matthew judged there would be six or seven feet of new snow in Lucite. There wasn't much chance of finding the lost party tonight, maybe ever, at least not alive. Snow, ordinary snow was one thing, but here was an onslaught of cold and deadly softness, as if a placid sea had superimposed itself over Middle Aspen Canyon to drip incessantly, flake by flake, into the village. In the dark the storm seemed to lose motion, but came on and on. Flood-lights along what had been a sidewalk were islands of brightness, but it wouldn't be long before they too disappeared into the white world of lost things. Flakes like these were scarcely falling but seemed to settle as though suspended in honey. They might not fall at all except for the infernal crowding of space and time. And quiet. Perversely, diabolically quiet. If snowflakes would only rattle like hail or thunder against solid things like heavily falling rain, if a storm like this announced itself with a crescendo upon the ear, ordinary people would take heed and seek safety. Thousands of skiers would never allow themselves to get trapped in an unbraced shaft if snow had in it the noise of elemental violence. But here, a gentle storm, soft sounds nearly musical, a peaceful kissing of flakes against coat and face. There was little wind now, thank God for that, but it would rise soon. And it too would be a quiet wind in this contoured world, but even so it would impose a terrible whisper upon a muted village.

Matthew shivered and waded on.

The day lodge was overwhelmed with people but not yet disorderly. The great round wall had been ringed with chairs, many of them piled high with ski gear. Most of the skiers were sitting, lying, or squatting on a tile floor, even that warmed by the mass of humanity. The only corridors through the crowd were improvised by the table tops cleverly strung out to provide elevated pathways to the restrooms, outside doors, and cafeteria serving lanes. The lodge seemed comfortable enough for the time being, but it would be oppressively close tonight when everybody stretched out, forming wall-to-wall bodies trying to sleep. That couldn't be helped, and at least the skiers seemed to be making the best of a bad situation. Knots of men had gathered, standing, chatting, joking. Some poker games were already under way, participants seated Indian-fashion in circles on the floor. A few men had radios tuned to Salt Lake stations. One announcer was saying that snow had blocked the road to Lucite and traffic was temporarily halted. Clearly the media hadn't been told all the facts. Matthew supposed it was a matter of getting the Forest Service, Weather Bureau and State Patrol together in one place so they could figure out the least disconcerting way to break the news.

Matthew walked the maze of tables until he saw who he was looking for, the slender black man noted earlier in the day. A member of a flight crew should know something about radios. The man was sitting alone near the outside wall, his head propped up against a chair containing his gear, minus the crew bag. Miss Nice-bottom might have taken it. He approached the man, stepping over and around prone figures.

"Are you on a flight crew?"

"Copilot, United. How did you know?"

"Saw you this morning with a flight bag. Your wife settled okay?"

"We're staying at the Bluebird Lodge. Ginger went back there."

"I've just come from the ranger station. We need a standby radio operator. Do you know short-wave and Morse code?"

"Some. I guess quite a bit."

"Will you help us?"

"Where?"

"Ranger station"

"Can I take Ginger there?"

"I'm afraid not. Sorry."

"Then I'm staying here. Ginger can find me here."

"Look, she's okay at the Bluebird."

"I said I'm staying here."

"Maybe I can arrange for you to see her at Bluebird. The ranger station isn't far."

"Okay, let's go."

As they trudged back toward the station, Matthew was thinking he had recruited a most unhappy man. Not a word passed between them. His companion was tense with the kind of tension that had transformed Jason and Matthew himself for an instant moments ago. It was like a virus, giving people not a fever of the body but a fever of the mind.

They were delayed at the sidewalk junction by a large group of men crowding around a jeep that had just stopped there with a load of snow shovels. A large man was organizing details and issuing instructions on what area each shoveler should cover. These would be the volunteers who would keep paths open between lodges and service areas. Snow throwers were still keeping the street open enough for one-lane vehicular traffic, but that lane was narrowing and deepening by the minute. The shovelers were animated and cheerful, probably glad to get away from the crowded lodge for a couple of hours, the duration of each shift. Each team was headed by a local skier who would know the village. The man in charge, a behemoth, held a Coleman lantern and a plastic-coated map of the village. After a consultation, he sent a group on their way with an exhortation. "Look out for that short fella. If he stops shoveling he'll disappear in forty seconds." After another group he yelled, "When you get to Middle Creek have yourselves a bath."

Matthew recognized the bishop's voice even before he saw the man. Jason had put him in charge and he was enjoying the role. "Those shovels are GI," he called out to yet a third group. "Bust your butts but don't bust them handles."

The volunteers seemed not to mind. Even Matthew was warmed by the crude levity after a grim day. But he noticed that his companion was unsmiling, his face and stance again showing the overbearing air of this morning when he had confronted the bishop. Matthew wondered if the bishop would remember or had even noticed.

The bishop was piling shovels back in the jeep when he recognized Matthew. "Howdy there. Not much skiing today."

"Where are your deacons?"

"Over at the Bluebird Lodge, they'll be orderlies for the medical center there. Who's your friend?"

Matthew explained.

"Well, at least he'll not likely get lost in all this white stuff." The bishop chuckled. Matthew felt Wendell stiffen, then heard him hiss an angry expletive.

The bishop seemed startled. He closed the jeep door and stood to face the black man, still holding the lantern, shifting it to better illuminate the faces of Matthew and Wendell.

"Hey old buddy. Can't you take a joke?"

"I like jokes."

"Then what's the matter with you?"

"I don't like that kind of joke."

"Oh, well then, I'm sorry."

"Also, I don't like bigots who think they're saints."

Matthew nudged Wendell. Come on. Don't make a big deal, we've gotta go."

To the bishop he said, "Better not yell too loud. Could cause an avalanche."

The bishop grinned, cheer returning to his face. "Where'll you be?" he asked.

"Ranger station."

"See you there later," said the bishop. Matthew figured he had already cleansed his mind of bigots and saints.

Chapter Eleven

Matthew awoke and looked at his watch in the dark. He had been napping for less than an hour. The canvas cot wasn't comfortable but it beat hell out of lying on the floor at the day lodge. It was cold here in the back room but Matthew would forgo the warmth of the wood stove for the quiet and darkness. The nap had cleared his head. He needed to think alone. Something was terribly wrong with Ellen. Of course something had always been wrong with Ellen, beginning the regrettable day he and Jason first met her in a Grand Junction bar. She had been too young for her age, too little-girl pretty, too eager to impress. They should never have messed with her, but the friends had had a few beers. Besides they were hard-up and feeling their oats after weeks in the mines. In no time she was drunk, confiding: "Lucky me! I just lost one boy friend, now I've got two." They took it as a promise and a challenge. All three were beyond the brink by the time they left the tavern. Ellen said, no, she didn't have any girl friends in Grand Junction to make it a foursome. "It's no big deal? That last guy took my cherry, and helped his brother rape me. I'm a cow. So what the hell? We're all friends here. You can flip a coin to see who's first."

Mathew and Jason drove a leisurely loop through Colorado National Monument and along the way took turns with Ellen in a sleeping bag in the back of the pickup. Afterwards they dropped her off at a seedy motel and cafe where she said she was employed as bus girl. The friends saw her many weekends after that, meeting always at the same bar. Then Matthew began to hear rumors about Ellen. Jason refused to discuss them. Finally Matthew told his friend, "We've gotta stay away from Ellen."

"How come?"

"I hear she's selling it around. We're candidates for clap or worse."

Jason had been furious. "Well, she isn't selling it, but that's no thanks to us."

"She's doing a strip Tuesdays and Wednesdays at the place on Highway Six."

"That's to earn a little money so she can stay weekends."

"Why would she want to stay?"

"She likes us."

But a couple of weeks before the friends would return to Golden, Ellen wasn't at the bar. They inquired of a bartender. "She left town with a trucker."

"What kind of trucker?" asked Jason. "Who saw her leave? Do you know if she said where she was headed?"

"Don't know," he answered. "Anyway what's the difference? Good lookin' kid like you can do a lot better than that little twat."

Because Jason insisted, they asked around other bars and pool halls. Nobody seemed to know or care, but they did hear a lament at one place. "Too bad, she shore looked like a nice little piece, and I never got any."

Jason had been saddened. "I'm not proud of what we did. We messed up her life real good, and didn't even try to help her."

"She was pretty screwed up before we came along," contended Matthew.

Matthew recalled that by the end of summer, he and Jason had been glad to draw their last pay check. The commissary was closing out jewelry, so Jason bought matching rings with petrified wood settings for his folks. Matthew bought a copper bracelet with a uranium gemstone that intrigued him. Jason chided Matthew, "That thing is probably illegal. The stone's giving off enough roentgens to mutate a walrus."

"I see lots of possibilities with this thing," Matthew had insisted.

Having been paid off they took the southern route back toward Denver. Something different by way of scenery, and they could observe the mineralized formations at Leadville and Climax. As they drove through rain into South Park they almost missed seeing a girl sitting by the road. "Hey, hold it," yelled Jason. "That's Ellen." Matthew was already braking when they passed the rain-soaked girl. He stopped and backed up. She hurried toward the pickup carrying a battered suitcase, a big purse looped over one shoulder.

"Gee, thanks," she panted into the open window. Then, recognizing them, shrank back. "Oh, shit. It's you guys."

"Come on, get in. It's raining." Jason leaped out to stand beside her on the road. He gave her a playful swat on the bottom, grabbed her suit case and tucked it under the tarp in back.

Ellen climbed in beside Matthew, grumbling about rotten luck in having bad pennies turn up again, but she smiled a weak smile. Her dark eyes were hard as polished agate, and wet hair wrapped her face like unraveled strands of rope. A light, sleeveless blouse molded her breasts and navel. Water dripped from the tip of her nose onto soaked Levi's. Her slightly flushed face had about it a scrubbed look of innocence.

For the first time Matthew had thought she could be more than just pretty. But he was troubled at seeing Ellen again. Perhaps sensing it, Ellen had patted his knee, leaving dampness there.

"Sorry to make such a mess of your truck, Matt."

"It's okay, kid. What were you doing back there in the rain?"

"I was riding to Denver with this guy. He stopped at the picnic table in the trees and started messing around. I pushed him off. He said put out or get out. I got out."

When angry, Jason used to make a muted sound somewhere between a swallowed expletive and an animal growl. Matthew heard it then.

"Where have you been?" he demanded.

"Where's it written that I have to register everywhere I go with you?" Her voice was way too loud. Then she relaxed and leaned toward Jason. The knuckle of her right hand brushed his cheek. "Okay, granny Jake. I went to Gunnison and worked in a cafe."

"How come you left without telling us?" It bothered Matthew that there was no banter in Jason's voice. He didn't like this conversation.

Ellen breathed deeply. "Oh, Jake, I have to get home."

"Where's home?"

Ellen's answer had been a long time coming. Glancing at her, Matthew thought she was in a kind of trance. She opened her eyes as if to speak, then closed them again. Finally she whispered, voice breaking. "I'm pregnant. I've gotta get something done."

Matthew remembered her frail shoulder trembling beside his. Tears mingled with dripping water from her hair and splashed on her hands, which were still tightly clasped together. Matthew had felt pity for the girl and perhaps some remorse. "Oh cripes, honey. it'll be okay. We'll see to it that you get home." Then he groped for words. "Ugh, I guess it could have been—I mean, almost anybody could..."

"Matt!"

Jason's voice had cracked through the pickup cab like a rifle shot. "Shut up, you son-of-a-bitch."

The pickup rolled on across South Park, no person making a sound except Ellen, who sniffed several times, then rummaged in her purse and took out a tissue. The windshield wipers seemed to beat time with the word preg...nant, preg...nant. Matthew had been furious at Jason and suddenly very much on guard. There was just no way the little bitch was going to pin that on either of them. Finally Ellen broke in with her small voice. "Look, don't worry. I'm not going to point a finger at anybody. Just drop me off in Denver and that's the last you'll see of me."

In one way, words are like numbers. It is combinations and interactions that mean something. But words are different in that some combinations stay forever in your mind. Matthew recalled each of Jason's words as their plans and dreams evaporated in the pickup cab to the tune of windshield wipers in the rain. Jason had laid his hands over Ellen's fist and gently unfolded her fingers. "Ellen, it's my kid." It had been as final as yesterday. Etch it in granite. "You'll never see the last of me."

Matthew opened his eyes to the darkness. It was a bummer to recall how Jason had thrown away his life. But the reality of this day, this hour, was even worse. After all those years and memories, it had come down to a hard cot in the ranger station at Lucite, Utah, and a hellish storm outside. It seemed an awful irony, but Matthew remembered the last day he had seen Jason at college as a rotten day, too. A cutting wind had blown out of the north along the Front Range, bringing sleet that iced the tarp in the back of Jason's pickup. The tarp cracked and groaned as they carried things out of the dorm to tuck underneath. Ellen sitting in the truck, not looking at Matthew or speaking, waiting for them to get it loaded. But she smiled almost a happy smile after Matthew went back in the dorm and brought out the uranium bracelet from Uravan and gave it to her, telling her why it was something special and why she had to be careful. He tried to make the scene a light one: "When you get mad at Jake, put this on and think about your old buddy Matt." Just before they pulled away, Ellen had put both arms outside the window, getting them wet, and cradling his cheek with her wrists and saying something so softly that it was mostly carried away by the wind. He thought she had said, "I'm sorry about you and Jason."

It had been a sad day, and maybe a tragic day all around. And now he had come here only to find that Ellen was trapped somewhere in this mess of a storm. Ellen, who had been sometimes crazy and sometimes beautiful as a girl. As a woman she was still crazy. Would she still be beautiful?

And whatever possessed her to want to send the boy away to Houston? No way that was going to happen. To have friends was one thing; to take advantage of them something else. Matthew refused to be exploited. If Ellen couldn't bear to be around the kid, then they should either send him off to relatives or send her back to the institution. Weird that Matthew should be discussed by Ellen and her shrink. Matthew wished the poor woman had forgotten him long ago, as she should have, or would at least forget him now. He fervently hoped he wouldn't have to see her. And he wished to hell he had never come to this goddamned place and that he could leave again right now.

Tonight there would likely be avalanches. The ferocity of the storm, coupled with the blocked road and lost skiers, had caused a fateful and possibly fatal disruption of control measures. If the snow continued, Jason would soon have to shoot Clementine Ridge with artillery otherwise the snow would build up enough to threaten Clementine Inn. The preemptive avalanche might sacrifice Jason's house, and Ellen and the boy would be in it. It was an awful mess. Matthew wished he could go back to sleep and forget the whole thing.

Even if the Clementine avalanche came down gently, the Wildcat slide would still threaten the center of the village. Matthew was no stranger to avalanches, but never had he been on the under side of one. He remembered a bitterly cold and snowy day at Arapaho Basin when he and Jason skied across a cornice behind West Wall and it started to move. It had been scary to watch the huge crack form under their skis. They lived to ski again only because the avalanche released behind them like opening a scissors. They simply zipped the snowfield apart as they traversed. The thunder and dust had been awesome. Matthew had been surprised and shocked when the boiling slide struck the canyon bottom, then snaked up the other side, chopping down trees as it rolled uphill. It had been frightening to see the monster move, as if with intelligence, to attack and destroy.

Jason and Matthew never skied West Wall again, but they had toyed many times with avalanches. Sometimes when they were traversing a questionable pack, a crack would strike its way through the snow. They would hear the deadly rumble but the slide would stop. Once, skiing across powder at the top of a ravine that they knew to be dangerous, they heard a muffled thunder and almost simultaneously an eerie whoosh. A powerful wind gusted out of the earth toward the sky and a foggy white dust enveloped them. An old patrolman explained it afterward: Sometimes a field of unstable snow, if disturbed, will simply sink upon itself like a tire going flat, expelling its air in a gush.

Another time, Matthew was skiing down a little-known gully at Winter Park. It was late and he shouldn't have been alone on such terrain, but Jason had deserted him to guide a terrified Missouri couple out of the steep Hughes complex, which baffled them, onto the catwalk leading to the base. Disgusted with Jason for missing the last run, Matthew had plunged down the lonely, unmarked shortcut. It was not more than six hundred vertical feet but narrow enough to impose a fierce discipline on any skier. Only quick, linked, carving turns, straight down the fall line, would do. There was hardly even a stopping place. It had been a thrill, but at the peak of his excitement, Matthew had sensed an unaccountable acceleration. Suddenly he realized that he was going faster through space than his skis were moving over the snow. It lasted for perhaps five fearful seconds, and Matthew knew as he passed again into stable snow that he had been perilously close to a grinding death. He had skied over a mass of snow in motion, a kind of pre-avalanche that moved with his invasion, then settled back peacefully after his passing.

Those were adventurous and foolhardy days, but Matthew knew better now. Deep snow on a mountain was something one didn't fool with. It was like the humming energy of a high-voltage line, and to draw it out of place was to release violence berserk.

Matthew shivered. He knew that if the snowfall persisted, even the ranger station would be threatened. Nobody at Lucite was really safe. But six thousand people! It would be a disaster to boggle the mind. He had heard of new ways skiers could protect against avalanche, like radar beacons and compressed air balloons. Even dogs were trained to sniff out skiers buried in the snow. But none of that would help now, not here in Lucite. Anyhow, at least his death would associate itself with an event of historic proportions He thought of the little graveyard below town and wondered what might have been the population of the village the last time Killvein struck. And how many would Killvein destroy if it fell on a population of six thousand?

Matthew sat up on the cot to peer out the window. An abyss. Of course, snow had long since risen above the windows of the ranger station. He pulled on his boots, opened the door and stepped into the main room of the station, blinking at the illumination. Jason was seated at a table along the south end, plotting snow depths, recording air currents, temperatures, and pressures from remote locations. An overhead battery of dials would tell Jason much of what he needed to know about avalanche hazards, but little of what he needed most to know: When the storm would end. Matthew walked past Wendell at the radio to the door and peered out into a sea of black. He extended an arm and felt the gentle sprawl of enormous flakes across his bare hand. Wendell said, "You better believe it's still coming down."

Jason lifted a haggard face from his work then and announced to no one in particular, "Wind's up to six miles per hour across the north ridge. The cornice above Clementine is getting deep enough to release. Unless the snow stops by seven I'll have to order a shot."

It was stated in a mechanical voice that seemed programmed by events. Jason the person had disappeared behind a stiff facade of Jason the ranger. There would be no more breakdowns during this emergency. His friend was emotional but Jason could also be very tough.

At 6:22 Edwin radioed to report that they had located the lost party, "at Bell's cabin in Wildcat Basin."

"Thank God. Are they okay?"

"Yeah. Jake, I'll call again in five minutes."

"He wants to tell me something," mused Jason.

At 6:30, Edwin called again and explained. The men had been playing poker. By the time he found them they were pretty boozed up, having broken the lock and helped themselves to liquor stored in the cabin. Getting the half-drunk gang through soft snow on snowshoes was a hassle for the rescuers, who were having an especially tough time with one big guy. He was belligerent and demanding to see Jason.

"Bring him right down here," Jason told Edwin. "Take the others directly to the day lodge."

"Jake, I've already sent him with the boys. I'm at Church Hill with Jerry about half mile from Clementine Ridge Road. We're going in to see if we can get to your house."

"I hate to have you chance it," Jason answered. There's no guarantee the avalanche won't release on its own before long."

"We'll make it quick."

"You might not be able to see the road. Look for the highline."

"We'll find it. I'll call every ten minutes."

"Take care, Ed." His voice carried a trace of huskiness. "Don't get lost up there tonight. You know we might have to shoot the avalanche."

Ed called at 6:40. "We're on the road."

"You're making good time."

At 6:50 he called to say that they had reached the summer condominiums.

"You're only seventy five yards from the avalanche zone," Jason told him.

"We're going on. Everything looks good here."

"But not here. Ed, some convection currents have been coming out of the valley, I think snow has concentrated along the east side of the ridge and on the cornice. Maybe you shouldn't go any further."

"We're not stopping now."

"Keep your voices down and stay close to the bank. If something starts you'll hear a wind."

At seven, they heard from Edwin again. "We've reached the east drift. It's too high, can't get on it from here. We'll see if we can go around."

"Hurry. I can only allow you to stay another fifteen minutes."

At seven-fifteen, Edwin told Jason he couldn't skirt the drift. "Jake, we'll have to tunnel through."

"There's no time. We have to get the avalanche down before I can risk that many men. Pull back to the condo. I'll send a rescue team to meet you there. The ski patrol will follow. When you converge we'll shoot the avalanche. As soon as it's down, go on in. Ellen and David will have signal emitters. I'll have them turn on the short-wave. We can follow that signal too."

"I'm sorry, Jake."

Jason radioed instructions to the snow clearing crews to form a rescue party. He called the artillery site. "Stand by for a shot on Clementine Ridge at 7:30.Use low percussion. We want a minimum slide and we don't want to jar Wildcat or Killvein."

He turned to the phone and dialed, speaking softly to someone at length. Matthew guessed it was Ellen.

Then there was a commotion at the door and a man barged in, head, shoulders, and upper back coated with snow. He was huge, taller and broader than Matthew, and quite obviously angry, the emotion setting his face in a contorted sneer. The chin and nose were effeminately angular, the mouth pouted. His red-rimmed eyes shifted aggressively about the room as he stood just inside the door, feet planted wide apart, swaying slightly. He pulled off heavy gloves, and a muffed touring cap with grey bill, shaking their covering of snow into a pile on the floor. He stuffed the gloves into one pocket of his parka, which was dyed a jumble of colors in wildly psychedelic fashion. He tried to push his cap into the other pocket but there was a fifth of whisky already there, so he simply let sail, the cap barely missing Wendell and landing on the batteries for the short-wave.

His voice was whisky-coarse. "Who's the Boy Scout in charge?"

Jason hung up the telephone and turned to confront him. But Wendell was the first to speak. "Hey man. We don't need that snow in here."

The man shifted his stare to Wendell. "You don't like it, boy, lick it up."

Then he glared at Jason. "You the Lone Ranger who's ordering people around?"

"I'm the person responsible." said Jason.

"Well look, you bastard. Name's Dain. I paid for a room at the Jackhammer. Now they've kicked me out. They said you ordered it."

"There's an emergency. Everybody's inconvenienced."

"Well inconvenience yourself but don't fuck with me."

"There will be a place for you in the day lodge, on the floor."

"Bull shit. None of the day lodge shit. I'm gonna sleep where I paid to sleep."

"If you return to the Jackhammer you'll be arrested immediately. Go to the day lodge and we'll leave you alone until this is over."

"Till this is over." His repetition sounded like a question. "What' s that supposed to mean?"

"You and your gang will be charged with criminal trespass of a posted area."

"Oh, go piss up a tree," breathed the big man, only slightly interested but dangerously furious.

"You'll also be charged with breaking and entering."

The big man stepped closer to Jason until he and Jason were standing only a meter apart. Matthew thought Jason would be physically attacked in a few seconds. A ski patrolman had entered the station behind the redhead A brawl inside Lucite's communications center could be disastrous. The three men would have to subdue the big guy and get him out of the station quickly. The featherweight copilot couldn't be much help. Matthew wanted to call out "Careful Jake, he's dangerous," but he knew it was futile. He saw in Jason's face and heard in his voice the stoic fury that always used to precede his brawling. Jason was ready for violence. There'd be hell to pay.

Dain was suddenly defensive. "We're entitled to take shelter in a storm."

"But not to steal wine and whisky. Call it larceny," Jason's left hand shot out to deftly grab the whisky. "And you won't be needing this anymore." For an instant, he displayed the bottle to the surprised eyes of the giant then quickly, with a sideways glance, tossed it to Wendell, who had risen to a standing position.

Dain mumbled menacingly, "I'll have your ass for that."

Jason's hands were on his hips, "You're going to have a lot more of me than you want."

The big man seemed startled by the anger he sensed in Jason.

"Look, don't worry about the booze. We'll pay the poor bastard for his booze."

"Well, you look. We're going to have avalanches here. They might have been avoided if you had obeyed the law. If any lives are lost, you'll pay with more than money."

"What you talkin' about?"

"I'm talking about manslaughter and jail."

It was too much for the big man. He slowly raised his right hand, finger extended, to tap the breastbone of Jason. His left, knotted into a quart-sized fist, swung upward. Matthew was yelling at Jason to look out, just as Wendell leaped toward the action, cat-quick in a blur of motion. There was an explosive crash, and a hoarse bellow simultaneous with the sound of glass fragments skittering around the concrete floor. A powerful aroma of whisky filled the room.

With mechanical precision, Wendell had smashed the whisky bottle across the thrusting fist of the Kansan.

Nobody moved for a moment. The big man was holding his wounded fist with his good right hand, blood running out to make a little river of red along his hairy fingers. But as the pain and surprise subsided, he turned to move menacingly toward Wendell. As the distance narrowed, Wendell raised a hand, a gesture as if to shake a fist, but it wasn't a fist he showed. His hand still held the broken bottle, bristling with jagged edges as long and lethal as ice picks.

The man paused and crouched, but before he could throw a punch, Jason was on him, one hand against his chest and the other at his throat. It was a quick powerful movement, thrusting the bigger man backward all the way to the east wall, crashing his head against it and pinning him there. Right hand violently pressing against the throat of the man, Jason talked, his flat, crisp voice a strange contrast to the savage words.

"In a half-hour, an avalanche is coming down on my wife and son. If it hurts them I'll hurt you. If it kills them, I'll kill you."

Dain dropped to one knee. His eyes were bugging. He was stunned.

Jason turned him loose, stepped back and stood very still for a moment. Matthew was aghast. Once in Madrid he had watched a matador kill a bull. This was the time. But Jason breathed deeply and turned away. "Take him to the Bluebird and get him bandaged. Then drop him off at the day lodge," he told the patrolman.

Chapter Twelve

By the time Matthew and Wendell mopped up the mixture of whisky and snowmelt and swept out the glass, Jason was on the radio calling for a relay to the Weather Bureau. He was told that Samantha hadn't checked in or answered the phone in her apartment. According to reports from both the southeast and southwest there wasn't any strong indication of weakening in the storm systems feeding the two fronts. Still no snow in Salt Lake, but a 30-mile-per-hour wind was blowing easterly, picking up a great deal of dust. Jason was told to expect winds to increase in Lucite during the night. "We judge the avalanche hazard as very high and increasing."

Jason was reading dials and updating his charts when Edwin called on the short-wave to inform him that a large rescue party had arrived at the condominiums on Ridge Road. The ski patrol were joining them, bringing doctors from Bluebird Lodge. The teams would be ready to move to Clementine Ridge within the ten minutes remaining before the shot. Jason asked about road clearance for the jeep. "Only as far as Wildcat Trail, so don't try to join us, Jake. Anyway vehicular traffic would be exposed to the Wildcat avalanche. You can help us most by staying at the station."

"I have to come, Ed. You know that."

"Okay, but you'll have to walk and don't delay anything, Jake. We should go ahead and shoot as planned before there's any more depth on that cornice."

'We shoot in sixteen minutes. Don't wait for me. I'll catch up."

Jason's back was to Matthew. After his conversation with Edwin, he sat without moving for a time. Matthew thought he might be making notes but there was no sound of a pencil in motion or paper disturbed. Only the wood fire, freshly stocked by Wendell, with its fierce frantic roar.

Occasional sparks would send bursts of flaming pine against the cast iron. Ordinarily Matthew loved the sound of a hot pine fire, but tonight it was not a pretty sound but somehow threatening and angry. Matthew could feel the danger gathering around. It even seemed dangerous for Jason to stand and walk to the door, open it and gaze into the darkness for a full minute. He walked back to the radio and called out a code that Matthew knew would have to be Ellen and the boy. Matthew felt a tightness in his chest and a lack of breath control.

The drift around Jason's house didn't affect the radio signal. The young male voice was loud and clear, and it responded quickly to Jason's call.

"I'm here, Dad."

"Have you been monitoring?" asked Jason.

"Some."

"Then you know what's happening."

"Well, I know the avalanche might hit here."

"David, listen carefully and do exactly as I say." Jason instructed David to turn off the gas and lights, then use tape to mask the windows above the heavy table in the spare bedroom used for an office. "There are signal emitters on the shelf under the radio. Take two, turn them on, give one to mother and put the other in your pocket." Jason added that David and his mother were to get under the table, but keep talking on the radio, and wrap themselves in blankets.

"Is mother with you now?"

"I'll call her."

"Jason, is something wrong?" It was Ellen. Matthew instantly recognized the. round inflections of her voice from years before. Even filtered through space and electronics, Ellen's voice was ageless and mysteriously lovely, bittersweet, melodious, wrapping itself around a listener.

"Ellen, we may get an avalanche. You and David have to take precautions. I've told David what to do. I'm coming to get you and I want you to leave the radio on until I get there."

"Jake, don't you dare come out in this storm."

"Ellen, I have to leave now."

"Jason.'" There was a sharp edge of urgency in Ellen's voice, something close to panic. "I couldn't bear to think of you out in this, with avalanches."

"But I need to come for you and David."

"Listen to me, Jake. If you leave that radio even for a second I'll scream terribly. I'll scream until you come back."

"You shouldn't worry that way."

"Will you stay there?"

"Yes. I'll stay."

"Thank you, sweet Jake. I don't worry about you. I'm afraid only for me. I'm not strong enough to lose you. Not even for a little while in a storm."

"I won't let you lose me."

"Jason, why is David taping the window?"

"If an avalanche comes it could push the window down on you and him. It mustn't shatter."

"Will an avalanche come?"

"Darling, I think so."

"My poor David. Jason, thank you for staying there for me and for loving David."

"Honey, you and David are going to be all right. You both have to get under the table now. Ellen, listen to me carefully."

The clock over Jason's head read 7:28.

"Wrap the blankets around you. Be sure your feet are tucked inside. Lay on one side and draw your knees up toward your chest. I want you to keep your hands and arms free. Tell me when you're all wrapped up."

There was a pause, then Ellen's voice again, further away but still clear and strong. "It's done, darling. All of me is inside, but it's not very comfortable. My head hurts, cocked this way. Jake, you officious dummy, why didn't you think about a pillow?"

"Cause when you get comfortable you get sassy."

"Jason, is Matthew there?"

"Yes. He came in this morning."

The clock read 7:29.

"Did you tell him what doctor Hendrix wants to do?"

"Yes. Matt says he'll help any way he can."

"Oh good. Matt is such a good fellow. Please tell Matt I've worn the bracelet all day to celebrate him coming to visit. Jason darling, you are a good fellow too. Thank you for staying there with me. I'd be frantic if you were out in the storm. You're good to me. You indulge me. Shame on you, Jake, for being too good to me."

Matthew heard a sharp thud from outside. He guessed it was the howitzer going off high above them.

"Ellen, baby. I want you and David to bring your hands up and cup them around your nose and mouth."

"Okay. I've done it. Do I sound a little funny now?"

"A little."

"Jason, there's a terrible wind outside."

The last sound they heard was a muted whistle as of a train far away or a breath sharply drawn.

The microphone dangled from its cord as Jason stood slowly and turned toward Matthew and Wendell. He was leaning on the back of the chair, seeming suddenly like an old man, feeble and peering. His back was straight but his knees were bent as if lifting or holding a heavy object. "Matt, I'll need my boots and a lantern."

"Stay here, Jake, at least for a while."

"Can't."

"Then I'll go with you."

"No, you have to stay here so I can go."

"Be careful out there." Matthew and Wendell peered through the open door after Jason. His lantern illuminated the great flakes for a way, then winked out and the black night layered itself between them. They were quiet, each with his own thoughts. Finally Wendell spoke.

"I can't believe this."

"It's no fantasy."

"I've never heard of anything so goddamn awful."

"It's hard for Jake."

"You figure the avalanche hit his wife and kid?"

"Yes. They're someplace under it now."

"Can they survive?"

"I think they're already dead."

"Why?"

"That wind. Ellen said she heard a wind."

The short-wave crackled. "Come in Jake. This is Ed."

"Jake's gone, Ed."

Matthew heard an expletive. "Go catch him and take him back to the station. He shouldn't be here."

"I tried. Nothing doing. What happened there?"

"The avalanche came down like a tornado. Airborne. Telephone the Bluebird. Have them clear out a room for a morgue. Also check the Clementine Inn. The slide might have carried all the way. We're going to tunnel in now."

Matthew hung up the mike and turned to find Wendell bundled up for the storm. "I'm going after Ginger," he explained.

Matthew knew there wasn't any way to stop Wendell, so he handed him a pass and telephoned the Clementine. Alice Morton said she heard the shot, then the avalanche. It appeared that some sliding snow had piled up against the roof on the west end of the lodge, but there wasn't any damage. If the avalanche carried as far as the lodge it had skirted around to the west of the ridge. "Jason saved us by shooting now. I hope Ellen and David are okay."

Matthew had to break off the conversation to take a call on the short-wave. It was a press wire service, relaying questions through the machine pool. He told them their figures were substantially correct; yes, about six thousand were trapped here. No, there wasn't any chance of getting out tonight. Two avalanches had come down, but there weren't any reports of casualties yet. Yes, there was no panic. No, they hadn't been warned that so much snow was on the way. Well, a statistician at the Weather Bureau predicted it but she had been overruled by superiors. "That's my understanding. I don't know all the particulars."

Those bureaucratic bastards deserved that.

"Well, yes. The snow ranger in charge wanted to close this morning but he was overruled, too. Lack of localized information and control are the reasons for this disaster and you can quote me on that."

"Quote who?"

"Unidentified volunteer in Lucite."

Matthew didn't want any notoriety but he was warming to the task as spokesman for six thousand trapped skiers. "Yes, there is potential for disaster. Of course, we don't want to alarm friends and relatives of skiers trapped here, but it's a bad situation. There aren't enough beds to go around. We don't know how long the food may last. Two other avalanches are threatening Lucite and we don't know when the snow might end."

The reporter asked if there were some feelings of bitterness because of the lack of warning.

"Well, some. These people are asking questions.' Matthew hadn't really heard any questions but he thought it was appropriate to unload a little.

The AP man asked if it would be all right to call every hour through the night. "Only till midnight," Matthew told him. "We have to get sleep here." Of course Matthew had no idea at all whether anybody in Lucite would get sleep. But he sensed that it would be useful to keep the media guessing.

The machine pool called then to tell Matthew that a relay station had been set up at the pool. Calls could now go directly from the ranger station to the Salt Lake terminal, so telephone contact could now be established again. It was agreed that only official and emergency calls could be allowed. Of course, messages from stranded skiers would instantly swamp the system.

The first direct call was from Denver, a Mr. Hayden. Matthew gathered that he was a high official of the Forest Service. He wanted Jason, but talked freely with Matthew instead. He seemed worried and knowledgeable and hungry for information so Matthew told him all he knew, including the suspected fate of Ellen and her son. Hayden said the Forest Service considered this a "Category One" emergency. "We'll launch an all-out effort to evacuate everybody. I'm going to call Washington now." He promised that a combined rescue force of Forest Service and military personnel would arrive at Middle Aspen Canyon early tomorrow. "Have Jason call when he can. I'll be here until about midnight, then I'm leaving for Salt Lake."

Matthew was somewhat cheered by both conversations. A world was out there beyond the curtain of snow, and it cared about Lucite. Jason called then to report that he had joined Ed's rescue party and would check in later. Matthew told him about the call from Denver, but didn't mention the reporter.

Wendell came stumbling back to the station. At the door he asked for a broom to brush himself off, shook his hat and parka, then entered glumly. Ginger had refused to come to the ranger station. She was a nurse and had volunteered to help in the improvised hospital. She had scolded Wendell that other women were separated from husbands, and admonished, "Honey, I may be better than they are but you're the only one who knows it." Recounting the remark to Matthew, Wendell grinned in spite of himself.

She wouldn't believe what Wendell told her about Jason's family. "Ginger insists that the woman and her boy will be okay. She says you need to believe in Armageddon to imagine that a man had to kill his loved ones to save others.. She says if it's here we're all done for anyway."

At 8:30 Matthew and Wendell were huddled around the radio, hoping for some word from the rescue operation. They had heard nothing since Jason called more than an hour ago. A voice from outside hailed the station. They rushed to the door. It was Olsen, the bishop.

Matthew pulled the man inside. Here was information. Olsen tugged off hat and coat, shaking them outside before closing the door. His face was ruddy as before, but the cheer had left his eyes.

"Cup of coffee?" Matthew offered as the Dane sat to pull off his boots.

"No thanks. We don't drink coffee."

"Were you with the rescue crew?"

"Just left."

"What happened?"

"I never saw such a mess. It tore the house to smithereens."

"What about the woman and boy?"

"We found the boy first. Looked like the wall came down on the table and him under it. The woman had been blown clean out of the house. She was under about twenty feet of snow and trash. We'd never have found her body except for that beeper that Jason made her wear."

"Both dead?"

"Oh yes. But at least it was quick. Didn't either of them suffer. Awful thing, with Jake Stemple right there helping dig them out."

"Where is Jason now?"

"He went with the bodies to the Bluebird Lodge. Said tell you he'll be here at the station in about an hour. Myself, I was wondering, since you're a friend of the family, if you might want to go there and sit for a while. I can take over here, and I'll get somebody to spell you before midnight."

"Spell me?"

The bishop frowned, puzzled momentarily. "Well, yes. I guess you wouldn't know this but here in Utah we don't like dead folks to be alone until they're buried. We'll have somebody sit with the woman and boy. I thought you might take the first stint." He paused then, looking carefully at Matthew. "Say, are you related to the boy?"

"No."

"I skied with Jake lots of times but never knew his family. David was a good-looking young fellow. It's a terrible pity for him. You couldn't tell much about the woman. She was pretty beat up, but the boy wasn't banged in the head at all. He was a tall kid, looks a lot like you."

Matthew wasn't listening. He was almost overcome with horror, and the talkative Olsen was telling him more than he cared to know. He felt a shaky nervousness, a sensation of body control gone awry. If he had a cup he couldn't drink from it, a pencil he couldn't possibly write. The mere thought of seeing Jason now was intolerable, and the idea of sitting alone with two cadavers, one of them Ellen, was almost more than he could bear. "Of course I want to go see Jake," he answered. Thanks for offering to relieve me here. It'll take a while. I've got to pull myself together before I can go anyplace."

The bishop put on his coat and hat. "That's okay. I should check the crews anyway. I'll be back pretty quick. Stemple wants both me and Ed to stay here at the station tonight." He paused again, looking around the room as if to be sure that the wrong ears wouldn't hear what he was about to say. "They're worried about another avalanche." He left then, slamming the door as big clumsy men often do.

Matthew poured coffee for himself and Wendell. "I guess Ginger knows by now," the black man said. "It's Armageddon. What a hellish thing to happen to that nice ranger."

The man from AP called again. Matthew brought him up-to-date. Sensing an unusual story, the man pried. "Isn't it ironical that the two dead are the family of the snow ranger who is supposed to protect Lucite?"

"I suppose you could call it that."

"Was the avalanche spontaneous?"

"How do you expect me to know that?"

"Or did they bring it down with artillery?"

Matthew's temper was hair-trigger quick. "What does it matter?"

"Wup. Sorry. It's just part of the story."

"Well, look. You've got your story, now go print it. Stemple will be here in about an hour. He's still in charge. You better not ask him about the avalanche. Is that clear?"

"I guess it would be, uh, indelicate."

After the conversation, Matthew felt better about seeing Jason. It was a sacred duty. His friend needed him. He wouldn't wait any longer. He bundled up. "The bishop will probably be around in a few minutes. Is it safe to leave the two of you together?"

"I just might lock him out," answered Wendell. "Anyway, what makes that hillbilly preacher think I couldn't take care of the station here?"

Matthew shrugged. "Don't hassle the big guy. He could charge you twenty bucks a day just to live."

"Oh sure, I'll be nice. Where the hell did I put that busted bottle?"

Chapter Thirteen

It was dark in the bedroom when Samantha awoke, and very quiet. She lay still for a moment, waiting for a clear head, feeling inside the kind of low that wraps around body and spirit after a bad dream. She seldom slept in the daytime, and always when she did she lost perspective as to time and place. Finally, it was Saturday. It had to be late in the evening. She checked the time, nine-thirty. She had stayed awake most of the night and slept most of the day. No, it hadn't been a bad dream, only a terrible morning. To be angry is one thing, but Buford had been so cold and sarcastic in his anger. It was unbearable to feel hated by someone, especially one's boss. A reprimand. The word hurt down into the pit of her stomach, and was nauseous there. Only the very lazy or the very incompetent got a reprimand. It was a word used by bureaus in the East or Midwest, unheard of in Utah.

Buford had said it was terrible. Of course he was right. It wasn't terrible to warn people, only terrible to warn people and be wrong. Maybe she should sleep some more. Sleep was paramount. Only sleep could end that painful scene in Buford's office.

Would there be a board of inquiry to weigh dismissal? What could she tell them? 'After I discovered the correlations and tested them for significance, I lost my head with fear.' Or perhaps, 'There was this beautiful, sensitive man who could be destroyed and so I went into a panic because it was important to save him and spare his conscience.' Truth won't help. One doesn't mix mathematics and emotions. A professional breakdown. They might pay attention to that. 'I was out of my mind with weariness, having recorded parameters for nearly twenty hours, non-stop.'

None of it would do. How awful to be wrong when one hates the message anyway. How shameful for one who despises incompetence to be so brash and presumptuous and trusting of one's own impulses. Why couldn't she have been un-dramatically and quietly wrong? Why must her error have been compounded by a silly feminine weakness for an attractive man? Jason must be laughing by now.

Her daytime sleep had not been a catharsis. Her thoughts had disturbed it time and again, and the phone had rung at least twice, perhaps more.

Well, she had to return to the world. She might loathe herself but she would confront herself. The world might think her contemptible or silly, or juvenile, but she would confront the world too.

Samantha struggled out of bed and went to make coffee, flicking on the television as she passed. She was sipping coffee when the program was interrupted by a newsman promising a "Lucite emergency report." His voice was more animated than usual. "Six thousand skiers remain trapped by heavy snow and avalanches at Lucite village. Telephone communication, cut by an avalanche, has not yet been restored. The Weather Bureau sees no letup. Meanwhile the surprise storm has claimed its first victims. The wife and son of Jason Stemple, Forest Service snow ranger at Lucite, were killed by an avalanche that struck their home at seven-thirty this evening. Due to heavy snow and drifts, the rescue party was not able to reach the site of the avalanche and remove the bodies until moments ago. More on this on Big Story at ten tonight. Now back to..."

Samantha threw her cup and saucer at the sink. By the time it landed with a clatter she was half way to the bedroom. She was dressed and headed out the front door almost before she knew what she was doing or where she was going.

She wasn't thinking as she rushed, only feeling the horror and the icy terror. My God. Jason, poor Jason. Six thousand people still in Lucite and his wife and son swept away. Jason, who couldn't possibly bear either calamity, now had both at once.

She was running. Where? Get hold of yourself: Must get a taxi. She hailed one. "Weather Bureau on Jackson Street. Hurry please." Her thoughts were racing. Did anyone help Jason? She had slept through a long, terrible, disastrous day.

She ran down the dark corridor. There was a bright light under the door leading to the bureau suite. If anyone was there the clack-clack of her heels would herald her approach. She burst in. Many drawn faces turned, startled at the abrupt intrusion. Almost the entire staff was there.

Impossible, Buford on a Saturday night. George Rose, off duty hours ago. Four meteorologists and a newscaster were gathered at the big wall map of western U.S. and Canada.

"What's happening at Lucite?" she breathed. "I heard..." She was out of breath and couldn't go on.

Everybody stared for a moment. "It's all true," George Rose was first to speak. They have at least ten feet of new snow. One avalanche blocked the road. Another killed two people. Thank God you're here. Nobody knows quite what's happening or what to do."

"What about the two fronts?"

"They're still very strong and pumping in moisture. Jason Stemple called for you several times today."

"Where is he now?"

"We don't know. His wife and son were killed in the Clementine Ridge avalanche."

"I know. I heard."

Buford spoke then. Samantha had never seen him drawn and worried this way. "There's a terrible dilemma at Lucite. The Wildcat avalanche has built up and it's threatening lodges in the east part of the town. It's risky to evacuate the area because there's no place to put the people. If the storm stops within a few hours, the avalanche may never come down. But if it should release without warning, there'll be more casualties."

You son-of-a-bitch, it's your fault!

Samantha wanted to scream at him, but there wasn't enough anger left, only a fear that kept catching at her breath and tightening her throat, and a heavy sorrow.

"What are you forecasting?"

"We don't know how this storm may behave. It's purely an anomaly."

"Buford, there's nothing mysterious about it. We read the vital signs just as we would for any storm. Now come on, let's get to work."

Samantha found herself organizing a major emergency forecast. One person would collate available data and assemble new information from the Gulf of Mexico, another off the California coast. Buford was to analyze land trends along the route of both systems and George would report on the Canadian low and local influences.

Samantha called the motor pool asking them to notify the ranger station that she was on duty and would remain at the bureau for the night. "They called for me several times today," she explained.

The Bureau was humming again. Skilled people were busy seeking answers that might save lives at Lucite. Finally Samantha was able to relax with a cup of coffee. She sought a quiet office and sat in the dark. Jason was on her mind. Her thoughts went back to the night death took the little girl, and the morning after. Jason had talked, by compulsion it seemed, of his boyhood on a farm in Kansas. He had told about his first pony, and the identical twin calves that confused everyone. And he made her smile with a description of his uncle's moonshine still that blew up when the mash got too sour. Then he told her about their old hired hand, and Samantha knew all the rest was only a prelude, because he needed a reason to tell her about the last hour of Randy Blake.

Perhaps Jason had never before told the story. Samantha thought so. She hoped he had told it to her because she alone would know what it meant to him. Though painful, the experience had about it the perverse glow of a Greek tragedy. Samantha would forever be haunted by the beautiful gray eyes of a youthful Jason, the suffering and bewilderment there as he watched his friend the hired man die under an overturned tractor.

"Lift it off, son," Randy Blake had begged him.

Jason had strained, moaning and crying. "Ataboy, son. that's better. I'll be out in a second. Good fer ya, boy. Just a little bit..." He passed out, and Jason ran for the house two miles away, only to hear a scream that brought him running back.

"Don't leave me, son. God, don't leave me. Lift her off, old buddy."

Jason would bend to the task. The tractor wouldn't move. "That's the way, boy. Feels better already. Heave, boy. Thank God you're here. Don't go away."

Each time Randy would lapse into unconsciousness, Jason would hold his face and weep. As he came awake Jason would strain at the wheel. Randy would smile, whisper encouragement, and faint again. The hired man died after an hour. Jason put his shirt under the pale head and ran crying for help.

"Some people thought it was my fault Randy died. While he still lived I should have gone for help, they said. But I couldn't leave him. He would have suffered more and died alone. He was an old hired man. He had been alone for most of his life. I couldn't leave him to die alone. I went through two harvests of hell watching Randy die, but I learned something from it. There comes a time when every person who cares about you needs you. And then it's not your help they need so much as your caring."

Samantha felt a hand on her shoulder then. It was George Rose. "We think we see a local change in the systems," he said.

Night of the Wren

The wren was hungry. He had uncovered a cluster of insect eggs, but they were scattered and hard to pick up in the darkness. He was busy at that when the alarm went off inside him.

Perhaps it was the gentle vibrations of flakes coming to rest nearby, or the extra warmth of air at the surface of snow. The wren cocked his head to listen and sample the air. From where it came didn't matter because the message was clear: *Go higher.*

He struggled out of the cavity and tried dropping down to the branch, but the branch was gone. He fluttered upward to find a shallow knothole. And as he settled there, his warm cavity with the squirrel hairs disappeared under the rising column of snow.

Chapter Fourteen

Matthew left Wendell in charge at the station and glumly set out for Bluebird Lodge following a trench deeper than the height of his head. It was just past ten-thirty. In a few hours the trench had narrowed by half. In the thickly falling snow, Matthew couldn't tell where the walls ended and the dark space began. Who cared? Snow on the ground, snow falling toward the ground, and more in the sky. Where one ended and the other began didn't matter now. It was all the same stuff. Snow covered the earth, the trees, the buildings, the street lights, everything else. What mattered if it covered the very air and space of Lucite?

Matthew's mood blackened as he trudged along the trench, his torch a halo of white puncturing only a little way into the storm. The snow no longer hung gracefully. The big flakes were starting to swirl. Goddamn wind rising, that spelled trouble. It meant drifts, concentration, cornices. The flakes were jigging, yes, the dance of the flakes, a frenzied, gyrating dance macabre. Soon the dance would end. Wind would push the flakes sideways. They would no longer pelt gently at the head and shoulders, but hurl themselves stinging and blinding at the face. They would drift and pile on the mountainside until gravity overwhelmed cohesion. Then they would crash toward the canyon bottom, rise again into the air, and scream down upon Lucite like a thousand witches airborne.

Matthew shuddered and plodded on.

A knot of shovelers had gathered just inside the front entrance to the Bluebird, resting and drying out before striking back toward the day lodge. Matthew inquired about the avalanche victims. "Down the hall. Room 24, just on the left."

The corridor was deserted, the floor strangely quiet. Of course, the rooms were packed with women and children who wouldn't be allowed in the hall because of avalanche danger. Avalanches had been known to rip a large building into two halves, almost always splitting it, like a walnut, at the central corridor.

Matthew knocked at room 24. Jason stepped out, closing the door behind him. The friends embraced loosely, their hands clasped together.

"You okay?" asked Matthew.

"I'm okay." Jason answered softly. His handshake was firm, his countenance a mirror of calm But his eyes appeared grainy and hard, opaque like a broken face of carborundum.

"Jake, I want to spell you and sit with Ellen and the boy." Matthew knew his voice was tremulous.

"Thanks, Matt."

"You go to the station now and get some rest."

"I can't rest. Matt. I've got to deal with the Wildcat avalanche. If you'll stay here for awhile with..." He paused, not saying the names. Muscles tightened across his face. "I'll get going."

"A shoveler could go with you."

"What for?"

"Well, somebody should go with you."

"Stop it, Matt! Nothing can help Ellen and David now. And I don't count."

Matthew watched Jason down the hall and out into the lobby. His hand was on the door knob. He was sweating. He didn't want to go inside. Maybe he could just stay out in the hall, but there was no place to sit. Anyhow he had just promised Jason to sit with the dead bodies. Jason was right to snap at him. Jason had perspective. What happened to his wife and son was heartbreaking. Worse, terrible. But if you called it that, how would you describe what could happen in Lucite before the night ended?

Matthew was getting hold of himself. Ellen and David were names of things. Too bad about the boy, but poor Ellen was maybe better off dead and Jason was better off having her dead. He felt sorry for Jason, but that's all. It would be silly, even counter, to grieve at grief.

Matthew felt better. He turned the knob. He didn't have to even look at the corpses. He would sit and think about, uh—the round bottom of Ginger, or the smooth white legs of Gloria. Or maybe take a nap. It wouldn't be long.

A single lamp illuminated the room. Even turned low, it provided enough light to outline white lumps on each twin-size bed. Someone had taken the morgue blankets, probably for use in other rooms. Only a sheet remained for each bed.

Matthew sat in a chair by the lamp, flanked by the beds. He looked neither left nor right. His eyes were glued to a heat duct in the ceiling. But it was melancholy, even oppressive to sit and stare so rigidly. And it wasn't working. Even though his gaze didn't leave the ceiling, images were seeping in from both sides.

Why couldn't they at least have left some pillows for the bodies? Almost the last thing Ellen said was, "My head hurts cocked this way."

And, Dear God, the face on the right wasn't even covered.

Without moving his head or shifting his gaze, Matthew saw that the face wasn't covered and it was so distracting that he could barely concentrate on the heat duct.

The duct was brown, a simple grill, with a lever to shut it off or perhaps a switch of some kind. Cobwebs laced the grill, but one of the damned faces was uncovered and Matthew thought of the mania that compels some people to hurl themselves off cliffs because they fear heights so. He couldn't bear the uncovered face. Not for any longer. The sheet was turned down. He would close his eyes, grope the bed and simply flip the sheet over the cold face. No, he would just keep his eyes on the duct as he moved toward the bed. One flip of the sheet and...

He looked at the face then. Thank God It wasn't Ellen. The lamp, being only a little higher than the bed, illuminated the forehead, nose and cheeks of the boy. Shadows deepened the closed eyes and heightened the lips. Matthew studied the fine, youthful face for a minute, maybe two. Finally, he touched the deep cleave at the chin and gently brushed back a tuft of errant hair at the forehead. He pulled the sheet up, spread it with care across David, closed his eyes and stood over the body for a time. Then he made his way back to the chair where he had been sitting between the beds. He picked up a small cushion and turned to the other figure. Ever so gently, Matthew raised Ellen's head, only slightly bending the stiffening neck, and placed the pillow underneath. He didn't raise the sheet, but he knew. Yes, Ellen was still beautiful as a woman. He felt along the hand and arm. The bracelet was gone. He dropped to one knee and laid his forehead on the bare mattress.

Some part of him was expelling words that come out muffled and hoarse. *"Ellen, Ellen. In the name of God."*

Then he was on his feet, lurching down the corridor toward the lobby. He wasn't walking or flying. A moving suspension, flowing toward the soothing blackness of the storm. The overhead lights moved past slowly and awkwardly. Why couldn't he make them go faster? "*Ellen, Ellen.*" Finally he was outside, lurching through snow that dragged at his feet, then running along the squeaky road. He wanted to cry out; suddenly he was yelling, shaking a fist, screaming. Faintly his voice echoed back.

He was on his knees again, hunched up and moaning. He felt cold. He pushed up both hands to brush away the snow from his bare head. It was dry. He looked at his hands. They were dry. He tilted was face to the sky and felt nothing. He opened his eyes to the blackness. Nothing.

It wasn't snowing anymore.

Chapter Fifteen

Close to midnight, Matthew arrived back at the ranger station. He hadn't wanted to leave the quiet room at the Bluebird, but the tall, somber man who replaced him insisted. "You've had enough for one day, maybe for a hundred days," he told Matthew in a low voice. "I understand the woman and boy were friends of yours."

"No. It was more," protested Matthew, the words springing without thought, an emotion offended.

"I'm real sorry about what happened. Seems like a terrible thing, but at least they're safe now."

His words jolted Matthew back to the living. The tall man had a point. Ellen and David were gone. They couldn't go again. But six-thousand people in Lucite still had to die, and some, perhaps hundreds, even thousands, might die here tonight. He remembered the little cemetery beneath Clementine Ridge. Spent eddies of the avalanche that buried Ellen and David likely came to rest there against the headstones. Symbolic that the headstones were boulders of birdseye porphyry, base rock of the silver veins that the miners picked, shoveled, blasted, sorted, and followed into the ground. The avalanche must have come down at night, otherwise the miners would have been safe in their tunnels. There was an odd irony in that too.

A grim-faced Jason greeted Matthew. He didn't seem relieved that it wasn't snowing anymore. "How does it look?"' asked Matthew.

"If the storm lays we may save the town. But the wind's rising. That's a worry. The bureau says the snow may start again."

"How can I help?"

"Get some sleep. Maybe spell me later."

It was cold in the back room. Matthew lit a propane lamp, turning it low. It would give a little heat and light without glare. There were four cots arranged head to head along two walls. Matthew undressed and occupied the same cot he used twelve hours ago. This time he slipped inside the sleeping bag and zipped it up, shutting out the cold.

After a while he began to feel oppressed and crowded. Of course David had been crushed to death instantly. He hadn't suffered the eye-bugging, helpless panic of smothering under the snow. Matthew unzipped the bag and brought his hands and arms outside. He'd rather be cold than shut-in.

He woke to the sound of voices across the room. He recognized the bishop, then Wendell, the latter's voice a parody of ghetto whine. Shit, who let those two in here together?.

Straining his eyes in the dim light, Matthew saw Olsen sitting on a cot preparing to turn in. Wendell was already in the adjoining sleeping bag. He must have been awakened by the bishop because he was jawing at the big man.

"We don't go around playin' grab ass in the dark."

"Just didn't know you were there, sonny. Sorry if I scared you," apologized the bishop.

"Man, you never scared me, but you damn near hurt me. Them's the family jewels down there."

Matthew thought he heard an unabashed expletive from the bishop, who was struggling to fit his monstrous frame into a sleeping bag.

Wendell must have heard too. "Whatcha mean, swearin', a preacher like you?" he goaded the big man.

"We don't have preachers."

"Who don't?"

"Mormons."

"Well, what are you then?"

"I'm a ward bishop. That's not the same as a preacher."

"You preach?"

"Well, I speak sometimes, or as we like to say, take up the time."

"In church?"

"Yes.

"Well, that's preachin', which means you're a preacher."

"Whatever you say. Call me what you want tomorrow, but tonight just get to sleep." The big man seemed a little irritated, but Wendell wasn't through.

"There had to be Mormon preachers."

"Why?"

"Well, my old uncle was never wrong, and he used to say that the stingiest dude on earth is a Mormon preacher."

"How's that?"

"He takes up all the good-lookin' females, just like a grouse does. Poor devils down the line gotta do without."

Wendell was laying it on a little thick. Matthew wished he would shut up and get to sleep.

'Well," said the bishop, "I've only got one wife and she's right fat. Nobody else wants her."

"How come Mormons stopped havin' lots of wives?"

"The Lord told the Prophet that the saints should quit it. We haven't practiced polygamy for better than a hundred years."

"Practiced. What you mean practiced? Sounds like something you got but don't do."

"Well, it's said that polygamy will be restored to the priesthood when we're worthy."

"What's this priesthood thing?"

"It's authority from God given to man."

"Any man?"

"Any who's worthy."

"Is this authority all that good to have?"

"Well, yes. It's the greatest gift a man can have on earth."

"And a woman?"

"Her greatest glory is to marry a fellow who holds the priesthood."

"This here priesthood, I want some of that."

"Okay, son, go to sleep." Olsen flopped his big body on the cot. It groaned and squeaked. He fidgeted for a moment, then sighed as if to signal that the conversation was ended. There was a long silence. Matthew could hear the deep, even breathing of the bishop, close to slumber, when Wendell spoke again. The bishop wasn't fully awake, so Wendell repeated: "How about lettin' me in on this priesthood?"

The bishop groaned.

"What about it?" repeated Wendell.

Olsen rolled over and sighed again. "I guess you know already. Just anybody can't hold the priesthood."

"Who can't?"

"Well, woman can't. Young boys can't. Sinners and apostates can't."

"What about black dudes?"

"Well, yes, the Lord revealed to the prophet a while back that black fellows can hold the priesthood."

"Why did he wait till just now?"

"I guess nobody knows for sure."

Another silence. Olsen was breathing evenly again, a prelude to sleep, when Wendell laughed hoarsely. "Well, there's gotta be a reason. I want to know."

The cot squeaked as the bishop threshed about, finally raising his head and propping it with an upturned palm. "Look, boy, why does this mean so much to you?"

"Watch that boy shit." The condescending note had disappeared from Wendell's voice. Matthew wondered if he might pounce on the big Dane.

Matthew interrupted. "Okay, break it up you two. Go to sleep. All that racket will bring down the avalanche." The lamp's light reflected from the eyes of both men as they turned surprised stares in his direction. They clearly hadn't known he was there. but they were quickly back at each other, with Olsen first to speak.

"I didn't mean it that way." Now the bishop seemed wide awake. "All we ever said was that black folks couldn't hold the priesthood in this existence. Now a revelation has changed that."

"What caused it to change?"

"Well, I think it's possible that the Lord decided to forgive the black race."

"How you mean that?" Wendell was patronizing again.

"As I understand it, there was a great war in the preexistence. The forces of the Lord and the forces of evil fought one another."

"That's a scary idea. A bunch of Spooks with burp guns. Who won?"

"The army of the Lord."

"Then what happened?"

"All those who fought for Evil were banished to Hell. The others were chosen to inhabit the Earth during our time."

"What's that got to do with the priesthood stuff?"

"Well," said the bishop, "this may not be true doctrine, but I was taught that during the war in heaven, lots of spirits were not valiant. They sat on the fence, so to speak, and wouldn't help the rest of us battle evil." The bishop's voice was rising. "The Lord, in his anger, cursed them with a black skin and sent them to earth to repent. Now that's only what I've learned. I don't know if it's the truth or not, but if it's true then I figure the Lord has decided to forgive and forget."

Again, a long silence. Matthew, wide awake now, was warming to the bizarre conversation. It was fascinating, but would there be any end short of an earthly little war right here in the back room of the ranger station?

Wendell unzipped his bag, slipped out, and swung to a sitting position, both feet on the floor. "You know what I'm thinkin'?" he asked, tone of voice promising a supreme revelation.

Nobody answering the question, he went on: "I'm thinkin' you white guys used to be black. You were the crazy dudes. You fought like cats and dogs and killed one another like flies. If you couldn't kill fast enough you invented new ways to kill each other faster. And when you' got low on folks to kill you screwed more to begat some more to kill.

"This here war in Heaven. I can believe every word of it, 'cause those guys would as soon fight and breed in Heaven as anywhere. But this time, man, you got your signals confused. The Lord, He don't like bloodshed, not even the blood of spirits. Wasn't that a sight, you rowdies fightin' and bleedin' and befoulin' all over Heaven. But the Lord, He don't like that. He don't approve of spirits that can't keep peace even in Heaven. So you know what he done?"

Wendell paused and looked around the cold room, including Matthew as part of his audience. It was an eerie scene. The flickering light of the lamp revealing Olsen lying on his side, woolly head propped only inches from the shoulder of the sermonizing black man. Wendell had one hand on a knee, his free hand moved upward to point a finger accusingly at Matthew, his stance and ghetto voice having taken on the flavor of fire and brimstone. "I'll tell you what the Lord done: He cast out the hate-filled warmongers. He took them polluters and violators of Heaven and hurled 'em to earth. And you know what else he done? He punished 'em by bleachin' the glorious pigmentation right out of their coverin'. That's right. The Lord, he cursed them wicked, violent spirits with just what they deserved, a white skin."

Wendell had risen to a standing position, still pointing the accusing finger directly at Matthew. He stood in stark outline for a moment, eyes shining, then slipped back inside his sleeping bag and zipped it up. He put his hands behind the back of his head and chuckled. The bishop giggled audibly. Matthew smiled at first, then broke out with a snicker. Wendell burst into a cackling laugh and the bishop roared.

Chapter Sixteen

Samantha was at the data map when they called her. "Mr. Stemple wants to speak with you from Lucite." She ran to the phone.

"Are you okay, Jason?"

"A little tired, that's all."

"How can I help?"

"Stay by the phone. I need you there."

"I won't leave."

"Thank you."

"Jason, I'm terribly sorry."

"You shouldn't be sorry. You were right."

"I don't mean that, Jason. And I don't worry about being right. I'm sorry for what's happened. And I'm sorry I ran away."

"Has the storm ended?"

"I don't think so."

"It just stopped snowing here."

"We thought it might. But it may start again."

"Why did it stop?"

"Jake, there's a strong wind in the valley. It's very dusty here, blowing east, gusting up to thirty-five miles an hour. We expected the winds to move toward the Wasatch and warm the system, possibly enough to stop precipitation for a while."

"For long?"

"We can't know for sure, but I'm afraid it's a temporary thing."

"You think it will snow some more?"

"I'm afraid it may."

"That's hard to believe."

"The systems are still powerful. Why is it so hard to believe?"

"Because of the amount of snow here and because of the situation here."

"Is it desperate?"

"The Wildcat avalanche will probably release if there's two or three more hours of heavy snow. Two lodges are in its path and they're filled with more than a thousand people."

"I know, Jason, and you can't shoot the avalanche."

"Out of the question. There's so much snow already we can't risk a shot without evacuating the people. Anyway the disturbance might set off Killvein slide and that would take the Jackhammer and day lodges."

"How can I help you?"

"This is unfair, but tell me what to do."

"Can you evacuate the people under Wildcat?"

"I hate to start that unless we know the ridge will avalanche. It's a dangerous movement, and no place is safe."

"Then I recommend you wait for a while. It's always possible there won't be any more snow." She was being irresponsible, but Jason would do that anyway. Samantha could scarcely go on. Jason needed her and he was reaching. If she could touch him, feel the shape of his misery with her fingertips, she could help him. In a man like Jason, love could heal agony. But she was professional. No letting down.

"Jesus, I hoped somebody would say that."

"Jason, is the station safe?" She was letting down but she didn't care anymore. Her voice was getting too soft, too much a voice for Jason, and people were listening, but she didn't care anymore.

"That's the least of my worries."

"But not of mine."

"Thanks for caring. We were fools not to believe you."

"Jason, I won't listen to that. You weren't ever a fool. I was the fool for calling you names."

"I'm glad you're staying at the bureau tonight. Do you have a place to sleep?"

Yes, he knew. Jason's voice was tender now. A voice for her. "You know if there's a place to lay my head I can sleep" She wanted the statement to convey some levity.

"I guess a girl who can sleep on the reception counter at Children's Hospital can sleep anywhere."

"I'm glad you remembered."

"Do you have a place to lay your head?"
"I'll find a place."
"Will you call me in an hour?"
"Of course."

Chapter 17

A burst of brightness and a sharp noise woke Matthew. He must have slept for hours, but it seemed only minutes. He was exhausted. The exhaustion and sleepiness were pulling him back into slumber when he heard muffled voices and remembered where he was.

The Coleman had gone out, but a wedge of light entered through the partially open door. Matthew recognized Jason bending over Olsen's cot, talking in a soft but urgent voice. Olsen was swinging to his feet.

"I'll get the crews back together. When did it start?"

"About half an hour ago.. We'll have to evacuate the Bluebird lodge."

Wendell unzipped his bag and was quickly on his feet. "Where's Ginger?" He looked wildly around the room then rubbed his eyes, boy-like, with both fists. "I'm going after Ginger."

Jason spoke to him gently, "Ginger's okay for now. You get some more sleep. We'll need you in an hour or so."

But Wendell was pulling on his trousers, 'No way, man."

They were gone then, shutting the door and shutting out the light. Snowing again. Dread squeezed Matthew's stomach like a hunger pain, a vise squeezing and cramping.

The walls of this canyon couldn't hold more snow. Of that Matthew was certain. It wasn't instinct or gut feeling. His engineer's training wouldn't allow him to grasp at straws of hope. This was a simple case of gravity offset by tensional and adhesive forces within the snow. Only friction, stretched to the limit, was keeping a million shattering tons of snow off the bellies and backs of thousands of sleeping people.

Matthew closed his eyes and lay back, pulling the zipper on his bag to hold out the chill and the fear.

There was a war. The mountain was hanging by its fingertips, slipping, turning, then suddenly it shot a white host out and down like a rocket on a sled to strike the advancing canyon at its feet and knees. The impact rent a great fault, the canyon roaring its agony, belching smoke and fire. Then there was a crack, perfect as if sawed, a seam, then a stream pouring forth, a gush of silver, glittering, beautiful, but floating there a stone of the dike. God, it was coming up from the cemetery. There were bones and pieces of people. Where were David and Ellen?

Matthew was struggling and kicking inside the bag as he awoke. In an instant he was on his feet and dressing. No more of this. Maybe he could help some way.

The main room had nearly filled with frightened people. A hush was on the crowd as they listened carefully to Jason standing at the big map, speaking softly, a pointer in one hand, cup of coffee in the other.

Matthew judged all the lodge owners were there, plus many of the ski patrol and ski school. Jason's every word was affecting his listeners.

The path of the avalanche couldn't be predicted with certainty. Most likely it would follow Wildcat Basin to the point where the draw bent sharply west. There it would spill beyond the containment and hook around the lowest place in the ridge. If it were airborne, it would be expected to cross the road four-hundred yards west of the horseshoe, and the center of the mass would flow within thirty feet of Bluebird Lodge. If the slide stayed on the ground, which Jason doubted, it would climb out of the draw further to the west and its mass would center along the west end of the lodge. Either way, Bluebird Lodge was doomed, but lodges to the east would be safer if the avalanche stayed on the ground.

Jason stopped and sipped his coffee thoughtfully, then described what must be done. He started slowly, deliberately, but as he finished his voice was faster and carried a note of urgency.

Bluebird and Eagle Lodges must be evacuated at once. Everyone would be moved to the basement at the Blue Spruce. As soon as this move was complete, all rooms at the Blue Spruce must be emptied also. It would put 900 women and children in the Blue Spruce basement. That meant standing room only, perhaps for hours, and the move itself was perilous. The avalanche could come at any time. There was a fifty percent probability it would slide by four a.m. if the snow continued. That was less than two hours away. During the move, people would be safer in the lodges than in the open, so the ski school would move groups of fifty at ten-minute intervals. Each group would hold hands during the movement. All street and walk clearing would cease during the evacuation. The ski Patrol and Olsen's entire crew, now 75 men, would stand by in the horseshoe parking lot.

The leader of each group would wear an emitter and count his paces, radioing every increment of 25 steps so rescue teams would know the precise location of each moving group. If a group were caught out in the open by the avalanche, they were to lie down, with hands around their mouths. The infirmary would move last, setting up in the east end of Blue Spruce Lodge.

Then Jason drew a circle encompassing all affected lodges. "Nobody will be allowed in this zone, not even any of you, beginning thirty minutes from now. Each lodge owner is to be the last person to leave his or her lodge. Now I think we should start." He paused to single out Bob Blake, manager of Bluebird Lodge. "Good luck, Bob, be careful."

Matthew joined Olsen's shovelers for the half-mile walk along the south road to the horseshoe parking lot. He wanted out of the ranger station and there was simply nowhere else to go. Wendell had made a dash for the Bluebird, promising a return to the station before the 30-minute curfew. Matthew didn't want to be alone with Jason. He couldn't possibly talk to Jason about David and Ellen, and he couldn't sit alone with Jason and talk about anything else. Surely Jason must have suspected what Ellen herself knew. How could a man as sensitive as Jason fail to see the cause and depth of Ellen's agony? Matthew couldn't talk of it now, so he fell in behind the rescue crew, a noisy group moving invisibly through the falling snow. The main road had been reduced to a steep-walled Jeep path no more than six feet in width. The trench was now deep enough to shut out all possibility of lateral sight. Even in full daylight one would see only a ribbon of sky. Matthew judged that there was perhaps three feet of packed snow underfoot, and the walls rose seven to eight feet above the base. Settling had occurred and of course some wall height could be attributed to snow displaced from the path, but it appeared that eleven to twelve feet had fallen in the canyon. The avalanche would start nearly 5,000 feet above the canyon floor. Add a foot of snowfall per thousand elevation and new snowpack at the top could be approaching fourteen or fifteen feet. Drifts and cornices would be much deeper.

Jason was right. Here was a danger to boggle the mind. The evacuation was as necessary as clearing the intersection ahead of a hurtling train, and it had to be done swiftly.

As the men came up to the unseen parking rendezvous, Edwin met them and directed groups of twenty each to snowbound charter buses for shelter during the watch. A few had been left behind to keep a clear path between the day lodge and Clementine and Jackhammer Lodges. Everyone else was here and would stay here until either the snow ceased or the Wildcat avalanche came down. Their chore now was to maintain a path between the buses and Blue Spruce Lodge. And wait.

Matthew sought out Edwin and Olsen in the big high-domed bus closest to the Blue Spruce. Edwin was on the portable radio, talking alternately to Jason at the ranger station and Neal Anderson, the ski school head, at Bluebird Lodge. The first group of fifty had been assembled and would move out in two minutes. Matthew could hear Neal issuing crisp commands but reassuring his charges. "Hold hands now. Don't be frightened. We don't expect the avalanche yet, but if it comes you must quickly lay flat in the snow." Then he was counting, "Point twenty five, point fifty, point hundred, point twenty five."

Jason had said it was 340 yards from Bluebird to Blue Spruce. Neal counted around to the third hundred, then twenty five again, then immediately announced, "We're at the lodge." Matthew judged quickly. Neal's steps were long by a mere inch or so. Pretty good job. Then the second group was coming and counting.

The world of Lucite was silent except for the count as it came in the radio. Even the great flakes couldn't be heard as they pelted against the mound of snow covering the bus. Only yards away there was a city of people, some this moment moving through the black night, but no sound penetrated the muted, insulated world of darkness and silence except the terse cackle of the radio: "Point seventy five, point hundred."

Then the cadence was broken. The point count didn't come in when it should. There was a moment of tension, finally the instructor's voice, "Point two hundred plus sixteen. We've lost a little boy."

"Well, he can't get out of the trail. He'll be scared as hell but the next group will pick him up. Move on."

Then another group was at the Blue Spruce and yet another was moving, counting. They picked up the lost boy at point one seventy-five plus twenty. The instructor complained of visibility. The falling snow was a blinding crescendo, and the walk way needed shoveling. People were slipping and falling and they were having to carry the smallest children. Then the group was at the Blue Spruce and the last group moved out from the Bluebird. It was slow in starting and slow moving. The point counts were noticeably farther apart. "Can you speed it up any?" Edwin was urging. "We still have to get the doctors and patients out."

"We'll try." Then the point count went on but no faster. Matthew thought the move was falling behind schedule because the snow was coming down even faster than before, fouling up the trail, but they couldn't halt the movement just to clean trail.

Edwin alerted the Bluebird to get ready to move out the hospital crew. "No straggling, everybody stays together and point count all the way."

Jason came on the radio then. "We're getting in trouble, Ed. We can't wait any longer. Everybody is to clear out of Bluebird immediately. Ed, keep a count on both moving groups."

The last words from the Bluebird were, "We're ready. We'll move out in about three..."

Wren's Reunion

The wren woke cold and stiff on his perch, but something else was wrong. Terribly wrong. The knothole was blacker than the darkest night, and the air inside still and stale. The way out had closed. Panic. But a tiny cavity at the top guided him higher, following the faintest current of air. His wings beat wildly against the loose snow. Nothing. No way out. Another desperate flailing, clawing this time. A tiny opening. Suddenly the snow began to move. Then all the snow was gone, followed by a moment of silence before a mighty rush of wind thrust the wren backward into the cavity, pressing him there. Barely audible, a crash rumbled from below, muted by the howling wind. Trees were vibrating, shaking, breaking. Finally the wren laid still on the floor of the cavity, spent but safe at last.

It wasn't long before he heard a soft call. Instantly he jumped at the opening, singing his joy toward the ledge. She answered, closer now. In a moment she was slipping inside.

Soon they were drowsy and dozing. The storm continued but the wrens knew now that the great white stars couldn't hurt them anymore.

An Episode of Avalanche

At 3:43 a.m. the beating wings of a wren set the Wildcat Avalanche in motion. It was quick and convulsive, with little more life span than a roll of thunder, for it came to rest only thirty-five seconds after the desperate vibrations of tiny wings pushed the first flake to rasp against others. A gathering, a tiny ball, a quick sharp drop, and the white world moved, gaining momentum, speeding faster and faster as if sucked hither by demons, sweeping along the ground through the blackness of night and storm, a monolith slicing a resisting universe, but suddenly malignant, changing the air through which it moved, pushing the air until an awful turbulence stirred within, a wind blast of explosive power. The vast column of snow began to rise off the earth, flying above the ground, no longer sliding but falling, hurtling against the air below, creating a wild wind in front and a howling vacuum behind, like the shockwave of Hiroshima.

The Wildcat avalanche was still partially airborne when it swept across the road some 200 yards west of the Lucite horseshoe.

Chapter Eighteen

Merlin woke and turned on the small light above his cot to check the time. After 3 a.m. He had slept well, considering. Probably the pills, or maybe the injection at midnight. But the pain in his foot was starting again. More pills? Naw. Suffer through for a while, then go back to sleep. He wanted a clear head, maybe figure out what was going on.

Hulda would be wild with worry. Hell, no help for it. At least he wasn't in too bad a shape, considering the trailer had smashed halfway through the cab of the Jimmy. That wasn't even what pinned him. Damn driveshaft had somehow pushed the five-speed right up through the floorboard, trapping his lower right leg and foot against the firewall. Shit, how it had hurt and how he wanted to scream when he realized he couldn't get out of the truck.

The way the leg felt now was nothing compared to how it had felt, smashed there in the truck. He wouldn't be able to drive for a while, but at least they hadn't cut it off. They had brought a doctor right away. Then after a while another doctor came. The second man Merlin recognized as a bone surgeon from Salt Lake. He had heard the two doctors whispering something about leverage space, light source and trauma. He had already passed out twice, but he vowed not to pass out again. Nobody was going to cut off a foot that would be okay if he could just get it out of that jagged steel and torn sheet metal.

But he must have Passed out again because he came to just as they lifted him into a station wagon. The foot was bandaged but still there. He could tell that from the shape of the bandage.

"How'd you get me out, Doc?" Merlin had asked.

"We found a little hydraulic jack in the car that ran you off the road. You're lucky."

"Are those girls okay?"

'Yes. But scared nearly to death."

"My foot. Is it okay?"

"A bit mangled. We'll operate in Lucite."

"Lucite. What about Salt Lake?"

"We can't get you there. The road's closed."

Three doctors had put him to sleep. He woke to a soft hand on his forehead, and a woman's husky voice, the words cool, the tone warm. "Shouldn't go around putting your foot in bear traps." A nurse. He must have been complaining about the pain. "When you do that it's bound to hurt a little."

Merlin looked into her face. Beautiful. Full lips, pouting. Big shining eyes. A black girl.

"Where am I?"

"Bluebird General hospital."

"Bluebird's a lodge."

"You're in the hospital part."

"Oh shit."

"Don't make light of our great institution." She reached for his wrist and began a pulse count. "We've never lost a patient here." She pretended to wet a finger, then touched his forehead. "No sizzle. Temperature under 110. That's good."

"My foot okay?"

"I wouldn't lie to you. It's kind of messy." Merlin breathed deeply.

"At least it's still there, right"

"That's something else. We've never cut off a foot here."

Merlin had grinned in spite of himself. "Ever sewed one back on?"

"Yours."

He was serious then. "Thanks for helping. When can I walk on it?"

"Ask the doctor." She leaned over him to attach a pressure gauge. "You're just lucky it didn't happen in the days before Band-Aids and Super Glue."

"How come you're takin' such good care of me?"

"I'm impressed with jockeys who smash themselves rather than two little girls."

"Have you known lots of us jockeys?"

"Well, not in a biblical sense," she had answered.

Now Merlin felt alone in the dark morning. Other patients were tucked behind curtains around the big room, which must have served as a dormitory in normal times. There were several sprains and two cases of broken bones besides his own. Late yesterday they had brought in a woman who was short of breath, with a dry cough. She was put on oxygen. Ginger told him it was a case of water on the lungs from the altitude. Others had been brought in through the evening and night, many treated and sent back to quarters. There seemed to be plenty of doctors, they kept changing, but there were only three nurses as far as Merlin could tell. Nobody had spelled Ginger, at least not before Merlin fell asleep at midnight. Merlin was glad for that in one way, but he did hope the girl was getting rested now. Gotta take good care of a humdinger like her.

He heard low voices from the hall. Ginger and a man were standing at the door. They kissed, then clung to each other, cheeks touching for a while. The man left and Ginger stepped inside the ward. She saw Merlin awake and walked toward his bed. Jesus, what a body, and a walk like Cleopatra.

"Would you believe we gotta move?" Her voice was cheerful but her mouth lacked the bright curving smile of the evening. There was worry in the almond eyes, maybe fear. Merlin was suddenly aware of a swell of sound and movement around the lodge.

"What's wrong?"

"Another avalanche." There was a catch in her voice. "You know anything about them?"

"You'd better not be where one is, I know that."

"Why would we move?" she asked.

"I guess it's the Wildcat slide. Could come right through here."

"Can it hit the ranger station?"

"No. That's too far over."

She brightened. "We gotta fix you so they can carry you out."

"Where to?" There was noise in the hall, and bustle in the ward. All the lights were on.

"The Blue Spruce Lodge."

"What you call that hospital?"

"Orthopedic Blue."

"Why blue?"

"Cause everyplace we go it's blue."

"Good hospital, is it?"

"The best. No bonded indebtedness. No accounts receivable. No avalanches."

"Who was the guy at the door"?"

"My husband."

"You worried?"

"Only about him, and you. Now lets wrap you up. Lots of commotion in the hall now. They were trying to empty the lodge fast. A stretcher was laid across two chairs. Ginger wrapped blankets around Merlin and eased him onto the stretcher. As he lay back the pain must have shown on his face. She held out both hands, "Squeeze." Merlin grasped the hands, cool, soft, slender fingers.

"Feel better?"

"Yeah. That beats the needle you carry. What you call that medicine?"

"Uh, just call it a double clutch prescribed specially for an old jockey." She pulled away then and picked up the cotton cord. "I'm strapping you inside those blankets. Arms in or out?"

Merlin held both arms high in the air. She had the first loop firmly around his chest in an instant and soon he was tied to both stretcher and blankets. "Whatcha think," asked Merlin, "that I'm gonna run away?"

"You couldn't outrun a maggot. It's still snowing like blazes. You're gonna stay warm all the way to Orthopedic Blue."

"When do we start?"

"We're last. That's because you are gonna get carried. Everybody else has to walk."

"You better go now."

"Can't. I talked myself blue in the face to get Wendy to let me stay."

"Why?"

"It's my job. I'm not really a skier. I'm a nurse."

"Wendy your husband?"

She nodded.

"What did you tell him?"

"That I had last rites for a couple of patients and a shot of cyanide for you."

The lodge seemed to be emptying out fast. Merlin noticed that for the first time he and Ginger were alone in the ward. "Everybody but you is at the debarkation place. They'll be here for us in a minute."

Most of the ward curtains had been pulled down, probably to serve as wrapping for patients. There couldn't be all that many blankets available.

Merlin wondered where Ginger had scrounged the three that he was now wrapped so tightly inside of. Ginger herself was standing at the hall door anxiously looking both ways, waiting for the bearers. She was wearing only ski pants and a shiny parka. It would protect her some, but not any too much. She walked back to Merlin's bed then and placed a hand on his forehead.

"Still no sizzle. I guess you'll survive the transfer. They'll be here soon, don't worry."

Merlin felt like reminding her Honey, it's you who's worried but that wouldn't be fair. Something to take her mind off the fear? "Hey, I'm hurting. How about some more of that pain-killing double clutch?"

Her hands were gripping his when they heard the avalanche. Ginger was startled, puzzled, but Merlin recognized it instantly. First a low whine, but no time for analysis before it became an incredible exploding scream. In a quick spastic motion, Merlin pulled the woman to him, locking his arms behind her before the floor shuddered and the walls seemed to bend around them. A shattering crash put out the light. A quick smell of smoke, Ginger screaming in his ear as they fell, a horrible thump, things crashing all around, Ginger muted now, agony in his foot, stabbing pain in his side, a blackjack laid against his head. Then a quiet, choking, hurting oppressiveness. Incredibly, his arms still locked around Ginger, limp above him. Trying to clear his head, can't shake it. Trying to breathe, can't. Scream for help. Can't. Choking, waking, breathing, choking. Then conscious, wide awake, pain again, but Ginger breathing against him. Thank God.

"Dear Heavenly Father, we ask you to bless us and help us. Thank thee for it. Amen."

Dark, an awful darkness, but they were alive. That was something. No chance to move. Getting cold, but pain gone now. All healed.

Chapter Nineteen

Sound of the avalanche didn't reach the bus until after Anderson, who was leading the last group, gravely reported: "Point two hundred" then shouted, "Down! Everybody down."

He might have said more but by then the wind was screaming into his microphone. Matthew never heard the wind directly, only felt a vibration rumbling up through the bus chassis, and heard a muffled crack, crack, like the splintering of wood in the distance.

Everybody in the bus was on their feet, Edwin calling Jason, "The avalanche just went by. It was airborne. We're moving out."

He tossed the radio to Matthew. "Try to reach Anderson, he was only seventy five yards from the Blue Spruce. He may be okay. Then try to call in Blake at Bluebird. Let's go."

Even as the bus emptied in a rush, a call came in. It was Anderson, his voice excited and unsteady. "I think it missed us but I can't tell for sure. Everybody's still on the ground. Some may be hurt. They're screaming and crying."

Jason came in with a quick command. "Stay there, Andy. Ed's on the way. Anybody heard from Blake?"

"Jake," it was Anderson again. "I think the slide went right through Bluebird." It seemed as if he was answering Jason's question.

Three tries brought no response from Blake. Matthew pocketed the radio, fished a flashlight from his pocket and stepped out of the bus. He would join the rescuers; no need to sit in the bus.

It was still snowing as if nature didn't know of the cataclysm at Lucite. It was an ironic snow because the falling flakes were the only commonplace thing left in this tortured place. Mathew's mind grappled with the thought that death was scattered from hell to breakfast up just ahead. The earth was shattered up there and the damned relentless bloody snow still piled up on the witless, rocky, death-haunted soil of this goddamn canyon. What about the miners? Those alive had left and those dead didn't have to. Why were these skiers so stupidly arrogant to learn nothing from the lesson of the miners? Those dead people up ahead, all stupid. The live ones stupid too. Everybody dumb shit stupid and maybe soon dead.

An angry Matthew was hurrying toward Blue Spruce Lodge when Wendell caught up behind him, running. "You okay?" panted Matthew.

Wendell, hard to understand, gasping. "Ginger. Up there somewhere. Please help."

They ran ahead together. Wendell sobbing with fear and exhaustion. He had run through deepening snow in the pathway from the ranger station.

They passed Blue Spruce Lodge. Women and children from the last group were moving inside the front door, single file. Faces tear-streaked, they were wet from lying in the snow, dazed with shock and fear. At the corner a small knot of boys, heads bowed, praying. It was the deacons and Olsen. "Amen." He pushed the weeping, snow-covered boys toward the lodge and joined Wendell and Matthew. "We've lost one," he told Matthew. "He stayed to help move the stretchers. We're afraid he's gone." There was a catch in the big man's voice.

"Ginger?" it was Wendell.

"The nurse your wife?"

"Yes."

"She stayed behind too! Dear God, let's go."

They found Edwin at the east end of the debris. He was waiting for them, having seen Olsen. "One of your boys, was he still at Bluebird?"

"Yes. Any news?"

"We' ve got to find out how many are under there."

"What about my boy?"

"I don't know. They're bringing out a body now."

Matthew felt Wendell stiffen at his side.

"We're afraid it's Bob Blake. He was probably in the boiler room turning off the power. They think the boiler blew."

Men came tramping along the trail, burdened, instructing one another in low voices. "Keep going. We'll take him on to the lodge. Then come back." Someone flashed a light. Yes, it was Blake, very white, dead, half-opened mouth still packed with snow.

Someone said, "They've picked up a signal. They're digging toward it."

Edwin and the bishop held a quick consultation. All members of the last full group were accounted for without casualties, thank God. But no one left at the Bluebird had been heard from or seen alive. There had to be two men with fractured legs from skiing yesterday and one woman. Another woman was ambulatory with frostbite and a third with pulmonary edema. Merlin Landis, the truck driver, was there. Those were all the stretcher cases. One doctor had stayed behind, plus the nurse, six stretcher bearers from the ski school, and a deacon. Luckily the remaining stretcher bearers had been waiting at Blue Spruce. All those at Bluebird, except for Merlin and the nurse, were under the overhang at the east door when the avalanche hit. Merlin's bed was at the northeast corner of the ward. He was probably there or close by. Edwin thought the nurse was probably with him.

Edwin put his hand on Wendell's arm. "All we can do is dig and hope. We've got a hundred diggers in there. You better stay here."

"Please, I have to go in," Wendell said.

Edwin looked carefully at him. "Okay, sure."

Olsen had a hand on Matthew's elbow. "Let's go." They hurriedly climbed the debris, stumbling, groping their way toward what had been Bluebird Lodge. They met rescuers carrying another body: young ski patrolmen, anguished. The dead man was an instructor, their friend.

"His head's crushed," they told Edwin. "One arm is gone and we couldn't find it. Jesus."

They trudged on through the awful roughness of snow, ice, rocks and pieces of trees. A brick wall loomed out of the blackness, a light shining on it, probably a beacon for the rescuers. It was a wall of Bluebird Lodge, a corner almost pillar-like, unattached at either end and jagged at the top with a layer of snow already gathered there since the avalanche. It was all they could see of Bluebird, a grim monument to the power of an airborne avalanche.

Rescuers were bringing out another stretcher. It was the woman with pulmonary edema. They had worried she must have oxygen. Nothing to worry about now. She was dead. Someone said, "They're digging out another one." The digging was concentrated about fifty feet downstream from the east end. A rescuer explained to Edwin, "Either the wind blew everybody or the snow carried them."

There was activity all around, the rescuers cutting parallel trenches no more than four feet apart. Matthew marveled. It was only half an hour since the avalanche and a vast field had already been systematically shredded by desperate men determined to regain their kind from the aftermath of avalanche.

They called then for the bishop. He hurried ahead and word came back: They had found the lost deacon. He was still alive but trapped in debris. Wendell grabbed Matthew. "I know Ginger's alive. Help me find her, Matt, please." Then after a while they carried out another body. It was the deacon. He had died in the arms of the bishop. Wendell collapsed in the snow. Matthew picked him up and held him erect, brushing off the snow, more falling in its place. Soon Olsen was back with them, weeping unashamedly. "I'm so sorry for the boy and his folks. I administered and prayed. That's all I could do."

Two more bodies, then the woman with the broken leg. She was still alive and conscious. By the time they carried her out she was talking hoarsely but plainly, the news transformed the nearly exhausted rescuers. suddenly they were shoveling, pushing, lifting with new speed and urgency, chanting, "Five still alive." But they dug up the young doctor next and he was dead, crushed by debris.

All the bodies had been found within a 40-foot radius, 40 yards from the site of the lodge, drawing most of the shovelers to the locale. In a short while they found another body, a fact telegraphed by the sudden concentration of lights and accompanied by cautious digging. The ninth body was found near the eighth. By 5 A.M. all the Bluebird occupants had been accounted for but two.

Chapter Twenty

Merlin came to slowly, struggling for breath, wishing for light. He might have been asleep only seconds, except now there was a pain in his head, numbing and heavy, as if one side was trying to split away from the other. It would take more than seconds for this kind of pain to build, so he had been asleep for maybe half an hour. Surely he had passed out, how in hell could anybody sleep in a predicament like this.

Ginger lay still as death over him. Merlin thought she hadn't moved. Her head was draped across his left shoulder, her right breast across his throat, the other pressing on his ribs. She was breathing softly, but Merlin couldn't remember that she had made a sound since the muffled scream as they fell.

He guessed she was badly hurt. Her body would have borne the brunt of anything falling on them and there had been lethal crashes all around. Something substantial and quite large had come to rest overhead. Maybe it had landed on their legs. Merlin couldn't move anything from the waist down and he felt nothing there, no pain, not even numbness. Nothing.

The stretcher was still under him. He pulled a hand away from Ginger's back and felt for the tie rope. Still taut. He was tightly bound to the stretcher, a pity, otherwise he might somehow ease out a blanket to slide over Ginger. She could get icy cold even though whatever had fallen over them seemed to have bridged out the snow. Merlin remembered her hands were without gloves. They would be the first to freeze. He fumbled for her arms and followed them down. His hands found both hers. Now to ease up under a sleeve and feel her pulse.

But his hand wasn't moving. Lord Almighty, she was gripping his hand: She was breathing and she could grip. Merlin wanted to sing with joy. He wasn't alone in the darkness. He was trying to whisper, "Dear Heavenly Father, thank you." Then he said "Amen," and the sound of it came into his ear.

"What?" a faint voice, very weak.

"I was praying."

"Yes, pray," a soft sigh, barely audible.

"Where do you hurt?"

"Head. Terrible."

"Feet?"

"Nothing." Slow, faltering.

"You cold?"

"I'll die…Wendy."

"I'm Merlin."

"Merlin." Her grip weakening. "Sleep."

"No, no. Baby. No sleep. Talk."

"'Can't talk."

"Don't sleep." A sharp command loud enough to fill the darkness. Her grip relaxed, Merlin slapping, stroking her fingers. "Ginger baby." Faint tension in her fingers. "Ginger baby, gimme a clutch." He felt her alive again. "A double clutch for an old jockey." Her right hand gripping his, then her left. Now together. Squeeze again. Strength coming back. "Clutch, double clutch." Stronger again. Then she quit. Her breathing seemed ragged. Merlin felt panic. He shook her arms, urging against her ear, "Ginger. No sleep. Stay awake." Her breathing smoother, her fingers moving against his. A grip again, then her voice, "Pray."

"Yes, you grip. I pray."

It was easy. Merlin hadn't prayed for years until now. "Dear Father in Heaven. Bless Ginger. Make her hold my hand. Thank thee for it..."

Merlin thought he heard something. A scrape, vibrating through the stale darkness.

Chapter Twenty One

Matthew and Wendell were taking a turn with shovels at the outside perimeter when Jason joined them. He spoke first to Wendell. "I'm sorry this happened."

Not looking up, Wendell answered, "I wanted to get Ginger. I shouldn't have listened to anybody."

It was unfair. Matthew glanced quickly at Jason, saw the pain in his eyes as he laid a hand on Wendell's shoulder. "You still have hope," he said gently.

Wendell looked up then. "Man, what am I saying?" He stood to face Jason. "Look, I'm really sorry. It's just this waiting. It's killing me."

"It's killing us all." Then Jason beckoned to Matthew. "Matt, come with me. I want to open a new dig closer to the wall."

Edwin and Olsen joined them. Jason led the way to the section of northeast wall still standing. "I want to go straight down at the corner."

"Jake, we shouldn't waste time with spot digging." It was Edwin. "The blow was too strong for anybody to stay in place. We haven't found a thing less than twenty feet downwind."

"we'll dig here," insisted Jason.

"Nothing doing, God damn it."

Tempers were thin. Everybody shocked and exhausted.

"Olsen, get me ten men," Jason ordered, ignoring the angry Edwin.

While the crew gathered, Jason aimed a strong spotlight up through the falling snow. It showed a series of notches in the bricks and splinters of wood fragments, some protruding. "Most of the roof blew off but it looks like a section broke loose and dropped straight down here at the corner. I want to see what's under there."

The men began shoveling at once, Jason, Matthew, and Olsen joining in. Edwin looked on angrily for a while, then left for the other site. He was back soon, pitching in with vigor alongside Jason. Matthew had noted that Jason often provoked fury in his friends but it never lasted.

Shoveling here was severely impeded by trash which seemed randomly mixed with the dense avalanche snow. Farther away from the ruin, fragments of the structure and its furnishings had been concentrated like stope from a mine, as if piled by powerful hands for picking through later. Here next to the corner, though, the building seemed to have been pushed downward rather than blown apart. Maybe Jason was right.

After half an hour of steady digging they were scraping on something. Shingles. A segment of roof. Matthew thought they might find corpses underneath. There would be consternation. The truck driver was obviously well known to permanent residents of Lucite, including many of the diggers. The black girl, terrible waste of life and such a beauty at that. Just no reason for her to be under that roof, she should have left when the first group evacuated. The roof segment was nearly clear. They could lift it soon. Matthew tossed his shovel away and set off to find Wendell, who should be kept away for a while. At least he shouldn't see the great slab that might very well had come to rest over the remains of his wife.

They were calling for men to help lift as Matthew cornered Wendell in a narrow trench at the first site. "You better stay here."

Then someone was yelling for a doctor and there wasn't any way to hold Wendell. They rushed toward the concentration of lights ahead, slowed by a stream of excited shovelers, passing the word: "They found 'em. They're both alive."

By the time Matthew pushed through the throng at the wall a doctor was saying something to Jason, the crowd becoming quiet but pushing forward, straining to hear. The woman, it appeared, had sustained a possibly severe concussion and multiple lacerations but no piercing wounds. The man suffered a slight concussion and a traumatized pelvis, possibly cracked or broken. There were no indications of frostbite or internal injuries. "I think they'll both survive. No reason why we can't move them."

The rescuers were transformed. The last two, both alive. It was as if the dead were merely battles lost. Two of their kind snatched alive from the coldest of graves. A cheerful murmur rippled through the crowd, already giddy from tension and weariness. A collective sigh of relief, even some banter. Someone said, "Honest to God, I thought maybe it was the lost arm, all of a sudden it moved."

Then a shout, "Hey, the snow stopped." A hundred faces looked around and up. It wasn't snowing, and to the east, a halo of color, a streak of brightness across the sky. The men could see around them the maze of trenches, the heaps of snow with debris protruding. Startled, they scrambled to higher places. The lights of Blue Spruce Lodge glittered beyond the lumpy avalanche, and to the west, lights of Jackhammer Inn, even farther a faint glow from the day lodge.

"By God, the storm is over."

The war won. The storm lifting. A ragged but exuberant cheer went up to bounce off the canyon cliffs and echo faintly. "We beat it. It's done." The men were slapping each other in relief, a concession to weariness and exhaustion. There were smiles and hand-shakes at the ebb of tension. They were seeking out Jason, touching his back and shoulders.

"Great work."

"Thank God you evacuated."

"You saved those people."

Wendell, dazed, eyes red, ringing Jason's hand, not turning loose. Edwin wedging in to hug Jason. "I was a damn fool."

Finally Matthew and Jason stood aside, and Jason turned his eyes away to the north. Matthew studied the fine face. Silhouetted against the faint light of early dawn, it didn't belong among smiles. Matthew thought he understood. Ginger's Armageddon had brushed Lucite and would be with Jason always. But the apocalypse was still to come.

Chapter Twenty Two

Samantha checked the time, surprised at her own stamina. It would be dawn soon and she had not slept at all this night. It wasn't so much a case of being tough, but a matter of having slept all day Saturday after staying awake most of Friday night.

The bureau was vastly overcrowded. It had been filling with people all night. Strange for the Bureau to be a gathering place during the emergency. Either the civil defense center or the armory were much more suitable. Why must everyone descend on the Bureau? She supposed it was kind of reverse dominos syndrome. The Forest Service had started it late yesterday. Their people came to watch the weather here, at headquarters they could do nothing. The Civil Defense brass came here because the Forest Service avalanche people were here. The Army and National Guard generals came here to be with the Civil Defense establishment. And of course the press and TV network people came because everybody else was here. But the State Police, the FBI, an Air Force cadre, the Governor, a man from Nader's Raiders, and a representative of ACLU, why here crowding the Bureau? The CAB man was probably necessary, but would they really need the bemedaled major from the Air National Guard?

Samantha marveled at the specialization of these people. What would they be doing when there were no disasters? And what would they do here? The thought was a little frightening. One narrow ribbon of highway leading up snow-bound Middle Aspen Canyon. She imagined an avalanche of bureaucrats and iron jamming the only road into Lucite.

There was bedlam all around. All telephone lines except the restricted one to Jason had been busy since midnight. Communications support equipment, mostly for the media, had been brought in about 3 a.m., and that was swamped, too. All offices full of people with questions. At first the bureau had been hit with something close to total confusion, but now a sense of mission and organization was subtly emerging out of chaos. One high-level Forest Service man, a Mr. Hayden, had arrived from Denver earlier and began to take charge. Another had flown out from Washington, checking in moments ago. An official briefing session had been arranged for all the federal brass. It would begin in minutes. Samantha would give the weather update; the Forest Service men would do the rest. Samantha's news had already shocked the Forest Service and the Forest Service news would shock the world.

Twenty people crowded into a small briefing room to hear it. Media and non-federal agencies were excluded, the only exception being the governor and his chief of police. Samantha, the only female, was introduced by Casey as "our statistician who predicted this anomaly. I'm proud that this section of the bureau has people of her caliber," he gushed on. "She has more than a pretty face. She has credibility..."

For God's sake, Casey shut up.

Embarrassed and impatient, Samantha came right to the point. "I can tell you now with certainty that the storm will end soon, probably within the hour." There was a shuffle of relief. Then Samantha continued, "But that is not altogether good news. We know now that the storm will not diminish but will terminate quite abruptly. We had dared hope for wind currents blowing up Middle Cottonwood as the front lifted. Ordinarily this would be the case. We did not want, or expect, a high wind, which seldom occurs anyway in the Wasatch. But no wind at all is more than disappointing. Frankly, it's scary.

"Here's the problem: We calculate that the Killvein Basin is brimful of snow. A moderate wind from the west could have displaced several surface feet of snow into the next basin, which will already have spilled its avalanche. Also, a gentle wind-packing would have stabilized the snowpack, reducing the probability or severity of any avalanche. But I must tell you, we know there will be little or no wind during or after dissipation of the storm. We forecast that the temperature of the air and snow surface will warm abruptly. Clouds will rapidly move out and the sun will be on south slopes above the canyon by a half-hour after sunrise. Just after 10:40 a.m. we expect snow surface temperature at the eleven thousand foot level to reach thirty-three degrees. Mr. Hayden will describe what all this may mean to the rescue effort.

"To summarize, the manner in which the storm is ending causes us to take little comfort in the fact that it is ending. The weather has not cooperated at all during this crisis. I'm afraid it will do no better now."

It was Hayden's turn. Moments after the briefing began, an aide had entered the room and handed him a note. He had been writing on a pad during Samantha's presentation.

He stood to face the group. His beginning was blunt and brutal. "We have experienced a second disaster at Lucite." Then Hayden read from his handwritten statement. "The Wildcat avalanche has released. It struck Bluebird Lodge while an evacuation was underway, but before the movement was complete. A group of twelve, including part of the volunteer medical staff, was enveloped. Luckily, two hundred and fifty people had been evacuated. They escaped without injury. None of the other lodges were struck by the avalanche. We have no communication with Lucite at the moment, as I have given our snow ranger permission to join the rescue group."

He turned to an aide. "Please read that to the press, but take out the part about the medical staff." Hayden turned back to his audience. He seemed perplexed, making two false starts, groping for words, in contrast to his crisp handling of the news from Lucite. Finally he shoved both hands into the side pockets of his crumpled business suit.

"This is something I hardly dare think about, let alone speak of. And what I am going to tell you must not be repeated outside this room except to your superiors.

"I'm sorry to tell you that we are face to face with the worst avalanche disaster ever in North America. Without going into detail about how things got so bad, let me assure you that they are bad indeed. There is very little chance that we can escape some grim consequences resulting from the following situation: Six thousand people are trapped in Lucite village. More than half of them are directly exposed to Killvein Basin, an avalanche course that buried almost a third of the population of Lucite the last time it filled. The population of Lucite then was about two hundred people. We expect the Killvein to slide again in a few hours.

"Unfortunately, we know very little about this avalanche except as we have studied its effects on the ecology of Middle Aspen Canyon." Hayden held up an aerial photograph and pointed as he talked. "The avalanche snow-shed comprises about two thousand acres lying along a depression on the face of Quartz Peak which is, in fact, a late tertiary cross fault. The wall of cliffs to the east are upthrust. The depression was caused by sinking of the west wall. This disjointed the east-west silver veins at their richest point, which explains the name of the basin. The ravine looks rather shallow, but when viewed as a catch-basin for snow it is vast.

"Several hundred years ago it brought down so much rock and silt that the avalanche dammed Middle Creek, causing a lake that lasted for several decades. One can still follow the water-line on granite bluffs above Clementine Ridge Road.

"There's not much to hold snow in the basin, but despite this the avalanche has rarely released. That's because a very large volume of snow is required to start and sustain the slide. We believe about twenty-two feet of fresh snow has fallen at the eleven thousand foot level on Quartz Peak. This is comparable to the depth in 1891 judging by reports of the avalanche that year. But there are differences in conditions between then and now.

"That year, heavy snow commenced falling around midnight. The surprise avalanche released twenty three hours later the following night. This time the avalanche is quite predictable. It will occur in daylight a few minutes after the surface of the pack warms to thirty-two degrees.

"So now you know when to expect it. Let's talk some more about the avalanche itself.

"In storms along the Wasatch, we usually get convection currents rising out of Salt Lake Basin. Even without wind, at high altitude there is a swirl to the east and a great drift along the cliff line of Killvein Basin. A storm like this one simply concentrates the snow against the rock barrier. Snow ranger, Jason Stemple estimates that there is now nearly thirty feet of snow piled at the greatest cliff height, about here." Hayden pointed to where rocks outcropped darkly in the photo. "Even though the course is not extremely steep, it can collect an awesome amount of snow over a large area, all of which explains the reputation of this slide.

"We think today's avalanche will follow the fault line, fanning out over the top of each containment ridge as it grows in volume. It will stay on the ground; the terrain is not steep or rough enough to force it into the air.

"The avalanche will envelop Jackhammer Lodge, here, and the Day Lodge, here, only seconds apart. As you see, it will also strike the east end of Clementine Lodge."

Hayden replaced the photograph with a large, framed map of the ski runs ."Momentum will carry the avalanche into the skiing area and probably about three hundred vertical feet up the north slopes.

"There are twelve hundred men in the day lodge, and another six hundred in Clementine Inn. We have nine hundred women and children in Jackhammer Lodge. With standing room only we can fit six hundred of them into the basement there. Unluckily, neither the day lodge nor the Clementine have basements. There is no place to move these people. When Killvein releases, the vibration will set off other smaller avalanches, including the Clementine Ridge cornice again, and possibly the Savage Mountain ski run from the north slope. Even the Wildcat slide is likely to run again because of remaining snow in the upper ravines. There is no place we can put the people who are now in the path of Killvein. They'll have to stay put.

"What can we do? Since we can't hope to save everyone, we have to try to save as any as possible. This calls for preparation, and to prepare for this avalanche we have to postpone it for as long as possible. In other words, we must be extremely careful to assure that the avalanche is not triggered prematurely.

"All man-made sources of air or ground disturbance must be kept entirely away from the vicinity of Lucite. We cannot allow aircraft flights, regardless of altitude, any closer than twenty miles in any direction Every bit of heavy equipment that isn't rubber-tired has to stay away from the upper canyon until after the avalanche, an unfortunate limitation because we must move heavy equipment into the area as soon as possible after the avalanche to open entry for rescue vehicles.

"Our computer analysis shows that for every minute of delay in beginning the rescue, we will lose as many as seventy five people, depending on severity of the avalanche. Of course, the escalation is geometric. So you see, we must move, and quickly, all available plows, throwers, backhoes, and bulldozers into the area on trucks. Rubber-tired units can be driven to the Helix Creek avalanche but snow removal cannot commence until after the Killvein releases.

"We will assemble helicopters at the lower equipment pool as soon as it's light enough to fly them in. A landing pad is being hand-cleared now. All Army and National Guard rescue personnel will have to he hauled to the lower pool by bus. Three sky cranes are available in Salt Lake; four more will be flown in from Idaho Falls and assembled, beginning at daylight."

Samantha was impressed by the intensity and detail of the Forest Service preparations and, as Hayden talked on, a little reassured. At least the avalanche, once spent, would trigger a massive rescue effort She knew a calamity was at hand but somehow she couldn't visualize the avalanche. It wouldn't come into her mind. Thousands of people buried by snow?

Preposterous. Jason wouldn't be under that. He would be skiing on top, carving the round single track that had always the heel following in the groove cut by the tip. If heads turned when Jason skied it was partly to see but mostly to study. His was not the airy elegance often noted in great skiers, but a stirring perfection of coordination between eye and foot, body suspended, moving only along the hill, skis faintly touching on snow, a gentle move to unweight, a soaring stretch, higher, then a soft flex ending a series. The mountain conquered by precision and grace.

Hayden was winding down. He had talked without interruption for nearly half an hour. 'To repeat, we don't believe the killvein will release until forty five minutes past ten, but all rescue personnel should be in position by eight thirty."

One of the generals was on his feet. "How can you be so confident about the time of release?"

"Something has to trigger any avalanche. If a shock, vibration or other disturbance doesn't set a large static snow field in motion then internal factors will."

"Internal factors?" The general frowned.

"Think in terms of a column of snowflakes." Hayden turned to a small blackboard. "I mean individual flakes piled one on the other with branches interlocked." He drew what looked like a tower of spheres, edges not touching, each radiating lines like little sunbeams as visualized in a child's drawing. "So long as the snow maintains this interlocking structure we're okay, because any movement within the column would encounter a large amount of friction as the bonds move and break. Snow in this state has enough strength to offset the stress placed on the column by steepness of the slope. It won't slide until something happens to weaken this column.

"As you can imagine, any warming of the snow-pack will reduce column strength because the ice crystals begin to break down as the surface temperature comes closer to the melting point. The column will bend downhill as bonds within the crystals begin to disintegrate. Loss of stability will take place just before the snow at the surface begins to melt."

A secretary entered the room and handed Hayden another note as he continued. "Tomorrow that critical temperature will predictably be reached at forty two minutes past ten. The avalanche will almost certainly release at about that time, unless it's disturbed sooner."

Hayden paused then, read the note quickly, and announced, "Jason Stemple is back at the ranger station. They located all of the party caught by the Wildcat avalanche. Three survived. Nine are dead."

A stunned silence followed, Samantha thinking it could have been much worse. Poor Jason. How awful when failure makes an equation with death. Was he prepared for this? Jason would somehow save Lucite. She believed it and she thought everyone in Lucite would believe it too, at least those who knew Jason. Jason wouldn't let Lucite die.

Hayden continued, "There's much to do so we have to adjourn. Question?"

"You mentioned differences between 1910 and now, but only described one. Are there others?"

"Yes, there is one other. Most of us don't think it's important, but ranger Stemple keeps bringing it up. As you recall we had two fairly long interruptions in the snowfall at Lucite. The first, occurring yesterday at about one o'clock, is meaningless. But we're not sure about the second one. The snow stopped for more than an hour at 12:10 this morning. During the interlude, some strong air currents elevated out of Salt Lake Valley and into the Wasatch. Wind swept in from Bonneville Flats west of the city and crossed Salt Lake, picking up quite a bit of red dust and small amounts of dry salt. Sandwiched between the snow that preceded the wind and the snow that followed, we have a very thin deposit of dust and salt. Jason, who discovered it, thinks it's a layer of weakness. If we had a way to trigger that last several feet at the surface without disturbing the lower horizon, Lucite would be saved. Our snow experts think he may be right, but it's purely academic because there's no known way of inducing a selective avalanche. Now, the meeting is adjourned."

Samantha remained in her seat as the men filed out. Soon she was alone in the room with her thoughts. Jason hadn't told her about the dust layer. The news had come with a quick thrill of insight and discovery. She knew at once what Jason would do, even though the thought of it took her breath away. It couldn't work. But maybe it could. Either way she knew that Jason would try.

Chapter Twenty Three

Daylight was filtering all the way down into the darkness of the trench-like pathway as Matthew and Jason trudged back toward the ranger station. Olsen's shovelers had gone ahead, moving some snow but mostly packing the way with their weary feet. It was easy going. For the first time in hours walking didn't require any great concentration and energy. There had been no conversation between them. Matthew was too exhausted and he thought Jason too pained to talk.

But Matthew wanted to know something. He was tired enough to sleep on his feet but he wanted to be awake when it happened.

"What's next, Jake?"

Jason didn't look at Matthew or change his pace. 'Killvein avalanche."

"When?"

"About three hours."

"What can we do?"

"Let's get to the station and make some coffee. Then I'll tell you." For the first time Matthew realized that Jason was also tired. They trudged on, Jason setting the pace, Matthew struggling to make his weary legs keep up. After a while Jason spoke again. "I loved the boy, Hank."

Matthew was startled. Of course Jason would have known all along.

Jason continued, "I guess you know that. I loved Ellen too. Nobody ever cared the way she did."

It seemed fitting that some words should pass between them. Matthew knew this would be the requiem for Ellen and David. He and Jason wouldn't discuss them again.

He asked, "Why didn't you tell me about David?"

"By the time I knew, David was my family. He was my son. Of course I couldn't stand to even think of giving any part of him to anyone else."

"But it was hard for you because of the way Ellen reacted."

"Yes. By keeping them together I caused them both to die a little. Yesterday they died all the way together. God, how that hurts."

"I'm really sorry about Ellen and David."

"I thought we might save Ellen with you here. There's nothing left to save now, and David is gone, too. We knew Ellen and David, so we can mourn for them. Now all these other good people are dead. We didn't even know them, but others will mourn. I've failed the ones I loved and they're dead. How many others have I failed, people I didn't even know existed? Matt, all I can do now is try to save the rest. There's no peace for me, no relief, no end of it until I've done everything I can do here to save Lucite." The strange, detached tone of Jason's voice was both dreadful and alarming to Matthew. He was not communicating so much as thinking out loud. Jason was suffering as only a deeply sensitive person in despair could suffer.

"Jake, it wasn't your fault. Those avalanches are over now."

"Not really. Not yet."

Matthew wasn't sure what Jason meant but they were coming up to the station and there was no time to pursue it. Anyway Matthew felt wounded and confused about David and Ellen. He had to think this out by himself and that would be difficult. He felt apprehension about Jason, and the specter of his own death blackened every thought.

At the station they quickly made fresh coffee and downed it in great gulps. Matthew felt better. Jason poured a second cup and was quickly on the radio, talking to Salt Lake City.

Matthew noticed it was getting brighter outdoors. He stood outside and lit a cigar, the first one for hours. Because of reflections in a world of white this was as bright a dawn as could be imagined. The sun cast yellow glow on the rosebud crown of Quartz Peak. Soon it would bring round golden light into the canyon bottom. If he should die today in Lucite, it would at least be a beautiful stage to die on.

Jason had called another meeting of lodge owners and rescue leaders. They dribbled into the station, taking hot coffee and standing around the walls. Wendell and Olsen were among the last to arrive. They had been visiting survivors at Blue Spruce Lodge, and after entering engaged in animated conversation in one corner. What a difference a few hours of crisis can make. Alice Morton had excused herself and sent a clerk in her place. They thought she had a hangover. All the other owners and managers were in attendance. Before the meeting there were respectful remarks about Blake, the first lodge owner ever to die by avalanche. Hamilton suggested they begin the meeting with a prayer. Someone asked him to say it. He began by thanking God that a greater disaster had so far been averted and asking his blessing upon those dead. He asked for a special blessing to guide the mind and actions of Jason, in whose hands the fate of all those trapped in Lucite now rested, and prayed for the deliverance of all. It was a long prayer sometimes fearful and beseeching, but Mathew knew it projected quite faithfully the mood of all those gathered at the station.

Jason told them what to expect of Killvein Avalanche. The only possible protection, he assured them, would be provided by structure and furnishings of the lodges. Everyone had to stay inside and be quiet. Loud noises or activity that might cause low-frequency vibration were forbidden. Regarding security within the lodges—all basements would be filled to standing capacity, priority going to mothers with children. Overflow people should move to rooms as far away from the direction of a threatening avalanche as possible. They would sit under dining tables. Windows had to be removed from the north side of the day lodge, a task that must commence immediately. The steel dining tables would be laid in rows on their sides with tops facing the avalanche. Men would crouch behind them. Because Killvein would not be airborne, a pocket of air at the junction of floor and table could keep them alive until rescued. That only applied to the day lodge. Jason quickly detailed special emergency arrangements for each lodge and pointed out that the ranger station could be knocked out by any secondary slide. No one should remain there, anyway they would need all available manpower at the day lodge to keep order once the crowd realized what was going to happen.

A second radio section had been set up at Blue Spruce Lodge. Wendell was to move the ranger station gear to the day lodge and establish contact with Salt Lake City from there. Edwin would be in charge.

"What about you?" someone asked.

"I won't be here."

"Where do you think you're going?"

Jason sat then and unzipped his snow boots. "Skiing."

"For Christ sakes, be serious." Hamilton was scolding him.

Jason pulled on a ski boot and began buckling up. "Well, Ham, tell you what. I'm going to carry my skis up Wildcat Ridge. When I get to the flat spot in the cliffs I'll put them on and traverse Killvein Basin."

"That's suicide," Hamilton breathed.

Edwin broke in, "Jake, if you want the avalanche down shoot it down."

"Pay attention!" said Jason, the tone of flippancy leaving his voice. "I want everybody to listen carefully. There's a dust layer about five feet under the surface on Killvein. I'll slice down to that. It might skim off the snow that fell after midnight."

Edwin was aghast. "You'll be a dead man, Jake."

Jason finished buckling his boots. He reached for his coffee cup and drained it, standing to zip his parka. "We may all be dead in two hours." Then he caught himself and looked around the room and grinned almost shyly. It was the first sign of levity since the storm began. He clearly didn't want to leave his friends on a grim note. "At least I'll bow out like a cowboy— with my boots on."

Quickly he gave his dazed friends instructions on schedules and signals; then he was gone, poles under one arm, skis under the other.

The gathering was stunned. Everybody in the room was looking at one another and shaking their heads. The consensus had Jason accomplishing nothing but his own demise.

"He's cracked," Anderson said. "Shouldn't we forcibly stop him?"

It seemed a silly question. Nobody could stop Jason once his mind was set and they all sensed, as did Matthew, that Jason's mind was indeed set.

Filing out, Edwin asked Matthew for help in getting the day lodge ready for the avalanche. Olsen would help, too, and so would the ski patrol. Wendell would be along with the radio soon.

When Matthew and Edwin reached the day lodge, they looked down the trench that ran north beyond Jackhammer Lodge to see Jason skating on skis, big powder snowshoes strapped to his back. He would ski to a point just above the junction of Horseshoe Circle and Clementine Road, explained Edwin. Then he would put on snowshoes and climb out on the divide between Wildcat Creek and Killvein Basin. Jason had a helluva climb ahead of him. "From here to those cliffs it's a vertical of probably three thousand feet." Edwin thought Jason could scale maybe seven hundred feet per hour. "It'll be nip and tuck whether he makes the jump-off before ten," Edwin told Matthew. "At least he's pretty safe on the ridge. If Killvein slides before Jake hits the cut, he may be the only one of us still alive by ten."

Jason disappeared at the junction of Clementine and Horseshoe Roads. It was 7:30. They watched a while, then he showed again, a tiny figure, dark against the shining snow, wearing snowshoes now, skis strapped on his backpack and a pole in each hand. He scaled a great snow dune with some difficulty, girdling it twice, then he was on Wildcat Ridge. A small crowd had joined Matthew and Edwin. Jason stopped to rest, turning to look back at Lucite. The village would be a fantastic sight from up there today. Matthew imagined Jason was seeing a vast lumpy snowfield with smoke trailing from the biggest lumps. Jason should spot the onlookers at the front of the day lodge. Yes, he moved a ski pole in a sweeping arc. They answered with wild but silent waving of both arms. It would be a relief to watch his ascent up Quartz Peak for the next hours because where there was Jason there was hope.

Inside the day lodge everyone seemed to be standing but there was little movement. Mostly the men had grouped into crowded knots. Some were standing in line to fill trays at the steam table but most had already eaten breakfast. In contrast to the night before, the men appeared dull-eyed and haggard. There wasn't any laughing or gaiety this morning.

Moments before, relatives of the avalanche victims had been called together and moved to Blue Spruce Lodge so men here knew now that people had already died in two avalanches. Edwin and Matthew climbed on a table with bullhorns. The groups disintegrating as men surged toward them. Discipline was breaking down. These men looked exhausted and apprehensive. They wanted information. Suddenly a crowd filled the floor, milling around. Edwin asked for quiet. Everybody began shushing. Silence came slowly over the hall.

On the bullhorn Edwin told them about the Clementine and Wildcat avalanches. He listed the names of the dead and took pains to point out that nearly 300 threatened people had been saved from the Wildcat avalanche.

"Another avalanche may come down. It could reach this far, so we have to get ready." He went on to ask everybody to stay calm, stressing that all who did as they were told would be okay. But he warned that military-like discipline would be required. Martial law had been declared for Lucite; anyone who failed to obey orders would not only jeopardize the safety of all but would be prosecuted to the fullest extent.

Edwin had exhausted himself shouting into the bullhorn, so Matthew took over to describe the rescue plan from Salt Lake. He pointed out that the government had moved 2,000 rescuers to the motor pool area below

Helix Creek, just a few miles away. Giant personnel-carrying helicopters would land there within a half hour to shuttle the rescuers into Lucite just as soon as the avalanche released. "The biggest snow-clearing equipment in the Mountain West has been rushed to Salt Lake City during the night. Much of it is already standing by west of Helix Creek. The rest is on the canyon road."

Workmen carrying ladders into the day lodge interrupted Matthew. Quickly they put the ladders in place and climbed to work at the highest window. Matthew explained that they didn't want glass between any avalanche and the men. Then he told them about aligning tables and taking shelter.

For the first time Matthew sensed that apprehension was turning into fear. Panic was a possibility. A crowd this size could quickly become a mob. Reassure, but carefully.

He asked for questions. There was a clamor as hands went up all over the pavilion, Edwin breaking in to command sharply: "We must have quiet. A sharp noise could bring the avalanche down before we're ready." He pointed to a questioner, "Go ahead."

"Won't the avalanche just push the tables over on top of us?"

Almost too quickly, Edwin tried to reassure. "Unless there's lots of rocks and trees, the avalanche would be expected to dam against each row of tables, then flow over. There will be a ton of guys behind each table. That's lots of beer and inertia. The tables are the best protection we have. I'm going to be behind one."

Matthew knew the questioner had a point. He thought the tables were a ruse, an illusion of safety to avoid panic. The avalanche would carry enough momentum to smash anything in its path. Against the Killvein holocaust even heavy steel tables would provide little more security than wigwams in a tornado. The occupants of Jackhammer and Clementine Lodges would be somewhat more secure, especially those in the Jackhammer basement. The day lodge people would be sacrificed. Hopefully the illusion of the tables would pacify them, but basically the day lodge people would be sacrificed. There was simply no place to put them.

Of course the day lodge people must never know that. There had to be hope, otherwise even the strongest might panic. The specter of a thousand berserk men stampeding toward the overcrowded lodges demanding shelter was more terrible to contemplate than the awful death blanket of the avalanche itself. Anyway, some would stay alive at the lee end of those tables. It was a better bet than fleeing in panic or standing defiant, snarling at the oncoming avalanche like a gopher run down by monster man. Matthew would be in the first row. He thought he might survive because he would know how and when to brace himself and cup his mouth. It would be a wild ride, but nothing would tear the protective cup away from his mouth and nostrils. If the rescue came quickly they would dig him up alive. "Uncle Matthew survived being buried in the Killvein avalanche." Yes, it was a significant place to be, whether he lived or died. It might be horrendous to die alone, but it didn't matter so much when so many would die together. On the other hand, it would be nice to survive, even to survive alone.

Edwin had been fielding all questions with the kind of answers that would give no one an excuse to bolt. He told them that every lodge was threatened by avalanche, if not the Killvein then another slide touched off by rumbles from Killvein. No place could be considered really safe, and no lodge was necessarily that much safer than others. Another question turned into more of a statement: "I'm not buying that. We're completely exposed here. What's between us and that avalanche?"

A nervous buzz spread around the hall. Edwin was losing credibility. Get their minds off it. Matthew glanced to the north; he could see the dark figure seeming not to move but illuminated now by the sun. He shouted quickly into the bullhorn. "Please give me your attention. There's something else. It's very important." The noise subsided. "We've given you the worst possible news first. Now please listen carefully. There may not be an avalanche."

He repeated, "There may not be an avalanche." The hall was much quieter now. "I want you all to look up on the side of the big mountain directly behind me. There was a shuffle, everybody straining for a clear view.

Somebody shouted, "Hey, there's a guy up there."

"What's going on?"

In a quick loud staccato, Matthew told them about the dust layer and Jason's plan.

"Can he pull it off?"

"We think so," said Matthew. "He may be the best powder skier in the world. At least we think he is. What's more important, he thinks he is." A faint chuckle rippled around the pavilion. There was a noticeable settling back, tension subsiding. Here was something to watch, a diversion and hope.

"I'm glad you thought of telling them about Jake," said Edwin in a low voice.

The men started dispersing then, organizing, calling instructions, beginning to turn over tables, occupied at that but all eyes returning to the solitary figure on Quartz Peak.

Visibility was better with upper windows removed. And now a sunlit Jason was in full view of all. The hall was quieter, its occupants not so fearful. They seemed captivated by Jason's adventure.

Chapter Twenty Four

Since her early-morning weather briefing, Samantha had been officially ignored. Nobody objected, though, when she twice used the precious radio to try to call Jason. Once there wasn't any answer. The second time the Blue Spruce operator responded but didn't know where Jason might be.

The Bureau was not so crowded now. Beginning at dawn they had sealed off the avenue for more than a block and brought in several motorized "efficiency offices" A long line was parked out front, bristling with antennae. The adjoining office complex of Wasatch Lumber Company had also been commandeered, but the Bureau was still the nerve center for the emergency. Ironically, most Bureau people had gone home and none of them were any longer involved. George Rose and Samantha were the only staff left. George had stayed mostly to feed data to other cities, Samantha because she couldn't bear to leave. Now she was sitting alone behind the glass wall in Buford's office. It appeared that contact had been reestablished with Jason, because the Forest Service men and military brass were gathered around the short-wave radio. After a moment they turned away. The Washington wheel, who had been introduced to her as Mr. Taylor, seemed to be in heated conversation with the military people. Then he and Hayden walked toward the office next to Buford's where a live Forest Service line connected with both Denver and Washington. Taylor was livid. In contrast to his calm of the early morning, he now seemed close to hysteria, cursing at the ceiling and storming at Hayden. "Goddamn Jock. Why the hell can't we put better people in these positions? That general may be sarcastic but he's right, it shouldn't take a disaster to find flaws in a system."

Samantha stepped out to accost the two, an unreasoned reaction. “What happened?”

Without looking at her, Taylor answered, “Your friend Stemple has deserted his post.”

“Jason did not do that.”

“Well, he’s gone. Without consulting anybody here.”

“To where”

“He wants to traverse Killvein Basin. The fool. He’s cracked up. We have no one in Lucite. It’s a terrible embarrassment.”

“What was he supposed to be doing?”

“We ordered him to move the station to Blue Spruce Lodge. It’s secure there.”

“You don’t know Jake at all.”

“I know he’s either insane or insubordinate. Now please, Miss, we have work to do.” He moved to brush past Samantha, but she grabbed his arm, clinging.

“Why would Jake traverse Killvein?”

“The ski patrol, the only people we have up there to talk with, says he wants to bring down the snow above the dust layer. That’s preposterous of course.”

“If Jason says he can do it he will do it.”

“It’s also suicidal. The man is completely insane at the moment.”

Taylor was trying to pull away, but Samantha had his arm tightly clasped in both her hands. “Miss Hendrix.” He was nearly dragging her. The exertion, the exhaustion, his hostility, Samantha was losing control.

She jerked his arm sharply, stamping with a loud “Oh! You rude son-of-a-bitch. I’m speaking to you.”

Samantha had lost all pretenses of controlling herself. She was close to tears and making a scene. Heads turned toward them.

Hayden enveloped the two. “Come on. Let’s go in the office.” Inside he closed the door. Samantha was startled to find herself still clinging fiercely to Taylor.

Calmest of the three, Hayden spoke first. “Miss Hendrix, why are you so distressed?”

“I believe in Jason Stemple.”

“But isn’t it madness to think of bringing down only part of an avalanche? Nothing like that has ever been done.”

"If it were madness Jason wouldn't try to do it. He is not a madman, Mr. Hayden. When you mentioned the dust layer this morning I thought he would try something like this."

Flushed and ruffled, Taylor had broken away from Samantha and seated himself. He spoke again. "In any case, Miss Hendrix, his behavior is completely irrational. The Forest Service won't tolerate that."

"Can't you believe that it's possible for Jason to be right?"

'Not in this case."

"Well, it doesn't matter what you believe. Today we're going to see if a skier can bring down only part of an avalanche."

"This is ridiculous. Please leave us alone."

Samantha started out, then stopped at the door. "Look, I'm a powder skier. I know how the Wasatch snow behaves, and I know that Jason is skillful enough and smart enough to control how deeply he disturbs the snow. Anyway, Jason has to try."

"Why does he have to do that?"

Samantha felt herself breaking again. "What else can Jason do? He has to try to save those people." It didn't make sense, but she was tired and it was all so hopeless and it was nearly over anyway. She couldn't trust herself to say more. She couldn't fight anymore and she couldn't take any more. Head bowed, she left the Forest Service people and returned to Buford's office, closing the door and placing her cheek against its cool, glassy varnish. She slid into a chair, mostly from exhaustion, but hopeful too of relaxing away some of the nervousness and tension. She should go home and rest. But Samantha could never bear the long wait alone.

Anyway, she had promised Jason. Why couldn't he have told her? He hadn't even so much as said good-bye. Of course, he couldn't tell anyone in Salt Lake; his bosses would have forbidden the traverse. And what person could say a finite good-bye? It was the wrong expression, especially for Jason

Samantha was trying to pull herself together so she could go to the radio. It was nearly half past eight. Release of the avalanche was only two hours away, and Jason would begin his traverse before then. *No, stay. There's nothing at the radio.* She sat with her thoughts. All she could do was wait.

Samantha had rested for perhaps a half hour when she was startled by a knock at the door. It opened even before she could turn around, and Hayden peered in. "Is it okay?"

"Sure. Come in. Sorry I cracked."

"Listen, Samantha." He hadn't called her that before. 'We've checked further into Stemple's idea. Our ski experts in Washington think it might work. For obvious reasons, it's never been tested, but everybody agrees that it's our only chance. Anyway, you're right of course, that's all Stemple can do."

Samantha smiled a thank-you.

Hayden went on, "Frankly, we thought Stemple was bent on suicide. We hadn't even stopped to think that it might work. Thanks for getting us back on the track."

"Jason is not a perfect man, Mr. Hayden, but he wouldn't ever stop trying to save those people."

Hayden nodded. In his eyes Samantha saw a quick understanding, an insight that seemed to elude Samantha herself. "Taylor is talking now to the president and the secretary of agriculture. There will be a press conference soon. Will you please come and represent the Bureau?"

"Yes, but I won't make a speech. I couldn't now."

"Maybe just take a question or two."

The conference was in the spacious board room of the lumber company. It seemed vast compared to cramped rooms at the Bureau, but it was filling fast as Samantha and Hayden arrived. Television cameras with their hot white lights were already in place. Reporters were flooding in, quickly filling the seats, then ringing the wall, two deep, pads in hand. Samantha was surprised to see New York Times and Washington Post newsmen there, plus half a dozen network people, including one from the BBC. She supposed the media had chartered jets from each city, bringing along foreign correspondents representing papers in London, Frankfurt, and Zurich. Of course the Swiss would be interested.

Taylor took the improvised podium, nodding at Samantha on the way. She read a mute apology in his eyes. Samantha felt only wonderment at her behavior. Never before had she been so physically angry, so within a heartbeat of hitting someone, and rude to boot. She dismissed the thought. There is savagery in everybody; during times of crisis it comes struggling out. Taylor greeted the assembly and read them a message addressed to the trapped people in Lucite. It had just been transmitted to the day lodge in the village. "I have had a telephone conversation with the White House. The Secretary of Agriculture is now reporting the situation at Lucite to the President. The President has asked me to tell you that he is deeply concerned about your plight and he pledges all the resources and power of the federal government to get everyone out of Lucite safely. Speaking for the Forest Service, we hope to have roads clear and traffic moving back down the canyon by nightfall. Meanwhile it is vital that all of you stay inside and keep calm."

Not a word about an avalanche, only alluded to: the President worried, the need for calm. Samantha thought the message artfully worded. In effect it said, *We're working at the highest levels to get you out. The avalanche thing is officially kind of serious, but not something for individuals to worry about.* Salt Lake City knew as surely as Lucite that there were vast security differentials within the village. A panic now might be worse than an avalanche.

Taylor went on to address the gathering. He described the rescue dilemma. They couldn't begin the rescue for fear of triggering an avalanche. Samantha thought he was quite candid regarding the problem, but evasive as to the possible devastation of Killvein and relative exposure of various lodges. He ended with the statement, 'Now, there's a new development that we're quite interested in. Jason Stemple, our Forest Service snow ranger at Lucite, and a powder skier of supreme skill, is snowshoeing up the face of Quartz peak. In about an hour he will ski across Killvein Basin, which is at the moment the most threatening avalanche course. His idea is to get the top one fourth of the snow depth there to slide out without disturbing the rest of the pack. If successful, it will reduce the avalanche hazard enough to allow helicopter evacuation of the most exposed lodges. Once that is done, we can clean up with artillery and clear the road."

Hands were in the air.

"What if the ski traverse is not successful?"

"One of two things will happen. Either we will have the desired partial avalanche or a somewhat premature full avalanche."

"What will be the effects of a full avalanche?"

"Nobody knows, of course. We have to plan as if it might hit occupied buildings, but that doesn't mean that it will do so."

"And what happens to the ranger?"

A hush fell over the room. Samantha thought she had never seen so many people so attentive. It was the kind of drama the media would love.

"It's a courageous thing he's doing, and of course there's some danger in disturbing such a large field of unstable snow. But our snow rangers are trained to place public safety above their own." He motioned for the next question.

"You didn't answer the question."

"Well, Stemple's life will be in jeopardy. But he's known as one of America's best powder skiers. If he can't pull it off, nobody can."

Samantha noticed that Taylor still hadn't answered the question, but the media as usual seemed content with having challenged the first evasion.

Questions were asked about the two nighttime avalanches. Taylor pointed out that 300 people had been saved by timely evacuation of Bluebird Lodge. He deeply regretted the loss of life, etc.

Could they release the names of the victims?

Hayden handed a paper to Taylor who announced, "We have just completed notification of next of kin. Here are the victims of two avalanches." He read the names. "The list will be mimeographed and made available to you."

Question: "The dead Stemple woman and boy are the wife and son of Jason Stemple, are they not?"

"Yes. We are all grieving with our ranger. But our people are trained to put duty above all other considerations." It should have closed the matter. Everyone could draw their own conclusions, but the questioner persisted. Samantha recognized him as a wire-service reporter who had been at the bureau nearly the entire night.

"I believe the Wildcat avalanche was more or less spontaneous?"

"Yes."

"And the Clementine Ridge avalanche—what triggered that?"

Samantha hated the question for its inference, but Taylor had to answer. To be evasive would only sensationalize the truth.

"Artillery fire."

"Who ordered the artillery?"

Taylor's face was white with anger. "I won't answer that. It's irrelevant."

The damage was done. Headline: 'Did Ranger Stemple kill his wife and son?' A fury built up in Samantha. *How dare that son-of-a-bitch ask such an indecent thing.* Poor Jason. She fervently hoped he would perish crossing Killvein. Take away the agony, give him the peace of death, save him from those who would make a sensation out of suffering.

Samantha was on her feet then. In control of her emotions, somehow cool. "May I address that question? I'm sure Mr. Taylor won't mind if I correct him here. Not that it's important now, but for the record, artillery was used to bring down Helix Creek avalanche. Clementine Ridge avalanche was spontaneous."

That would confuse the hell out of them. Never in her life had Samantha told such a blatant lie. As she sat again, Taylor glanced his gratitude. Samantha could lie, Taylor couldn't.

One of the generals began describing technical and material aspects of the avalanche. But the crowd was melting away. They had stories to file. There was a war in Africa, another contested election in Florida, and a sensational ship hijacking out of Singapore. But the drama in Lucite would be the lead story around the world that day.

Chapter Twenty Five

Matthew wondered how long since Jason had stopped to rest. After forty-five minutes he had gained maybe a third of the vertical distance to the entry chute. So Edwin had underestimated the speed of climb.

It looked easy from the day lodge, but Matthew knew it wasn't. Jason kept disappearing, then turning up again, always higher, indicating some rugged seams and undulations in his way.

A thousand eyes were now on Jason. At times he seemed not to be moving at all, but suddenly he would be higher on the mountain. Some of the men had brought out binoculars. Matthew borrowed a pair, watching Jason push through the brushy upper branches of a grove of aspen trees. It would be something like walking through willows. With the glasses he could see for the first time that Jason was sinking three or four inches each step, telegraphing lightness of the snow.

Matthew shifted the glasses to Wildcat Ravine on Jason's right. It was choppy and wrinkled in spots. Tree stubs protruded, with bare wood flaming yellow, and some trunks showing long gleaming gashes as if split by lightning. Up higher branches of the ravine, deep snow loomed in white cliffs as if cut that way. But the main ravine was a great sore, roughly inflamed by the aftermath of Wildcat avalanche, like a stomach vomited but not yet emptied.

He picked out Jason again. Finally resting, leaning forward on ski poles planted at the toe of the snowshoes. Matthew swung the glasses to the west, across the great white ocean of Killvein Basin.

The fault line, so noticeable from the airliner only 24 hours ago, had mostly disappeared. Only in a few places the highest cliffs jutted dark brown above the snow. From ridge to ridge, the Killvein Basin was quite literally brim-full of snow. Trees and rocks had disappeared, obliterated as if by a single swipe of a great white brush.

Edwin spoke at his elbow: "That's what the old miners called a Killvein White. I never expected to see it in my lifetime. I didn't even believe it."

Matthew fixed the glasses on the place where Jason planned to begin his assault on Killvein Basin. It was just down-grade from a ravine that cut into the fault line, isolating a great needle of rock rising grandly above the snow level. The needle was capped with a cornice of its own. Jason would probably rest for a moment under the great rock before beginning the traverse, perhaps his last, perhaps the last descent most men in the day lodge would see. It would be a fast trip, a quick strike across about 300 yards of snow field. Jason would aim for a cluster of fir trees along the east slope of Clementine Ridge. The path would drop sharply by probably 400 vertical feet, steep enough to power Jason against the press of snow at his chest and shoulders.

It could work. The key would be to create a sharp fracture, a line of weakness from which the downhill layer could break away. 1f it did work, the maneuver would save Lucite, because a six-foot layer would do little damage. But if the snow below slid, that above would be expected to do the same, so Jason would likely be dragged under. Matthew tried to shut the thought out of his mind. Anyway it would be spectacular to watch. And Jason, the skier who despised grandstanding on skis, would have the most attentive audience ever for his last traverse.

The sunlit morning was lovely in rounded blue sky and dimensioned light. High above glittered as alluring a field of virgin snow as any skier could ever imagine, but within it—like a tsunami in solid-state—lurked a killing machine. The leopard, the diamondback, the Amanita mushroom—why were dangerous things so often beautiful? Here loomed the stuff of avalanche. There was nothing aggressive in it, only a mindless reaction; a slow spring without rage or rancor; just a witless strike; beauty gone berserk; a vast snow field out of place. The life span of even the most dreadful avalanche could be reckoned in seconds.

By nine o'clock the sun was touching the canyon floor, illuminating all but the bottoms of the maze of snow trenches that connected points of habitation. The tables in the hall of the day lodge had been turned on their sides in a bristle of crescents pointing at Quartz Peak. It reminded Matthew of an inverted theater. He thought that shaping the lines into arcs was probably not necessary but it couldn't hurt, and maybe they would create a kind of natural flow to divert some snow of the avalanche.

Anyway, it gave an illusion of belligerence and strength that was somehow impressive. Anything that could help morale in the next hour might be critical.

With all the north windows removed it was getting very cold inside the hall. A white halo of frozen breath hovered over the men, but their spirits seemed better now. Moments ago, Edwin had read them a message from the President. It brought no cheers, only a glum murmur. The cold air, however, was a kind of catharsis. The men felt themselves almost outdoors, and less confined. But they seemed most diverted by the progress of Jason, who was now only about a thousand feet below the great needle.

Matthew marveled at Jason's stamina. His friend had climbed steadily for nearly two hours, rarely resting. He couldn't have slept for the past thirty hours, and had apparently taken nothing but coffee during the night and morning.

It was not a dangerous climb, only hard and taxing. By contrast, the traverse would be a piece of cake for Jason, but dangerous beyond reason. Only the courage of desperation could drive a sensible man across the taut white field. Jason, reasonable, never a fool, desperate now, but he also had his skill. Once the avalanche started he would need to surface in an instant. If he did that, he could swim for a ways and maybe even survive by maintaining a diagonal to the safety of the ridge. But if he allowed himself to be sucked downhill he would be churned under by turbulence or blown off his feet by wind. It would mean a hellish death by laceration.

All the same, Jason had two chances. Maybe the snow would slice away at the point of fracture as everyone hoped. If it didn't, if Jason felt the snow tugging him down, he could speed up, float out, and ski for his life toward the western eddy of the avalanche.

Matthew was sitting on the one table still upright, left that way for public address use. Edwin had been called to the kitchen. He was back now, tapping Matthew on the shoulder. "I'm afraid we've got trouble."

"What's wrong?"

"Some men just raided the kitchen and took all the cutting knives. We think it's the gang that got lost on Red Diggings Road. A big redhead with a bandaged hand was the leader."

A ski patrolman hailed Edwin then from near the steam table. He was moving through the crowd. They read his lips, "I've gotta talk to you."

Coming closer, he motioned toward the front door, indicating he wanted to see them outside. As they were working their way toward an intersection with the patrolman, Matthew saw the big man, Dain, in intense conversation with a small group about twenty feet from the door. He thought maybe the movement of Edwin and the patrolman might have kept the group from bolting through the main door, which was guarded only by one of Olsen's men, checking passes. Outside, the Patrolman told them in a low voice that Dain and his gang were going to break out. A few minutes ago, they had tried to enlist members of a Topeka ski club to join them, arguing that the avalanche was sure to come through the day lodge. The only safe place would be Blue Spruce Lodge and they aimed to make a dash for it. Most of the club members had wives in other lodges that were already overcrowded. They refused to join the break-out. There had almost been a fight. One of them reported the incident to the ski patrolman, warning that the gang was desperate. "This guy, Dain, intends to be the first one out of Lucite so he can get across the state line and back to Kansas. He thinks he'll be charged in the avalanche deaths. The guy has friends in government there and says they won't extradite him. We'd better be careful, Ed, I gather he's pretty mean."

"We know," said Edwin. "And they've got knives now. But if we let them bolt there may be a disaster here."

Matthew asked, "Does anybody in Lucite have a gun?"

"Only the deputy, he's at the Jackhammer."

"Go after him," Edwin told the patrolman. Then he turned to Matthew. "Well, let's find some clubs and get those bastards."

"It'll be dangerous," said Matthew.

Edwin motioned toward Quartz Peak. The figure of Jason, higher now, appeared to be within a half-hour's climb of the big needle.

"Let's go after them," said Matthew.

Just then they heard a commotion inside the lodge and somebody was yelling for Edwin, "East door."

"Jesus," muttered Edwin. "We forgot the east door."

The two rushed through the snow trench toward the east end of the day lodge. Matthew remembered that the antenna was there and Wendell had set up the short-wave near the door.

No one was outside yet but the door had been flung open. Just in front of the short corridor leading inside they found Wendell. He was standing with his back to the door. He held a chair in one hand and a length of pipe in the other. Four men crouched in front of him, including the big redhead, his good hand holding a 15-inch butcher knife and a meat cleaver.

They were jockeying for position on Wendell. They seemed startled at the opposition but respectful of the pipe, apparently part of the antenna base.

Matthew urgently looked around for a weapon. Nothing. He whispered to Edwin, "get us some clubs," but even as he said it he knew there wasn't so much as a snow shovel nearby. He wanted to call to Wendell, "They'll kill you, look out," but Dain was already holding up the bandaged hand and snarling.

"You're the son-of-a-bitch that did this." The bandage looked soiled. "I've got plenty of reason to kill you. Now move."

Wendell stood his ground. "Get back. Nobody's leaving here."

The crowd had fanned around several feet behind the four men, shocked by the scene.

Matthew and Edwin stood defenseless at the door. Only Wendell, slim, bristling with outrage and hostility, blocked the way.

The redhead started sidestepping to the right, moving away from the pipe and toward the wall at the butt end of the door. Wendell countered by thrusting the chair in his direction. The other men rushed. Wendell swung the pipe. One man went down, then the other three were on Wendell in a quick rush so menacing that it brought a gasp from onlookers. Wendell was down struggling, then they were lifting him to fling him away, when a great shout seemed to freeze the action.

"Turn that fella loose."

It was Olsen, charging through the crowd, pushing and shoving as men struggled to get out of his way. Then he was free of the crowd and his bulky figure imposed itself between the violence and the door.

"Turn him loose, I said." The command was both urgent and threatening, and carried the authority of surprise.

They dropped Wendell to the floor, and stared at the big Dane, a formidable hulk, standing like a great scarecrow, with long arms wide as if to assure that no one tried to outflank him. Knives had been dropped in the rush to move Wendell aside. Now the men picked them up and leaned toward Olsen. The great hall was so quiet that onlookers could hear the gang panting from the excitement and exertion of rushing Wendell.

Except for the redhead, they seemed to waver. Matthew sensed that this was more than they had bargained for. The knives were meant for intimidation, not mutilation. A ski vacation had turned into a nightmare, but murder? Dain sensed their indecision. He was urging, "We're in too far to stop now," his eyes were only on Olsen. "Every one of us. That avalanche will be down in ten minutes. We'll smash the radio. Nobody's gonna know a thing about this."

He raged at Olsen then, "You stupid bastard, get out of the way or we'll cut you to pieces."

The man stunned by Wendell's pipe was on his feet then and grabbing for Wendell. The big redhead commanded, "Okay, rush him."

But he was too late. Olsen was already charging, shoulder first, running low like a fullback. He smashed against the group, knocking people down and sending Wendell flying into the redhead. Cat-quick he was on his feet, lifting a man over his head with both hands, flinging him at the crowd. Then there was a rush, Matthew and Edwin from one side the crowd from the other, quickly subduing the redhead, threshing about. In moments the other three, battered, were against the wall, held there by a hostile ring of men.

Matthew looked around for Olsen. He was sitting on the floor, ashen, Wendell bending over him. Edwin urged the crowd, "Please get back. He's hurt," and calling for a doctor.

Wendell telling Olsen, "Hey, you're gonna be all right."

Olsen smiling weakly, "I don't feel all that great."

Matthew saw the blood then. Olsen was stabbed and bleeding badly, but talking to Wendell. "That was a brave thing, son. I never saw anything so brave." His voice was trailing off toward weakness. Wendell looked around helplessly.

He saw Matthew standing near. "Give me a hand."

Matthew stripped off his parka. Together they laid Olsen gently back on it.

"Look who's talking," Wendell telling Olsen. "You just saved my skinny ass."

There was little power in Olsen's voice, but it was measured and clear. "What I was saying last night. I used to believe that but it didn't sound right when I said it."

"Take it easy. No need to talk."

"When I said it out loud it seemed like an excuse to put somebody down."

"I know. Good people can't hate without reason."

"You're going to be at the right hand of God. I know that for sure." Olsen's voice trailed off.

They were struggling to cut back Olsen's clothing to find the wound. "A doctor's coming to fix you," said Wendell.

"Better call some elders too." Olsen might have read the fear in Wendell's eyes. "Stop the worry. I'm gonna be okay."

A covey of parka-clad doctors were around Olsen when they carried him away.

The gang was still cringing against the wall, the deputy arrived panting. He had run from the Jackhammer, where he had been guarding the door. Edwin instructed him to get help and take the redhead and the three men they suspected of stabbing Olsen to the ranger station and handcuff them to pipes in the back room. The others would be kept under guard in the day lodge.

Chapter Twenty Six

During the fight and its aftermath, Jason had gained another 200 feet. Matthew could now see both Jason and the needle through the binoculars. It would soon be over. He gazed again at the peaceful white sea of Kilivein. In less than half an hour an avalanche would thunder down. It might be a partial slide, but nevertheless an avalanche. Matthew reasoned that the viewers in the day lodge probably wouldn't know until the avalanche had traveled nearly to Clementine Ridge road whether it was full or partial. Too bad, because the difference could spell life or death in the day lodge.

Wendell was on the radio giving Jason's position to Salt Lake, and Edwin was calling each lodge, telling them to put everybody under cover. Jason would begin the traverse in minutes. Killvein would slide immediately. If it was full depth they expected its tremor to destabilize both Savage Mountain Run and Goose Gully. They might slide instantly but most likely their release would come about five minutes after the Killvein slide. If telephone contact were lost, all lodges would know that the avalanche had struck the day lodge. Because of the chain reaction hazard, no rescuers were to venture out from other lodges. The first shuttle of helicopters would land three minutes after the avalanche. They would deposit military rescue forces on the avalanche snow between Clementine and the day lodge. It would be better if everybody already in Lucite stayed under cover and out of the way.

Edwin would man the radio from the time Jason began his run. He knew the terrain and could best describe the development and path of the avalanche. Based on his information, the control center at Salt Lake would chart the movement of the slide so they could estimate areas of greatest destruction and determine where to begin rescue efforts. Matthew had a grim thought that areas hardest hit would be the last excavated. In the statistics of the rescue, dead people would mean nothing for hours. Only the living would count. If the avalanche veered east the first shuttle of rescuers would descend on Clementine Inn, where they could save a lot of people quickly. If it veered to the west, Jackhammer Lodge would yield more live people per minute than Clementine Inn. Either way, diggings at the day lodge would not be comparatively rewarding.

Jesus! Even as Matthew cursed his morbidity he feared his logic.

Jason was at the high needle. He had refused to carry a radio, protesting its added weight on a hard climb. Matthew knew the real reason: Jason wanted to be sure that no one would try to order him back from the mission. He carried instead a small mirror. He would signal with a flash, sixty seconds before moving into the traverse.

The brilliant sun shining from behind Matthew out of a cloudless sky would be a help for Jason, assuring him a strong signal that he could move across the darkly shadowed evergreens on the north slope and guide into perfect position at the day lodge. It would be like aiming the beam of a spotlight.

They saw the flash then, sweeping across the day lodge, up and across again and down.

It was twenty-two minutes past ten. The temperature of the snow would not be quite warm enough for spontaneous avalanche. That was perhaps 30 minutes away. Jason had picked a perfect time for his traverse. The top layer was ripe for movement. Surely it would flex and slide across the salty red dust like a blanket on ice. No need to think any differently. They had done everything possible to protect against the violent paw that threatened to sweep down upon Lucite.

Thousands of Americans were cowering here. Even their government couldn't save them. Of what use to these people was Fort Knox with its billions in gold? An elite force of America's military might was poised only a few thousand yards away. But here in this Wasatch canyon lay thousands of citizens of the world's most powerful nation, cowering pathetically in basements and under tables, behind fragile, puny walls of brick and steel; grist for the mill. There was not a thing worth putting up to hold back a great avalanche.

Jason appeared to be standing motionless. Onlookers from the day lodge might imagine he was drawing some deep breaths or having second thoughts. But Matthew knew he was lacing the straps of his poles into his fingers, an intricate weave that would give him great holding ability but still allow him to instantly turn loose of the pole if sucked into the avalanche.

He had shed his backpack and thrown the snowshoes aside. It was time. The seconds were used. Jason raised his poles and dropped them once, twice. Then he was plunging down toward the watchers, instantly sinking out of sight, a narrow rising column of powder marking his intrusion into Killvein and moving tornado-like across the great snow field. Thinner at the edges, the column slashed a sparkling diagonal across the rock-laced edge on toward the dangerous heart of the basin, cutting scissors-like, leaving behind a flaring ditch. It was a perfect route. If the upper layer were taut, here was the place to cut it.

On and on the column sped toward the dead center of the great dead sea of Killvein Basin, only to disappear into a sudden white screen that obliterated the basin, even the mountain and the sky. It was a great white fog, an explosive white-out—A snow cloud, not drifting against the sky but expelled in a burst, boiling upward. Matthew heard a roll of thunder, then a dull echo. The cloud stopped rising. It seemed suspended. Then it began to billow down toward the bottom of the canyon.

"Lord Almighty," someone gasped. "Here comes the avalanche."

Chapter 27

To Samantha it wasn't suspenseful so much as sickening. Every word from the short-wave was a hammer pounding in her chest. Eight people were gathered at the short-wave, including a secretary who was frantically recording the monologue in shorthand.

They were trying to get used to hearing Edwin, his rather harsh inflections bringing bursts of electrical interference. He was describing Jason's progress across Killvein in a flat, almost monotonous voice, colored only by weariness. It was incredible. Samantha was here and safe and she could scarcely breathe from terror and excitement. It was either the deadly calm of desperation or a virtuoso performance from Edwin. If only he would round out the harsh vowels to get rid of the static. They must have every word.

"He's eighty yards in. A hundred in. The powder is very light. It's rising about twenty feet in a stringer. Now he's about fifty yards from the center of the basin."

There was a five-second pause.

"Something's wrong here." Another pause. "Uh, huh....." Edwin was so engrossed that he was forgetting to talk. "The snow just blew up across the whole mountain." Shorter pause. "It sounds like thunder, but it's not an avalanche. The snow just blew up in the air instead of sliding down. Now it's starting to fall back. Looks like a lot of it will drift down right on top of us. Do you read me?" For the first time there was color and excitement in Edwin's voice.

"We read you," it was Hayden. "You say drifting?"

"Yes sir. The snow is just kind of sifting down."

"Holy hell!" Even Hayden was excited. It was the first time Samantha had seen emotion in the man. "We must have an implosion of the entire horizon."

Another pause. Samantha hearing rumbles of excited conversation at the other end. Then Edwin's voice came back. "Yeah, several of us have seen it before. The cloud is because all the air blew up out of the snow. We don't think there's going to be any avalanche."

It was a thought too revolutionary, too startling, and too attractive to dare to grasp.

"God bless you, Ed." Hayden was explosively joyous, grinning into the microphone, then turning to one of the generals.

"Are your helicopters up?"

"Yes, when the traverse started."

"Better call them back. We'll need to send them in empty to evacuate the east lodges."

"You sure about this?"

"Yes. Killvein has spontaneously compressed. It's a fantastic bit of luck. Now we can go in and get those people out."

He was calling Lucite again. Edwin telling him, "Sorry, I can't hear. There's pandemonium here. The men just learned there won't be an avalanche."

Hayden grinning broadly, shaking hands with the governor, hugging Taylor and Samantha. Samantha was surprised to see the extent of relief in the man, who had seemed the least excitable. Maybe it was proportional to the degree of pent-up anxiety.

There were smiles and handshakes all around and much back-slapping. And as the group drifted away from the short-wave, Samantha slipped closer to the radio, picked up the mike and called for Edwin. She was relieved when he came in promptly. "Ed, can you please tell me anything about Jason?"

Chapter 28

The snow settled and the mountain began to take shape again. Matthew searched with binoculars for the dark figure of Jason. It would be much harder to see him now because the tops of trees, previously covered, jutted out along the side of the ridge.

He reasoned that Jason would be okay. It must have been a helluva sensation, like a roller coaster plunge into pale darkness. But Jason surely knew instantly as the snow blew up around him. He would have skied on through the white sea with little fear of obstacles, so he might be a long way from where he disappeared.

Watching for movement, Matthew swept the glasses across the traverse route. Nothing. Down through the trees along the inside of the ridge. Nothing. Back to the spot where the column was last seen. Nothing. No pole, no hat, no motion, nothing dark except tree tops to break the great expanse of white. The compression and shower of snow had even healed the gash left by Jason's intrusion.

Edwin was searching now. Salt Lake was raising questions.

"Hey. There's a flash." Someone caught the reflection directly in their eyes. "Again." They all saw it this time. Jason was somewhere at the apex of Clementine Ridge, already halfway down. His signal seemed jerky, erratic. It danced along the front of the day lodge, swept away, then returned to a staccato of dot-like flashes. A collective gasp of relief swelled from the crowd, cut short by a sudden hush. Dismay. The message came like a rippling wave toward Matthew and Edwin. Olsen had lost too much blood. The doctors couldn't save him.

Too bad, thought Matthew. He was a good and decent man. "Jake will hate that," he said to Edwin. Edwin didn't answer. Then Matthew remembered that the Dane and Edwin were also friends.

Matthew called loudly for Wendell, who pushed through the quiet crowd. After they relieved him at the radio, he had left to be with Olsen. He was back now, a moist veil across his eyes and a stark paleness below them.

Grim faced, Wendell took note of the flashes from the mountain, nodded satisfaction, but said nothing. Matthew thought maybe he couldn't trust himself to speak. Poor guy had been through all the hell a body and mind can stand in the past few hours. But he would have to come around because his expertise was needed now like never before.

"What kind of signal are we getting from Jake?"

The urgency in Edwin's voice brought sharpness and focus into the eyes of Wendell. After a pause, he had a slow answer: "I'm not too sure. On the high seas those kinds of short bursts are a signal for caution. There it was again. I think he's warning us about something."

Edwin interrupted "Jake can see the north slope. We can't." He turned quickly back to the radio, calling Salt Lake. "We see Jake now. He's about half-way down. He looks okay, but he's signaling that something's wrong. It's like he's saying 'hold everything'; For God's sake, keep those helicopters grounded until we know what's happened with the other avalanches."

By this time, most of the men were milling around in the trenches outside the lodge. Edwin picked up the loudspeaker. His warning was not loud, but stern. "Everybody back inside the building. There are still avalanches up there. We may have to reverse the tables."

All except the shoveling crew began sifting back into the windowless building. It quickly became crowded and cramped again, but not nearly as cold as before.

Somebody noticed that Jason had renewed his descent, and called attention to the tiny dark moving figure. There was much finger-pointing, excitement, exclamation. Matthew heard a shout behind him, "Just look at that dude ski," an exuberant reflection of what Matthew himself was thinking. It was vintage Jason, no longer plummeting ever deeper into powder, churning up rising plumes of white as during the traverse. Now he was floating the dense pack, lifting, skis gliding, sinking, steering a splendid carve down the rough, steep fall line. It was stirring to the eye, but left an icy apprehension in the mind of Matthew. When Jason Stemple skied like that he wasn't showing off. He was anxious about something and in one hell of a hurry to get down.

In only a minute or so Jason disappeared behind the snowy mounds north of the day lodge, then appeared again in the trench leading toward the remains of Bluebird lodge. Anticipating his return, shovelers had cleared the path, and stood waiting, walls of snow looming high above the tallest head. As Jason rounded the bend he was inundated by the men, who rushed along the trench to pull off his skis and hoist him onto their shoulders. They carried him for a hundred yards or so back toward the day lodge. Only minutes ago they watched him begin the dangerous descent into Killvein. It seemed incredible that he was back again and alive.

Approaching the lodge, Jason saw Matthew and Edwin near the door and made his way toward them. He was smiling weakly through the onslaught of admiring handshakes and backslaps. As he approached Matthew could see a deadly weariness in his eyes. but at the same time, a grim concern. He embraced Edwin, then Matthew.

"The downhill layer slid. The rest blew up. It felt like a bridge falling in," he answered their question.

"What were you signaling when you stopped up there?" asked Edwin.

"We've still got big problems, Ed. When Killvein dropped, the rumble de-stabilized Savage Mountain. I could see the cornice from up there. It looked okay before I hit the traverse. Now there's a twenty foot gap at the corner. The section is braced against the big rock needle on top. You know that won't last long. Is anybody at the patrol house?"

Edwin paled. "We sent a dozen patrolmen over there to wait out Killvein. I'll go get 'em back." He turned away.

Jason locked onto Edwin's arm with an iron grip. "Nobody's going in there. Call on the radio. Tell them to get out quick. Their lives depend on it. Half should take the east trail. The rest are to head in the direction of the horseshoe. Tell them I said to run, don't walk."

"But, Jake. They're across the creek and uphill from the slide."

Jason stabbed a finger in the direction of the short-wave. "Damn it. Do as I say. Get on the radio. I want those men out fast."

By the time Jason finished, Edwin was on the radio. Jason lowered his voice and said to no one in particular "I guarantee that slide will take the patrol house." He shook his head as though to clear his thoughts, then turned to Matthew. "Thank God, there's nobody in the ranger station."

Matthew interrupted. "I'm sorry to tell you this Jake." He quickly described the attempted breakout and the stabbing of Olsen. Jason's head drooped. Matthew saw tears in his friend's eyes for the first time ever. Blow after blow after blow. Now this. Jason was crumbling. Matthew wanted to comfort him, but didn't know how. Edwin was off the radio now.

"They've got the message, Jake. They're clearing out." Jason was sitting on the table's edge, white-faced, not listening.

"Uh...Jake," said Edwin. Those guys locked in the ranger station..."

Matthew shushed Edwin and pulled him aside. "For God's sake give Jake a minute. He needs to get hold of himself. Forget those sons-of-bitches in the station."

"They're right in the path of the avalanche. They're helpless. I'm going in," insisted Edwin.

"No you're not going under that avalanche." Matthew grabbed the much smaller Edwin by the collar. "You're staying right here until Jake is fit to decide. Now simmer down." Matthew's action surprised even himself. He hadn't manhandled anybody in years, but here he held Edwin almost in a hammer lock. Edwin was objecting. They were swearing at one another when both realized at the same time that Jason was trying to break up the scuffle and demanding to know something:

"Who has the key to those handcuffs?"

The deputy came toward them. "I've got the key."

"Give it to me. I don't want any dead heroes here. Nobody is going into that ranger station."

The deputy handed over a single key on a ring.

"That means you too, Jake," ventured Edwin, now quite contrite having tried Jason's patience and tested Matthew's muscles.

"Don't worry. I've seen that dead-man's cornice barely hanging there. Now if everybody will leave me alone, I haven't had a chance to piss in three hours. Then I'm gonna find a place to lay down for a couple of minutes. When you hear the Savage slide wake me."

Jason disappeared into the crowd. It seemed like such a natural request that neither Edwin nor Matthew tried to stop him. For his part Matthew, exhausted beyond belief, was just glad to have Jason back and taking charge again.

Wren's requiem

The world of the wrens was an anxious place. Earlier a white curtain had enveloped and showered them. After it settled into silence, the wood was gone.

She had sneaked into a crack in the rocks, ruffled her feathers, and waited for the wood to come again while he hopped along the stony ledge, not waiting but searching here and there.

Abruptly, both wrens turned toward a faint sound from across the valley which started as a whistle, then exploded into a thunderous splintering and crashing. An avalanche was pouring off the mountain through groves of aspen, ripping at branches, tearing them away, leaving trunks as smooth as power poles; the strong ones erupting upward from out of the earth, hurled into a churning mass of rock and snow, then gulped inside, as though pulled by a giant tongue. The massive avalanche enveloped and obliterated a house at the base of the mountain, crossed the creek and moved uphill toward the wrens like a writhing snake.

Then motion slowed and stopped. For a moment, noise raged at the wrens. Then that ceased, but across the way a raw wound had cleft the mountainside.

The mountain suffered there in silence.

She clucked her surprise. He launched a barrage of high-pitched sound, his cry for the mountain. It was the loudest racket a tiny bird could manage and It went on and on to kill the dreadful silence. Then he too ceased and squeezed in beside her.

Finally, the wrens perched there together in gloomy contemplation.

Chapter 29

Suddenly Matthew woke. He was sitting at a table with his head propped on one elbow, but he couldn't remember sitting down. He was too weary to move or think. He didn't know that he was half-asleep when the face of Edwin came galloping toward him, bouncing and grimacing. He tried to stir, but could only stare at the face moving ever closer. Then Edwin was shaking him, screaming. "Wake up, Matt. For God's sake, wake up!" He was shaking Matthew again. Matthew's eyes focused onto the mustache of Edwin. Finally the words came clearly into his ears. They were high-pitched, despairing, with an edge of panic: "You gotta come, Matt. Jake is in there under the avalanche."

The dreadful impact of Edwin's words propelled Matthew to his feet like the thrust of a spring. He was running toward the ranger station, center point of the avalanche. Edwin was beside him. They were shouting in the direction of the avalanche, screaming for Jason, but the only sound coming back to them was the plop of snow sheets dripping from shaken trees into patties of crushed ice on rocks below. It was the death knell of a spent avalanche.

Still running in the trench, they came up against the wall of the avalanche, blocking their way like a dike The tortured snowpack was icy, chunky, dense, seeming somehow colder than the fluffy undisturbed fields behind them. "God Damn," breathed Edwin. They stood and stared, neither wanting to say what he was thinking. By now others were running up behind them, men with shovels.

There was consternation all around. "They say the ranger's in there." Matthew and Edwin were still staring at the deadly wall in shock when

Matthew realized that other men had already started digging trenches across the avalanche stream.

Someone pushed a shovel into his hands. "Help us, man. Point the way to the ranger station." Mathew pointed and began digging furiously. Beside him, Edwin had a shovel too. Neither of them was the least bit tired anymore.

Chapter Thirty

Merlin could hear a chopper taking off. It was at least the fifth or sixth flight out. There had been much coming and going. He figured they were bent on complete evacuation of the east village. Even now the corridor was full, waiting for another load that would move out in minutes.

He felt better but very tired. He would have slept, like Ginger, but for the helicopter noise. He would be home soon. Shit, seemed like he'd been gone forever. Merlin and Ginger were on adjoining cots in the southwest corner of Blue Spruce Lodge. He knew it was the southwest corner because the sun had been slow to work its way around to their end of the room. It had shone for a long while on the sheet-covered corpses at the east of the room before dropping a beam across Merlin's bed. The other person they had saved from the avalanche was asleep next to Ginger. The black girl hadn't stirred for hours. Her head was heavily bandaged. She had slept soundly, even through the racket and screaming when they announced that the avalanche threat had ended. She slept through the landing and thunderous takeoff of the big helicopters. Then through a short visit by her husband, who looked even more whipped and tired than Merlin felt. Merlin had tried to ease his mind. "She's breathing good. She's gonna be just fine."

Wendell had noticed that Merlin was holding Ginger's hand. He looked a question at Merlin, and their eyes met. "She asked me to," said Merlin.

"Thanks," said Wendell. "The doctor said by keeping her awake under the snow you probably saved her life."

"If she'd died under there I would've too."

"Take care of her, and yourself."

"Sure."

Now there was almost too much sun across Merlin's face. He wanted to shade his eyes but hated to turn loose of Ginger. She could wake any second. Finally he couldn't stand the glare anymore. He brought the hand up to shade his eyes.

"Hey jockey," very softly.

Merlin turned to look. Her eyes were open.

"I thought you were gonna hold my hand."

He reached out. Felt her slim fingers curl strongly around his. Ginger was okay.

"What's all the racket?" she asked.

"Helicopters are taking everybody out. They're coming for us pretty soon. 'We get a ride all the way to Salt Lake. How you feel?"

"Not in a hurry."

"You want to stay here?"

"This orthopedic blue?"

"Sure it is."

"I like it here."

"Why?"

"Well, who's gonna hold my hand down there in Salt Lake City?"

"You' re crazy, but sweet."

"Hey, I think you better think that after what happened."

"What happened?"

"Can't you imagine the stories the big boys are tellin' about us?"

"Stories?"

"Why honey. I laid on top of you for the longest time last night."

"Hell, that's nothin'. Be different if it was the other way around."

"I like it better that way."

"Wish I'd known."

"Anyway, what was that hard thing?"

'Well—I guess the granny knot you tied in the rope."

Ginger giggled. "Good thing I never knew that."

"Why?"

She laughed, full throated. "Honey, that's what really kept me alive."

Merlin was speechless, blushing warm.

Ginger giggled again. "I guess we're well."

"If you are, you better get up and run."

Her hand was squeezing his when orderlies came to put them on stretchers. There wasn't any chance for conversation on the helicopter. It made too much noise. But they were close to each other and Merlin's hand found hers. He propped his head on a pillow so she could see his lips. "I'll die without your double-clutch."

She couldn't have heard but she understood. Her black eyes smiled first, then her lips, teeth sparkling, a glowing beauty, a tawny beauty, a smile to last a lifetime. Her lips moved and he read, "I'm glad. But don't really."

At Salt Lake City Hospital, Hulda was waiting inside the emergency entrance, wetting his eyes and cheeks with moist kisses and tears. "They said you wrecked to save two girls. We're so proud of you."

"Hulda, listen carefully." His whisper was hoarse and too loud. "You've gotta get me out of here quick."

"Honey, is something wrong?"

He pulled her ear down close to his face. "Yeah. I'm horny as a goat."

Hulda laid her finger three times across his lips as if to say, "Shame on you."

Merlin closed his hand into a loose fist. It felt empty.

Chapter Thirty One

If they must do a post-mortem on poor devastated Lucite, the office of the Civil Service Commission in Salt Lake City seemed like a fitting place. It occupied two drab floors in the old Mormon welfare building on 59th Street and tenth. Matthew found a tree to park under so Gloria would be comfortable with her book. "If the sun chases you out, come inside." He kissed her. "I'll save a place."

"Darling, I hate legalistic stuff, you know that."

"It may not be as dull as you think. I hear this SKOF outfit may show. If they do, there'll be some fireworks."

Gloria stared vacantly at Matthew for a moment, closed an eye and wrinkled her nose. "You mean those grouchy people who are always bitching about skiing in national parks?"

"National forests, not national parks. There's a big difference."

"Doesn't matter. My husband refuses to teach me how to ski so I may as well join the club. Then I can bitch too."

"We're both lucky I didn't bring you last winter. You'd probably have windmilled at Lucite and hit the ground hard enough to destabilize the avalanche. We'd both be dead."

"So I'm clumsy—and fat."

Matthew smiled and muzzled her cheek. "You're not a teensy bit fat."

Gloria waved him off in mock disgust. "Just leave me the keys. If the shade moves I'll move."

In the hearing room, Edwin quickly left a huddle of friends, many of whom Matthew recognized, and came toward him. Ernie was there, chatting with Wendell and Miss Nice-bottom. And so was a stocky guy with a gas company cap who Matthew assumed was Merlin the truck driver. A woman, plump and pretty, stood by his side.

Edwin's handshake was firm and affectionate. "Thanks for coming, Matt. I figured you'd get here one way or the other."

Matthew looked around the hall, which was filling fast with mostly strangers. A brunette woman, noting the stir over Matthew's arrival, left her conversation with a tall elderly man and came toward him. Though dressed rather severely, nothing could hide her fresh bursting beauty. She smiled, and held out a hand. "It's time we met. You're Matt, the ski monster."

"Samantha the soothsayer," he bantered back. "You call a snow storm in July, I dig out my long underwear."

"You're so kind. At the Bureau nowadays I'm only known as the blizzard bitch."

Edwin was occupied again, so Matthew took Samantha to one side and lowered his voice. "Glad we got to talk before the action starts. What are they saying in Salt Lake about this inquiry?"

"There's lots more local interest than you would expect from a subcommittee, especially considering that none of the senators are well known here. People expect the hearing to just dramatize what went wrong without shedding any real light. They're likely to make Utah look bad, or at least incompetent."

"I hear the Stop-Killing-Our-Forests lobby has been invited."

"That's mostly why the locals are apprehensive. Having survived the avalanches, and prospered from a fine season of late skiing, the last thing Utah needs just now is opportunistic agitators from the east. Aside from Park City, national forests are the only places we have to ski."

"What do the avalanches have to do with SKOF?"

"Their main strategy is to discredit the Forest Service because it allows and regulates skiing. So when something goes wrong that gets public attention they charge incompetence. Almost surely today they're going to attack the way Jason handled the crisis at Lucite. I think we can counter most of what they bring up. The toughest problem is controversy about Jason's role in the death of the guys who killed Frank Olsen.

"I hear their families have been out here raising hell."

"True, and others, including politicians. One of the senators is from Kansas, and he's likely to be hostile. Some of the media seems to be on their side. That's mainly why there are so many curious people here. It's horrible, but some believe that Jason out and out murdered that one guy.

"I guess it all boils down to today. Will Jason lose his reputation along with everything else?"

Samantha averted her face. Matthew could see she was deeply moved. When she looked up her eyes were filling with tears. "It's heartbreaking. Of course that's why we're all here isn't it? To fight for Jason."

Matthew reached out to embrace Samantha. An odd emotion tightened his own throat, and he hadn't wept since childhood.

The gavel sounded.

Matthew and Samantha sat side by side on the bench reserved for character witnesses who may or may not be called upon. There were only four, so it shouldn't take long. Across the way, a government lawyer sat beside the Forest Service executive known to Samantha. Next to him, but keeping a disdainful distance, was the representative of SKOF. Chairs occupied by six senators formed an arc facing the committee chairman and witness stand.

The Chairman, senator Hoag of North Dakota, introduced the subcommittee as Hopson of Alabama, Clintridge of Nebraska, Cooper of New Hampshire, Shoemaker of South Carolina, Golden of Kansas, and Harrison of Indiana. Matthew noticed that none of them hailed from a western state where skiers use national forests.

Senator Hoag went on, "Our task is to uncover facts that might be useful to the committee as a whole, and the U.S. Senate, as we debate whether changes in federal administration of the national forests may be necessary. We are not here to determine guilt or innocence, only to assemble facts. However we are empowered to take votes on resolutions that may be introduced by senators in attendance."

He pointed out that the State of Utah was offered representation, but declined. "Utah feels it's a federal matter," he said. "The State doesn't claim to be among the entities damaged by the avalanches that struck Lucite, last winter." Then Senator Hoag lowered his voice and smiled slightly. He continued in a conversational tone: "I'm told, in fact, that the avalanches were actually a boon to Utah. Within days after the slides, record numbers of skiers from around the world descended on Lucite for a shot at skiing the greatest powder fall in 60 years. Much of the influx was due to special promotions designed to offset bad publicity from the avalanches. I'm happy to report that federal disaster funds assisted in the effort. Promotions centered on the beauty, excitement, and safety of Utah skiing. And they made a strong point that, according to the Hendrix cycle of 60-year storms..." Hoag paused and motioned toward Samantha, "no person can reasonably expect to ski such powder snow more than once in a lifetime."

Then the senator read from a prepared statement: "We are not inquiring into the performance of any federal agencies involved except the Forest Service, which lies within the jurisdiction of this committee. A question we hope to shed some light on: Did Forest Service employees fail in their responsibilities to prevent the tragedy at Lucite. And, if so, are any modifications in employment or supervisory practices warranted.

"In fairness to all, and especially to the reputation of snow ranger, Jason Stemple, the answer is not easy. An unlikely, in many ways incredible, series of events plunged Lucite resort deeper and deeper into crisis. To bring everybody here up-to-date, and to assure that we are all on the same page, I have asked Mr. R.J. Taylor, regional manager of the Forest Service, to summarize the crisis up until the disappearance of ranger, Jason Stemple. This latter event, we shall examine in considerable detail this morning."

Taylor stood. Beginning with the three weather fronts converging, he recounted the events as they unfolded. The wrecked truck. The Helix avalanche. The lost ski party. The Clementine avalanche. The deaths of Ellen and David. The fight at the ranger station, the security measures taken, the preparations for the Blue Bird evacuation. finally Jason's last traverse and the death of Olsen. The crowded room was deathly quiet as everyone listened with rapt attention. It occurred to Matthew that, although Taylor had somewhat glossed over the Clementine avalanche, here was the relentless march of fate; the kind of story that doesn't gently unfold but hammers the senses. When Taylor finished, the audience appeared somewhat dazed and deeply moved.

A surprise witness then came forward, accompanied by an armed and uniformed sheriff who brought his own chair and seated himself a few feet away. The prisoner was introduced as Mr. Casey Stroud, of Kansas City. Mr. Stroud, said the chairman, was under arrest pending trial as an accomplice in the murder of Frank Olsen at Lucite. Matthew remembered Stroud, a dark stocky man with a bright scar on a jutting chin, as the most hesitant member of the gang that attacked Wendell, then Olsen at the day lodge.

"Mr. Stroud, I understand you witnessed the murder of Frank Olsen in the Lucite day lodge, but claim to have taken no active part in it."

"That is correct, sir."

"You also witnessed the confrontation between Jason Stemple and Burt Dain just before the Savage Mountain avalanche."

"Well, you might say I saw part of it and heard part."

"Please describe those events, beginning with the arrest of you and three other men in the day lodge."

"Well, the deputy handcuffed us all together then made us walk ahead of him and a few others through the trench to the ranger station. Burt, he was really mad, and swore at the deputy all the way."

"What about the rest of you. Was the avalanche on your minds?"

"The rest of us went quietly. It was like a nightmare. We couldn't believe that somebody had stabbed the big guy. We were so sick and scared that we didn't even think of the avalanche."

"Continue, please."

"They took us to the back room at the ranger station. The deputy unhooked the cuffs one by one and locked our free hands to a pipe that ran the length of the room. It got pretty messy because Burt kept pulling away. So they had to tackle him and drag him over to the pipe. It was quite a scuffle. Burt was a big guy. After they handcuffed us there, they went away."

"What did you do?"

"As soon as they left, Burt made us try to pull away from the wall. We tried several times, but nothing doing. The pipe was well attached. So we quit. That's when Burt really got mad. He called us yellowbelly, said if we'd cooperated we could have broke out of the day lodge. He said the stupid big fella who interfered was stabbed deeply and that's what he deserved and we should have killed the chicken shit black guy, too."

"Sounds like he felt no remorse at all."

"He didn't. Burt said the same kind of stuff to the ranger when he came in to the station, and that's probably what got him killed."

"Describe what happened."

"The ranger, I never heard him come or anything. All of a sudden he was just there among us and he had a key to the handcuffs. He looked awful tired, and he was out of breath like he had been running to the station. Burt started carrying on about the stupid guy who got stabbed and the black guy. The ranger said 'shut up you son-of-a-bitch.' Then he told us to listen carefully...that an avalanche could hit the ranger station any second. He quickly unlocked both Mays and Hanford, leaving the cuffs dangling on the pipe. I was at the end of the line. To get to me, he had to unlock Dain first, but he only unlocked the cuff on the pipe, then he locked that on his own wrist and he said to Dain, 'Okay killer, you're goin' with me.' He told Mays and Hanford to run like hell toward the day lodge.

"Before the ranger could undo my cuff, Burt made a fist with his free hand, the one without the bandage, and hit him like a sledge hammer in the stomach. The ranger gasped loudly and doubled over. Of course he dropped the key. Then Dain kneed him hard in the face and he fell. He looked unconscious. Dain drug him across the floor to where he could pick up the key. He began fumbling with the key to try and unlock his cuff. Finally, he got free, and headed for the door still holding the key. He turned at the door and came back toward us. I thought he was going to unlock me but that wasn't what he had in mind. He still had his ski boots on. He came over to the ranger and tried to deliver a kick in the head that would likely have killed him."

Stroud paused, shook his head meditatively, and grimaced. "That Burt—when he got mad he was about as mean as they come. Everybody who knew him knew that. Anyway, he was standing awkward and the ranger had pretty much come around by that time. The ranger ducked the kick, grabbed the boot and put such a twist on it that I think he broke Dain's leg or twisted it almost a full turn at the knee. Burt screamed, then flopped over and fell on his face."

Stroud bowed his head and shook it, as if trying to erase a recollection.

"Was that the end of it.?"

"No. I didn't see the end. But I heard it."

"What happened?"

The ranger drug Burt through the door and into the main room. "I could hear Dain swearing at him, and now and then he would groan in pain. The ranger must have pulled Dain up into a chair."

"How do you know that if you could only hear what was happening."

"I saw it on the way out."

"Go on please."

"There was some more scuffling and movement and sound of a struggle. Then I heard the ranger say, 'See this?' He said it just as plain as day.

"Did Dain answer him?"

"It sounded like he said something like 'no, no God'."

"Then?"

I heard more scraping and grunting and groaning. It sounded like Burt was choking. He was trying to talk but I couldn't make out any words.

"Things got real quiet for maybe half a minute before the ranger spoke up again. It was cold back there, and I was already scared. But his words put a real chill on me. I'll never forget what he said."

"Tell us precisely, if you can."

"I heard the ranger say, 'You made me into a killer so it would be easy to kill you'.

"I could hear Burt trying to say something, but mostly chocking again. When the ranger spoke up next it was a lot louder. He said, 'listen to me you son-of-a-bitch. I'm not a coward who kills with knives. I kill with avalanches. I'm real good at that'."

Stroud hesitated. "The ranger talked on but that's the jist of what he said."

"Go on. It's important that we know exactly what was said."

"Well, the ranger's voice got kind of wild then and he said, 'I don't need to slit your throat and whack off your balls to kill you'."

Stroud paused and looked around the room. "I'm sorry to repeat that here, but it's what the ranger said."

"Can't be helped. Continue."

"He said, 'the avalanche will slit your throat and rip out your balls for me, I don't need to do It'. Stuff like that. He was talking like a madman but his words, again, came out just as plain as day. He kept telling Burt to listen for the avalanche."

"Did Dain try to answer him?"

"I don't know. That's when I yelled for help."

"And then?"

"Right away the ranger stuck his head in the doorway. He was really surprised. He had forgotten all about me. The first thing he said was, 'My God. We gotta get you out of here.' He came right over and unlocked my cuff and told me to get out as fast as I could run.

"I started through the main room past Burt. He was sitting in the chair. It looked like the cuffs had been locked behind the chair. A rope was tied around his throat, holding his head straight up. I paused just long enough to ask: 'What about you and him?'

"The ranger grabbed me by the arm and shoved. He came close to screaming: 'I said get to hell out of here'. I left then in a high run."

"But you didn't go back to the day lodge."

"No. I was afraid they might kill me there. I veered left in a narrow trench and kept running and falling until I came up to a first aid station, sopping wet. That's about the time I heard the avalanche. After the avalanche was cleared and I could move around, I gave myself up to the police."

"Have you told this story before?"

"Nobody asked me about it. I think everybody figured I'd left the station at the same time as Mays and Hanford. I didn't say anything because I thought some people might think I'd done wrong not trying to get back to the day lodge and spread the word that the ranger was going to kill Burt."

"Do you think you did wrong?"

"No. Burt got just what he deserved. He was the cause of all our troubles. Can you believe he was going to run off and leave me locked there?"

"Do you think the ranger killed Dain?"

"No. I believe the avalanche was what killed him, just like the newspaper said. The ranger just helped things along."

A titter arose from the onlookers.

Chairman Hoag excused Stroud and called Edwin to the stand.

Edwin was tense as a coiled rattler. Clearly he hadn't fully come to terms with the stresses and tragedies of Lucite, and the loss of Jason.

The chairman began: "We are especially interested today in the events that preceded and immediately followed release of the Savage Mountain Avalanche. You need not go into the murder of Bishop Olsen, which has been well documented in grand jury testimony for the upcoming trial. Please relate as accurately as you can the chain of events, beginning with what happened when Ranger Stemple returned from his traverse."

"Well, Jake told me right off that the Savage Mountain Avalanche was about to spill, and there was enough snow to cross the canyon. He said to evacuate the Ski Patrol House. I said I would go over there and he said no way. Call them on the short-wave. While I was on the radio, Matt told him about the murder of Frank Olsen, and about the handcuffed men in the ranger station. Jake was really distressed about his friend Olsen. I said I would go get the men out of the ranger station. He wouldn't let me go and took the handcuff keys, saying he didn't want anybody entering the avalanche zone.

"He said he had to lay down and rest for a few minutes. That seemed natural." Edwin paused, his voice faltering. "Jake disappeared then and I never saw him again."

"Did he take a nap?"

"He said he was going to, but I don't know if he did."

"When did you realize that he had gone over to the ranger station?"

"Not until I saw one of the prisoners running toward the day lodge. He didn't have any handcuffs on so I knew Jake had gone over and turned him loose."

"What were your thoughts at the time?"

"Thank God, Jake has unlocked the prisoners so they can save themselves. I was hoping to see Jake any second, thinking *come on Jake. Get out of there.* The prisoner, name of Mays, said that another prisoner, Hanford, had taken a trench to the right. He said the guy, Stroud, was somewhere behind him and that Dain and the ranger were handcuffed together and Dain was acting up, so they may take a little longer. I waited just a minute or two, then started toward the station to find Jake. I was about half way there when I heard the avalanche and saw the powder plumes rising. With Jake missing, it was a terrible sight."

Edwin's voice was getting ragged. He was breaking down again. He blew his nose, the only sound in the crowded hall.

The chairman waited a moment, then resumed. "What did you do then?"

"From where I was, I could see all the way to the avalanche. There was no Jake in sight. So I ran back to the day lodge and told Matt that Jake was under the avalanche and we had to go get him. We didn't even think about shovels. We just ran toward the ranger station. Other men came in behind us."

"How long did it take you to get there?"

"Just a few minutes. We were running as fast as we could."

"Did you see any sign of the snow ranger?"

"None. When we came up to the avalanche it seemed like a wall had closed over Jake and just zipped him away. I think we all knew we'd never find him alive, but we began digging. By the time we got to where the ranger station used to be, we couldn't find any part of it. We searched around on the avalanche snow until we came to where the chimney had floated up out of the pack. I sent a man back to the day lodge to call in the helicopter crews and we began digging as fast as we could. We had poles but they weren't much help because there was so much trash and solid stuff in the snow. Just before the helicopters came in, we hit a corner of the station. After the crews pitched in, the digging went faster and we quickly found the body of the big redheaded guy."

"How long after the avalanche was that?"

"Less than an hour."

"Was this body still inside the ranger station?"

"What was left of the station, yes. The body itself was pretty battered, too."

"Was he wearing handcuffs?"

"Only on one wrist. The other arm was free.

"How long before you found the body of Hanford, the other dead prisoner."

"Not until early in the afternoon. He was nearly a hundred yards downstream, and out closer to the west edge of the avalanche. This body was in better shape than the first one."

"How do you account for its location?"

"We tried to piece together what happened. It looked like maybe after Jake unlocked him he went a ways toward the day lodge with the other guy, then thought better of that, came back and started down the trail toward Clementine Lodge. I reckon the thought of being arrested again was more scary than the avalanche. Of course, when he first heard the avalanche he knew he was trapped but it looked like he still tried to run away."

"Was the body of Mr. Dain, when you found it, still somehow attached or hooked to a chair with a cord around his throat as Mr. Stroud has described it?"

"No. We found him sprawled in what had been the main room, with only one handcuff attached as I told you."

"If, as you say, Mr. Dain was no longer restrained before the avalanche, why do you suppose he didn't try to run, or at least get out of the ranger station?"

"We're not doctors in the ski patrol, but working in avalanche country you learn a lot about trauma and death. When we dug him up we saw right off that he'd been killed instantly by piercing wounds. But it was pretty clear, too, from blood flowing to bruises on his knee and face, that he had sustained injury there before the avalanche. It had been a mystery until Mr. Stroud's statement this morning. His description of the fight between Jake and the big redhead seems to mesh with our hunch that Dain probably couldn't even walk, let alone run at that stage. We figured there had been a fight in the ranger station just before the avalanche."

The chairman pressed on, "It would appear from what we've learned today, that Jason Stemple, having survived the fight with Dain, confined Dain to a chair and threatened him with death. Then he unaccountably set him free. What on earth really happened?"

"I don't know sir. I do know that Jake would never kill a helpless man, or any man."

There was a stir. The chairman recognized the senator from Kansas, who asked: "Is it not true that just the night before, Stemple threatened to kill Mr. Dain?"

"Well, yes. But he was under a lot of stress at the time. It was Dain's fault that an avalanche was about to come down on Jake's wife and son."

"Wasn't it also Stemple's fault. He could have induced the avalanche before it got big enough to threaten the Stemple residence?"

"He didn't do it because Dain and his cronies were out there lost. Nobody in their right mind can blame Jake for the death of his family."

The Kansas senator relinquished the microphone. The chairman continued:

"Did it surprise you that during the fight the snow ranger was able to subdue such a large and apparently violent person as Dain?"

"Not a bit. Jake was a powerful man. He was in damn good shape, and he knew how to fight. I was only disappointed that he didn't kill the guy. He had plenty of reason to."

Again Senator Golden was on his feet. "Mr. Mesa, U.S. government employees don't go around killing people for any reason except self defense."

Edwin swallowed, saying nothing.

The chairman continued: "Was it the avalanche or ranger Stemple that killed Mr. Dain?"

"It was the avalanche, sir. Everyone who examined the body of the redhead agreed on that."

"Have you any idea what the ranger did, or where he went, after he freed Mr. Dain for the second time?"

"I think he tried to drag or carry Dain out of the ranger station. Failing that, maybe he set out to get help. That seems most likely. Of course, we don't know at what point the avalanche came down."

Again, Senator Golden demanded a microphone. "Mr. Mesa, you've just told us the snow ranger was powerful enough to subdue Mr. Dain? How can you expect us to believe that he was not strong enough to drag or carry him out of harms way?"

Edwin was coming to the end of his rope. He flushed in anger, and lashed back at the question: "At that stage senator, Jake hadn't slept for two days. He'd helped dig up a dozen men and women both dead and alive. He'd just climbed three thousand feet on snow shoes and skied off the most dangerous snow field I've ever seen. He'd had two fights with this hulking son-of-a-bitch from your state. God knows how tired or bad hurt he may have been." Edwin paused a moment, opened his mouth to continue, instead bowed his head.

His questioner shook his head, gestured palms up toward the chairman, then turned to face the other senators as though seeking support to continue the questions. They looked straight ahead, stony faced. He shrugged and sat abruptly.

A buzz of whispers and exclamations rose out of the audience. The chairman waited patiently for silence, and for Edwin to raise his head. Then he continued, as though the outburst had never occurred.

"Tell us about the search for Mr. Stemple's body."

"We shredded the avalanche snow for two days. It wasn't in there."

"Do you believe that he somehow survived the avalanche and left the area?"

"No. I can't believe that anybody in there survived the avalanche. It appeared most likely that Jake's body was carried all the way to Middle Creek where the avalanche crossed. As the snow settled, the water rose quickly underneath and floated the body out. It's way downstream somewhere under silt that the avalanche dams caused. God knows where. I'm sorry to say we may never find Jake's remains."

Edwin was teary-eyed.

"You may stand down, Mr. Mesa."

The chairman next called up the SKOF representative.

Claire Trevor was a small man with a clipped Bostonian accent. His beginning was softly spoken but as his message became more aggressive, so did his voice. "Mr. Chairman and distinguished senators, what I have to say here today may seem negative to many of you, particularly in light of widely-held admiration for the late Jason Stemple. Please believe, however, that the organization I represent is not against anybody or anything. Rather we are a single-mind organization, positively in favor of the sanctity of the national forest system. Given our mission, we must speak out forthrightly at this time, because it is clear that during the crisis at Lucite, the Forest Service has once again shown that it cannot be trusted to manage a resource as valuable as our national forest system.

"We believe that Ranger Stemple, through faulty judgment, abetted by faulty service policy, made a series of decisions that exacerbated the crisis at Lucite. As a result, five avalanches needlessly ravaged the area, destroying hundreds of acres of remaining forests, and exposing fragile slopes and formations to the accelerated erosion that is now taking place. Even worse, of course, Mr. Stemple was clearly the direct cause of two deaths, his own and that of Mr. Burt Dain. Further, his negligence may have indirectly caused other deaths during the crisis.

"For this, we hold the Forest Service, his employer, responsible. They should have predicted his erratic behavior, provided him with better guidelines, or supervised him more carefully.

"We have to ask ourselves (a) what kind of person was Jason Stemple, and (b) is this the kind of personality who is suited for the work of snow ranger?

"For an answer to these questions, we must look closely at the progression of events at Lucite. Given the circumstances, it is tempting to sympathize with Mr. Stemple, as most people do. But we must view this the way a computer might, without emotion. Applying the precision of science, I see a plain, logical, almost inevitable progression toward disaster.

"I reviewed the employment and service records of Mr.Stemple and found a significant detail in an early job interview. When asked if he had ever been involved in a fatal accident, Stemple said that a tractor once crushed an employee on the farm where he lived. Prompt medical attention might have saved a life. But young Jason delayed seeking help because the critically-injured man begged not to be left alone. In this incident, we see emotions overwhelming pragmatism. As a youth, Stemple faced the acid test of responsibility, and withered before it.

"After he was hired by the Forest Service, Stemple proved to be a competent, reliable employee, but emotional, and excessively given to his humane impulses. He was a gifted skier, a conscientious person, very influential among his colleagues and fellow workers. We see an excellent snow ranger until he faced the unexpected storm at Lucite. It was another acid test. Clearly, when a wrecked truck blocked exit from Lucite, the responsible course would have been to quickly move the truck or shoot down the threatening avalanche. Out of concern for the truck driver, Stemple delayed doing either, thereby causing the dangerous entrapment of thousands of people for whose safety he was responsible." Trevor paused, looked around, shrugged, and lowered his voice. "How do you weigh the life of one man against thousands?

"It was predictable. The course of events proved once again that a so-called bleeding heart does not belong in a position where the greatest need is a hard head. Mr. Stemple failed. But he was an intelligent man. He realized his mistake and resolved not to repeat it. But again, out of concern for a lost party, he delayed so long on a second avalanche, that it finally came down on his wife and son, killing them both."

Trevor paused again for effect, seeming to enjoy the impact of his choice of words on the audience. "Some might call this a crass irony, or a macabre bungling.

"Then, Mr. Stemple suffered a pure failure in judgment. He ordered an evacuation too late. Nine people died And so we have his own agony piling on disaster. Overwhelmed, he appears to have attempted a dignified suicide. Although his courageous traverse of an avalanche field may have saved lives, even that failed in a sense, and worse. In his absence, or perhaps because of his absence, a dear friend was murdered.

"In all this, we certainly have a motive for the apparent neglect or violence that contributed to the death Mr. Dain. I imagine that many among us, perhaps most, would have been driven to act in a similar way. But that is precisely my point. The job of the Forest Service is to seek out the kind of person who will not crumble when face to face with disaster. In studying the crisis at Lucite, and Mr. Stemple's part in it, we detect a lack of stability. Clearly, in any future crisis of this nature, a personality such as Mr. Stemple's could be expected to behave in exactly the same way. We hold the Forest Service responsible for failing to perceive this."

Trevor sat.

Hulda Landis, wife of Merlin, took the stand. Her face appeared blotched with anger, but her voice was self-assured and her message was blunt: "I usually talk too much and embarrass Merlin. So today I'll keep it short. I speak for myself and two kids. We thank The Lord that Jason Stemple was the man in charge at Lucite when the storm came. Three times during the crisis he saved the life of the man we love; our husband and father. I say this to the United States Forest Service: Thank you for having the good sense to hire as fine a man as Jason Stemple." Then she directed a shaming stare toward Trevor. "And to you, sir, I say go after the Forest Service if you must." She paused, stamped her right foot loudly, and continued. "But don't you ever dare tarnish the name and memory of Jason Stemple again!"

The audience tittered and the chairman gaveled.

Hulda gathered herself and glanced down at Merlin. "Okay, Dad. Have I carried on too much?"

Merlin didn't look up, but lifted two fingers in the sign of a V. That's when Matthew noticed something startling. The other arm couldn't move because Merlin and Miss Nice-bottom were holding hands.

In contrast to Hulda's homey message, Wendell's came across as crisp and composed: "I say this respectfully, but after listening to Mr. Trevor, I feel I must speak out. I recognize that SKOF is a powerful organization. You have the power to assassinate the reputation of a deceased person. You have the power to humiliate his memory. But you do not have the power to lower the profile of Jason Stemple in the eyes of all those who feel only respect and gratitude toward him.

"As evidence of Jason's good work at Lucite, I offer you one beautiful life. Ginger..." He turned to his wife. A hush descended. It was the quietest moment of the day. The black girl released Merlin's hand, stood elegantly, and smiled at Wendell. Her eyes sought out the senators, as Wendell continued, "You all know the story, so I need not repeat it. For this gift I can only thank God—and Jason Stemple."

It was Matthew's turn.

"I am an engineer, a businessman, and a long-time friend of Jason Stemple's. You would perhaps expect me to come to his defense. So let me say at the outset that I am known as a pragmatic and objective person, more inclined to lay blame than heap praise. I am here because I learned something about Jake and about myself during the crisis at Lucite. The decisions Jason had to make at Lucite were life-and-death decisions that in fairness cannot be criticized by anyone who did not have to make them. It's easy to believe that Jason's performance as a person or professional had somehow to be compromised by his humanity and generosity. I confess to you, and to Jake, wherever he is, that I used to believe so myself. After being at his side during almost every moment of the crisis, I don't believe it anymore. I know that his strength and will, and the decisions he made, averted far greater disaster at Lucite.

"Precious lives were lost there, including those of the Stemple family. I knew them well and had reason to care deeply about them. I think of Jason, Ellen, and David in terms of love—because they were united in life by its bright and dark shades. In death they are still a family, united now by love's eternal happiness and peace."

Mathew pulled himself together to leave the podium, as the chairman called on Samantha. Her eyes were bright as she came toward Mathew and suddenly she held out her arms. They embraced for the second time that day. She whispered quickly in his ear, "I love you for saying that." She released him and continued on to begin her statement:

"As our chairman has told you, I am the person who predicted that three fronts would converge on Lucite with devastating effect. I take no pride in this because if Jason is deemed to have failed at Lucite then I am equally at fault. I failed to convince anyone of the storm's approach. I should have gone into the streets and screamed the danger.

"Do others share culpability? It is tempting to slice the blame and pass it around like pieces of pie: Not once did The Weather Bureau, from which I have now resigned, provide any useful information to guide the ranger's decisions. What about the chain of command? When Jason ordered the ski area closed, superiors countermanded his order. That was after a nasty little collusion with ski area operators. What about the public service company, who sent a truck into the eye of a storm on a busy ski day? And the lodge owners, who refused to cooperate with Jason?

"But as Jason's friends, we hold that there is no blame to pass around. What happened at Lucite was an act of God. The disaster played itself out. It tested the will and skill of many and revealed human flaws and weakness in us all. True, we saw ugliness as has been described. But some of the most wonderful and unselfish traits of humanity came together at Lucite, helping us avoid a far greater calamity.

"Jason Stemple did not face those avalanches alone, but he rose above the rest. Now it appears that his reputation alone, and his life's work alone, is on trial here. Jason was a proud man, he was wonderfully competent. That is why this small circle of friends—there could have been many more—are here today. We are determined that Jason will not be remembered for some macabre bungling, as stated by Mr. Trevor, but will be recognized in death as the good and true person that he was in life."

Samantha sat again by Matthew, who patted her arm.

The chairman announced: "Ii is past noon. I think we have enough information for now. Are there any more statements?"

A well-dressed man in the audience stood and raised a hand. "I have a point of information and a comment."

Samantha remembered him immediately as the one who had raised questions in the briefing about artillery and the Clementine avalanche. The chairman nodded, and the man continued.

"As a news reporter for AP, I was the first to cover the Lucite crisis. The Clementine avalanche is widely believed to have been spontaneous, but that is not true. It was brought down by artillery fire ordered by

Ranger Stemple, who well knew that it would cause the death of his wife and son.

"In retrospect, it is clear that the preemptive shot saved hundreds of lives. Out of concern for the ranger's feelings, his friends have suppressed information about this, but in light of Mr. Trever's statement, it's time the world knows the truth."

He paused, then continued. "That's my information. Here is my comment: Only a man of great courage and devotion to duty could have ordered that shot. It seems a pity that The SKOF statement acknowledges Ranger Stemple's heart of gold, but ignores his nerves of steel."

Isolated clapping was starting among the audience as the newsman continued. "I say to SKOF, if you want to discredit somebody, it's unwise to base your case on a man who, in his lifetime, was a credit to humanity."

Applause burst out and the audience stood as the chairman gaveled for quiet.

He recognized the senator from North Dakota whose deep, strong voice rose above a shuffling of papers. "You said resolutions would be in order. I submit the following: "Be it resolved that this committee, after hearing the facts in the case and the opinions of many, wishes to commend the late Jason Stemple for his performance during the avalanche crisis at Lucite, Utah. Evidence before us indicates that Ranger Stemple died in the service of his country. He deserves the highest honors that the Civil Service Commission of the United States can bestow."

The last part of his statement was nearly drowned out by another swelling of applause from the audience.

The chairman called for order and tallied the vote: five in favor, one abstaining. Then another hand raised slowly, to more applause. It was that of Senator Golden.

The chairman was about to declare the hearings convened when he was interrupted by the senator from Nebraska: "I have one quick question: Ms. Hendrix said she is leaving the Weather Bureau. I'd like to ask what will she do next?" The question caught most of the audience on their feet preparing to leave, but the hall became quiet as everybody looked toward Samantha.

She took the proffered microphone. "With the help of Jason Stemple's many friends and admirers, a foundation devoted to helping disadvantaged children learn to ski has been established. It is called the I CAN SKI FEDERATION in memory of a tiny, dying girl who Jason befriended and introduced to skiing. I will be privileged to serve as the president."

She smiled then. "Thank you for the question, senator, and of course, contributions are welcome."

The senator smiled back at Samantha, "To start things off, I pledge one hundred dollars."

"You always were stingy, Henry," grumbled the chairman with a grin. "Put me down for a hundred fifty."

The gavel hammered. "Meeting adjourned."

As Matthew turned to leave, he noticed Merlin and Miss Nice-bottom moving along just ahead of him, still holding hands.

Chapter Thirty Two

Gloria looked up at Matthew's approach, taking her glasses off. She seemed grave and thoughtful. With her Texas tan and hazel eyes she was also glamorous. His bright Houston wife glittered here in Salt Lake, a city weary of a cold winter and a windy spring. They kissed. "Were you getting hot?" asked Matthew.

"Not from the sun. Maybe a little, thinking about last night."

Matthew chided her, "You were supposed to be reading."

As Matthew got into the car, Gloria put an arm around him. "I was reading and thinking. You know I read about lots of things. But since Friday I only think about bed."

Matthew glanced at her sideways, incredulous. "You're putting me on."

"Please, darling. I'm pretending this is the real old-fashioned honeymoon with an end of innocence and all that."

Matthew smiled. "If it really were the good old-fashioned kind this would be a hell of a way to spend it. Anyhow, we're going now."

Gloria nodded, stretching and smiling. She was quiet while Matthew groped his way through Salt Lake City one-ways seeking an avenue along the foothills that would intersect with the road up Middle Aspen Canyon. Gloria was thoughtful that way. She knew he didn't like anyone to break his concentration.

Once on the road to Lucite, though, she asked, "How did the testimony go?"

"It wasn't really testimony. We didn't have to swear on a Bible. It went good. We cleared the air as far as Jake's reputation is concerned. That was important to all of us. We want the world to remember Jake the same way we do: A good and decent man, generous with everything including his own life. At the end, the senators commended his performance during the crisis. I'd like to hope that he's alive somewhere and will learn about this. But in my heart I know that Jake is dead.

"Well, darling, it does seem to me your friend deserved some blame for letting those prisoners die, maybe even killing the one guy. But I know you care deeply, so I'm glad his reputation is clear now. What makes you so sure that he's dead. They've never found a body. Wasn't there some doubt?"

"Oh yes. of course. Some people think Elvis Pressley is still alive, and they had a body. I know Jason is dead because he the same as told me that he was expecting to die that day."

"Then why can't they find the body?"

"They didn't look the right place. I've never told anybody this. Until they find his remains, Jake is still on the payroll, and his salary goes into the new children's ski society we contributed to. Besides I'd rather think of Jason lying in a snow bank than under the ground. That's more like where he belongs The snow is melting fast now. They'll find the body soon."

Matthew looked sideways at Gloria and smiled, "Don't panic. We won't go looking for Jake's remains today."

"I wouldn't put it past you. Anyway where should they be looking?"

"When you dig for avalanche victims you always search downstream from their last known location. In Jake's case, they should have searched upstream because that's almost certainly where Jake went down."

"Okay. How do you know?"

"Two items of equipment always stored in the ranger station were never found. One was a kind of low-percussion device sometimes used nowadays to set off avalanches. It's called an Avalauncher. The other was a second pair of snowshoes.

"Jake set three prisoners free. About six minutes passed between the time the first prisoner appeared at the day lodge and the avalanche came down. We learned this morning that by the time the prisoner arrived, there had already been a fight between Jake and the guy, Dain, who died in the avalanche. Jake broke the guy's leg, dragged him into a chair, and told him to get ready to die. At that point, Jake was about as destabilized as the avalanche course, but he was no killer. He hated Dain and wanted to make sure that Dain knew what was to come. I suspected this all along. A prisoner still in the ranger station verified it at the hearing today. After the last prisoner left, Jake freed the big guy from the chair, knowing both of them were about to die.

All this didn't take long, a minute or less. Leaving Dain in the station, Jake strapped on the snowshoes, grabbed the Avalauncher, climbed out on the snowpack, and started uphill. He got into position for a good view of the cornice, and aimed the gun. Knowing Jake, I think it was a magnificent moment for him. In the middle of that beautiful, bright morning, two killers—Dain and the avalanche—were at his mercy. He could orchestrate their destinies as well as his own. He paused for a few seconds, not to analyze what was going on, of course, but to relish that glorious power. Jake never had a second thought. After he pulled the trigger, he let out a yell and charged like a maddened bull, snowshoes and all, toward the avalanche. That monster writhing down the mountain could do nothing worse for him than a favor.

"The only thing Jake ever feared in his life was the pain of others. I know he died just as fearlessly as he lived.

"If I were a betting man, I'd bet a hundred K that when the snow is all gone they'll find Jake's remains about two hundred yards uphill from the ranger station."

Gloria slid across the seat to Matthew. She laid her cheek on his shoulder. A delicately manicured hand stroked his thigh. "Thanks for telling me that. You make me love Jake, too, and I never even knew him."

By that time they were entering the depths of Middle Aspen Canyon. Gloria seemed thrilled by the towering rock walls around them. Even Matthew responded to the beauty of the place, so different now from ten weeks ago.

Snow still coated the highest peaks, appearing to be quite deep along north slopes. It was winter up there, but springtime adorned the creek banks with willows and grass and walls of dancing aspen leaves, their reflections metallic, sometimes nearly white. At intervals, water from melting snow pulsated down the canyon sides like suspended brooks that spread fan-like when enveloped by the mountain breeze. They stopped at times to listen, the music of the water a chorus of melodious rumbles like a hundred high-pitched drums. Coming out of the darkest part of the canyon, the road crossed a bright south slope where the sun would hit the greater part of the day. Here the harsh outlines of the mountain were softened by bunches of low-growing wild flowers, splashing ragged color across the ridges.

Lucite was a strange place now, so different From the white contours that Matthew remembered. The empty parking lots looked muddy. A few cars were scattered around the buildings, but it appeared as though most lodges were closed for the summer. They drove around the horseshoe, Matthew identifying the lodges for Gloria as they passed. He pointed to the site of Bluebird Lodge, noting with silent satisfaction that even the foundation had been razed. Nothing remained. The wound left by the site would heal by the end of summer, although Matthew guessed someone would rebuild the lodge.

They picnicked at the place where the road ended, far up near the head of the canyon just below the waterfall. There was little conversation between them: each had their own thoughts, and anyway the roar of the water filled the little glade where they rested, and noises of the forest were all around them.

Summer serenity and peace in Middle Aspen Canyon. Here was a catharsis to lay against the terror of the winter storm. Matthew was glad now he had come; he had been tempted not to. This would be a good way to remember Lucite.

"We should go now," he said finally.

"I love it, Matt. Can't we stay awhile?"

"No. There's something I have to do while the light's good."

He drove up Clementine Ridge Road, finally coming to a place where deep ruts stopped the car. Apparently a truck hauling debris had gotten stuck there. They walked on, hand in hand, Gloria carrying a paper bag from the picnic basket. "For the animals," she explained.

The concrete footings of what had been Jason's house jutted above the uneven ridge. Gloria sat at a corner as Matthew walked back and forth across the hill below the house, concentrating to the south and west. It took only twenty minutes to find the bracelet, which had been lying upside down. The copper band was badly tarnished but the stone itself glistened after a quick wipe with Matthew's handkerchief.

He heard Gloria squealing at the antics of a chipmunk she was feeding. He walked back and sat beside her, holding up the bracelet.

"Matthew, it's beautiful. Whatever is it?"

"Jake and I called it the commitment rock. Because the setting is a salt of uranium. it's very radioactive. It shouldn't be worn for more than a thousand hours during any person's lifetime. Naturally a woman would wear it only for people she really cares for on very special occasions."

"Oh Matt, can I have it?"

"No. It belonged to Ellen. I gave it to her."

She looked intensely at him, a question in her eyes. Matthew went on. "I bought it at a trading post when Jake and I worked in the uranium mines. I had in mind this girl I was trying to make time with." Matthew was deep in thought, barely aware of Gloria.

"I thought I'd give it to her along with a bunch of roses and a little note saying something silly like: 'When you're not with me you have to wear this.' But the day Jake and Ellen were married I knew that Ellen hadn't gotten any presents at all. I realized the bracelet was a little personal for a wedding present, but I didn't have anything else so I gave it to Ellen."

"Did you love Ellen?"

"I came to love Ellen."

She reached out and took the bracelet. "we'll keep it always, for Ellen."

Matthew nodded.

"Matt, you told me that a part of Jason died during the storm. I've thought that about you too. You used to be, well, you were cynical. My mother used to say you were definitely crafty. You know I never agree with mother about anything, but darling, you had a kind of nihilism about you when you left Houston. It wasn't there anymore after you came home. Maybe it wasn't that, but really, Matt, do you know what I mean?"

"I guess I do. Gloria, baby, I'm afraid nothing sinister in me died here."

"Well, maybe something different came alive."

Gloria threw out some more bread to the chipmunk, which was creeping ever closer in fearful jerking movements.

"Was this the place where the avalanche killed Ellen?"

Matthew nodded.

"I thought so," said Gloria.

The chipmunk was sitting on its tail, holding a bread crust between little paws, beady eyes glaring at Gloria. "You darling little beast. Matthew, let's catch him and take him with us."

"He's too smart and quick. I guarantee you'll never catch him."

"Matt, why was Ellen so dreadfully sick?"

"I'm not sure she was altogether sick. I think she was just sad and haunted because she thought she was selfish."

Gloria was staring at him questioningly with her hazel eyes. Matthew said, "Your little chipmunk there, look how happy he is. He's taking your bread and he's happy. He's not being foolish about it. He doesn't love you for feeding him, he's not even grateful."

"Does that have something to do with Ellen?"

"In a way. Animals, all of them, are happy when they can take something. They don't give except in the sense of survival. The problem with people is that some were born to give. They're miserable unless they're giving something away. Maybe those are the ones who have come the highest above that chipmunk. And then there are the people who can't bear to accept a gift because they fear the giver has paid too much for it. Bring these two kinds together and you have misery on both sides of the scale. A lot of the agony in the world stirs around and around in those people."

Matthew took Gloria's hands in his. "Come on, baby, let's go."

"Matt, I never knew you to talk that way or to feel pity for people or to be sad about them."

Matthew helped Gloria down from her perch. "Okay, something came alive," he answered softly.

They had to walk slowly back to the car because their arms were around each other and the ruts were deep.

Epilogue

Reprint from The Albuquerque Dispatch, June 14

Denver, CO – The U.S. Forest Service reported today that the body of Jason Stemple, the Snow ranger who's heroism is widely credited with saving many lives during the avalanche crisis at Lucite, Utah, has been found by a hiker. The formal search for Stemple's remains was suspended nearly two months ago. The spokesman said Stemple was either thrown uphill by the force of the avalanche or unaccountably made his way uphill in deep snow before the avalanche struck. At the time, he was wearing snowshoes and apparently carried an explosive device of the kind often used to bring down avalanches. His body came to rest under densely packed snow, laced with saplings and brush.